THUNDER IN DEUTSCHLAND
THE MUNICH MASSACRE

The Beginning of the Age of Terrorism

By Don Eudy

D1520100

Some of the characters and events written about in this work are fictitious. When historical characters and actual events are portrayed, the words and actions are fictitious and are a creation of the author's imagination. When historical figures are portrayed, their words and actions, except in rare instances, are fictitious, although care is taken to portray them in as accurate a fashion as possible. In most instances, the characters and events depicted in this book bear no similarity to real persons or events.

ISBN-13: 978-1500361310 Printed in USA

Dedicated to my parents: My father, D. C. Eudy, and my mother, Voda L. Carmical Eudy. The two people who helped me through life and who wanted to see me succeed more than anything else.

BLACK SEPTEMBER AND THE MUNICH MASSACRE

The thunder that erupted in Deutschland at the Summer Olympics in Munich on September 5, 1972, consisted of less than 500 rounds of ammunition being fired, but it ushered in a new age that was characterized by a violent method of attaining objectives—terror. There were no innocent non-combatants now; everyone in the enemy camp was considered a potential target.

Napoleon's campaigns in Europe to spread the ideals of the French Revolution had brought about the concept of a People's War, where everyone in the nation was a part of the armed struggle. In the new "Age of Terror," innocent people became the preferred target. Their deaths generated the most outrage, brought the most publicity, and pushed the affected government to settle the dispute as quickly as possible.

The idea grew among the displaced peoples of the Middle East that there was no longer a need for extended periods of combat with many deaths among the troops of the belligerents in order for one side to declare victory. A well-chosen incident where the slaughter of innocents was so repulsive that everyone demanded a solution was more likely than anything else to bring about the desired results in the shortest time. Nothing could demonstrate the desperation of the oppressed as well as terror.

According to declassified files from the United States Department of Defense, Department of State, FBI, and CIA, the deaths of the eleven Israeli athletes at the Summer Olympics in Munich, Germany on September 5, 1972, signaled the beginning of the "Age of Terrorism."

PROLOGUE

They struggled against the cords and tape that bound them together but could not free themselves. Later, the teeth marks on the ropes showed how agonizing their efforts must have been. The nine Israeli Olympic athletes watched the drama play out through the windows of two helicopters where they were being held hostage at a NATO airfield and realized they were not going to survive the ordeal.

Wrestling Coach Moshe Weinberg and weight lifter Yossef Romano had already been killed at the Olympic Village when they resisted. Of the nine others taken hostage, weightlifting judge Yakov Springer, wrestler Eliezer Halfin, and weightlifters David Berger and Ze'ev Friedman were being held in the first helicopter. Wrestling referee Yossef Guntfreund, sharpshooting coach Kehat Shorr, track and field coach Amitzur Shapira, fencing master Andre Spitzer, and wrestler Mark Slavin were prisoners in the second helicopter.

The Palestinian terrorist group, which the hostages learned went by the name of *Black September*, had already set several deadlines for killing them, but extended them each time. The German government offered a large sum of money for their release and also offered to trade German officials for the Israelis, but to no avail.

Two of the Palestinian terrorists, the leader Luttif Afif, known as Issa, and his second in command Yusuf Nazza, called Tony, left the helicopters to inspect the airliner they had demanded to take them to Cairo, Egypt. The hostages felt they might have some hope of survival if the Labor Government of Golda Meir would relent and release the more than 200 Palestinians held in Israel in exchange for them.

The trip to Cairo was their last chance, but they all knew that none of the previous administrations had ever negotiated with terrorists who kidnapped Israeli citizens. So they resigned themselves to the fact that they were going to die. One of the German officials who had been allowed to visit them at the Olympic Village in Munich later remarked that he marveled at their calm dignity in the face of certain death.

Their imminent death became even more evident to them when they saw Luttif Afif and Yusuf Nazza come running back from the airliner. The terrorists discovered that the promise of a flight to Cairo was a trap. There was no crew on board the jet. As the two scrambled for the safety of the helicopters, a firefight broke out and the hostages watched as three of the terrorists fell.

It soon became apparent to the hostages that the assault had failed, and now they watched nervously as Luttif Afif glared angrily in their direction once the shooting became sporadic. During the next hour and a half they struggled desperately to try and free themselves from their bonds. They stopped when the terrorists checked on them, but resumed as soon as they left.

Suddenly it was calm. Then they heard the noise of a vehicle with a large engine moving in their direction. Yosef Gutfreund, who was tied sitting in a chair, could see that it was an armored vehicle. They realized the German authorities, in their haste to resolve the situation, had given them a death sentence. They reconciled themselves to the fact that they were going to die in the next few minutes.

The door of the first helicopter opened and the four tightly bound Israelis watched as Luttif Afif appeared in the doorway. He lowered his assault rifle toward them and pulled the trigger. After he exited, he threw a grenade into the helicopter. One of the other terrorists killed the five remaining hostages in the second helicopter with his assault rifle.

The death of the eleven Israeli athletes on September 5, 1972, heralded the arrival of a new era. It was marked by the use of violence against innocent civilians to achieve political objectives. "The Age of Terrorism" had begun.

CHAPTER ONE

An invitation to Riyadh, Saudi Arabia

William Smith, from Wild Horse Canyon, Kentucky, was on his way to the Middle East. He had been given a new assignment by his mentor, Simons Grebel, a retired CIA agent. Grebel's friend from *Mossad*, Yitzhak Kahan, wanted him to recruit someone who had no connection to the state of Israel to travel to Egypt, Syria, and Jordan to assess the sentiment for war there. He wanted an opinion other than the normal intelligence that came across his desk. Grebel offered the job to Bill Smith, his young friend who was completely undocumented. There were no official records to show that William Smith existed. His identity consisted only of forged documents provided by Yitzhak Kahan.

Smith's mother had gone to live with her aunt to escape from her alcoholic husband. Bill was born at home and had no birth certificate. He never attended school and no official documents about him were on file anywhere. After his mother died he left the isolated area outside of Wild Horse, where he had grown up, and traveled around the South working part time jobs that required no identification. He performed a small job for Simons Grebel and continued working for him and Yitzhak Kahan doing things that no one else wanted to do. When this new assignment from Yitzhak Kahan was offered to him, there was nothing else he could do except go.

He had no money and no other offers. He had left all of the money he had acquired working for Grebel and Yitzhak Kahan with Ana-Marie Fontenot, the young French girl he became engaged to while he was in language school in the city of Amboise outside of Paris. He promised to marry her, but that was before he

met Rebecca Lundstrom in Tel Aviv. Ana-Marie thought he had
died while he was working in Vietnam for Yitzhak Kahan, and if
she ever found out he was alive and hadn't returned for her, it
would cause her even more pain. Bill knew that he could never
marry anyone except Rebecca now. He and Rebecca decided it was
best if she left Tel Aviv and went back to the United States while
he was gone. She had an opportunity to work at one of the
foremost medical facilities in the country, the Mayo Clinic, in
Rochester, Minnesota, near her home.

She would be about ninety miles from Blue Earth where
her mother lived alone. Bill and Rebecca would be married when
he finished this assignment, but he would not have any contact
with Rebecca while they were apart. That bothered him the most.
He had a feeling of dread when he thought about leaving her. He
was afraid he could lose her while they were apart, even though
she had told him repeatedly that she loved him and wanted to
marry him. On the day of his departure, they kissed goodby and he
walked out the door of Simons Grebel's house, and turned and
waved to her as he boarded the taxi.

He looked back at Rebecca's beautiful face all the way to
the end of the street and then stared out the window during the ride
to the Tel Aviv airport. He would be traveling as a representative
of the Compton Oil Company with headquarters in Houston,
Texas. He would fly from Tel Aviv to New York and from there to
Houston. Then he would fly back to New York and on to London.
Yitzhak Kahan had supplied Simons Grebel with plenty of cash in
American dollars for his recruit, Bill Smith. *Too much*, Bill
thought. It would be difficult to conceal that much currency.

But Yitzhak always wanted whoever he sent to be his eyes
and ears to have enough cash available, if the need arose, to buy
someone off. If his asset had enough money, he reasoned, it might
save his life. So Bill had purchased a backpack to carry it all, and a
small suitcase for clothes and the rest of his items. He had three
passports and supporting documents with him, but on Grebel's
advice he decided to use the passport that Yitzhak Kahan had
given him for an earlier assignment in the name of Charles Harper.
He would travel to London and on into Egypt using this identity
and go to Jordan and Syria later.

Bill wondered if any of the steps being taken to protect him were worth it, since he considered himself such an insignificant figure when it came to gathering intelligence. But his mentor Simons Grebel thought he was worth investing in, so he went. He looked forward to the trip to London, although he wasn't going to stay long this time, just a few hours to change planes. When he arrived at Heathrow he found that his flight had been delayed because of weather. He would have to catch another flight the next day. As he walked away from the counter, he noticed two young Arabs walk up to the check-in desk of Saudi Arabian Airlines.

The young girl talked with the clerk while the young man gazed around the lobby. The carrier, Saudi Arabian Airlines, had recently opened a route from Riyadh to London via Beirut and was experiencing difficulties in confirming and handling reservations promptly. The passengers displaced from this latest flight were upset, and Bill edged closer so he could hear the exchange between the ticket agent and the girl. They had been bumped and were trying to find another flight to Riyadh. They would have to wait and catch a later flight, the agent said. The flights were always overbooked and they were among the last to purchase their tickets. She complained loudly, but to no avail.

Bill sauntered up to the desk after they left and asked the clerk who they were and where they were going.

"I can't give you that information sir," the agent replied.

"Too bad. I can make it worthwhile if you're willing to overlook such a small infraction and give me their names and destination."

"And how much would that be?"

The agent was temporarily alone at the desk so Bill extracted a one-hundred-dollar bill and then added another when the agent made no response. He took out a third one-hundred-dollar bill and folded them together and placed them in the agent's hand before he could say no. The clerk made no response, but walked away after turning the log of passengers on the waiting list around slightly so Bill could read it. The names on the list were: Faisal Abdul al-Saud and Khalisah Amtullah al-Saud. Their destination was Riyadh, Saudi Arabia.

If they were who Bill thought they were, they were part of the Royal family that ruled Saudi Arabia. *I think it would be wise to go to Saudi Arabia instead of Egypt, if I can arrange it*, he decided. He walked in the direction the two young Arabs had taken and encountered the girl standing alone by a cart containing their luggage. He looked across the terminal and saw a young skycap in the distance pulling a cart loaded with luggage in her direction. He intercepted him and asked if he would perform a small favor for him.

"I'm in a hurry," the skycap responded.

"I'll make it worthwhile if you'll help me."

"What do you need?"

"I want to meet that girl up there at the end of the terminal. You're going in that direction anyway. Just run into her cart and knock part of her luggage off, then keep going. Apologize and tell her you're late and can't miss the flight the luggage is going on. Then I'll load her luggage back on the cart for her."

"That's too much. Besides, I could get in a lot of trouble for doing something like that."

"How much is it worth for you to do that?"

The sky cap paused and then said $500, thinking that Bill would leave him alone since the amount was so high.

"Done!" Bill quickly handed him five one-hundred-dollar bills. The skycap looked stunned, but stuffed the money in his pocket. Bill watched while he crashed his cart into the girl's cart, apologized, and headed in the other direction.

Bill hurried toward the girl who looked to be almost in tears. No one had stopped to help her so Bill walked over and began loading the luggage back without asking. He stepped back and admired his work while she looked at him warily. When he turned around, she thanked him and Bill thought he caught a glimmer of admiration in her eyes, so he asked her a question.

"Where are you going? Maybe I can help you get your luggage there."

"Riyadh," she replied.

"Let's see. I think I can help you locate your gate and move your luggage there for you if you'd like. Where are you coming from?"

"Oxford."

"The University?"

"Yes."

"Student?"

"Yes. Look, thank you, but we can get a skycap if we need to, and my brother can handle it when he returns."

"Where is he?"

"In the men's room."

"An older brother?"

"No. He's younger."

"Well, I won't bother you anymore if you don't need my help."

"You didn't bother me. I am grateful for your help. But..."

Her brother walked up before she could finish, and glared at Bill without saying anything.

"Faisal, this is..."

"Charley. Charles Harper."

"He loaded our luggage back when it was knocked off, and offered to help us move it to our gate. But since we've been bumped from our flight there's no need."

"I see. Well, yes. It seems that we'll have to catch a later flight, so there is no need for your help. Excuse me. Mr. Harper, is it?"

"Yes."

"I really don't think my sister should be speaking with you."

"I apologize. I was only trying to be helpful."

"Faisal, please. Don't embarrass me. I am perfectly capable of deciding who to talk to. Go get us all some tea, please." Faisal wandered off to buy the tea, keeping both of them in view.

"I hope I'm not causing you trouble."

"No. It's all right. I speak with boys all the time at the University. It's funny. Until now, we haven't had an argument all year over who I've talked to. You see, at home in Saudi Arabia, I'm not allowed to talk to any males unless one of the men in my family is present. Outside the country we try to follow that policy for appearance's sake, but I generally talk with whomever I want to at the University."

"Is that right? Then how did you get to go there?"

"My father went to Oxford."

"I see."

"And I am his only daughter. He isn't like the older generation who want to keep women veiled and in the home. He wants me to be removed from that kind of cultural restriction. Our patriarch, Abdul Aziz, whose name my father bears, wanted women to be able to read also."

That was nice of him, Bill thought, *since he admitted to having over 200 wives.*

"You came here with your brother so you would have a male family member with you then?"

"Yes. I attended the Women's University at home until he was old enough to come to Oxford with me."

"Interesting. I would like to hear more about your country. But should I leave you alone now instead?"

"You can do whatever you want, I suppose. Where are you going?"

"Egypt."

"To do what?"

"I work for an oil company back in the U.S."

"We're going to eat now. Are you hungry?"

"That was my next stop."

Faisal and his sister Khalisah were indeed the children of one of the wealthiest families in Riyadh, who were descended from the founder of modern Saudi Arabia, Muhammed Ibn Saud. They had the same mother, but had older siblings born to different wives of their father, Prince Faisal. Bill remembered reading that the country was not only named after Muhammed Ibn Saud, his family continued to rule it by decree, without a constitution or a legislature. It had been characterized as "a country ruled by 2,000 cousins." Ibn Saud had defeated all of his enemies, and the money from the oil deposits allowed them to run the country as they wished, according to the conservative teachings of his ally, Muhammed Ibn Abd al-Wahhab.

They found a nearby place to eat and Bill ordered his favorite, fish and chips, even though he knew they would not be as good as those in a pub. Khalisah's brother warmed up to him after a few minutes of conversation, and they talked about soccer and crew, which Faisal was involved in at the university. He was slightly built, but seemed to be strong enough to handle an oar.

"You're not the coxswain, are you?"

"No. No. I pull my weight. Do you play a sport?

"Well, I like them all. Haven't played any sport except as recreation. I have hunted most of my life."

"What have you hunted?"

"Mostly deer. But also turkey, and even bear on occasion."

"Have you ever played cricket?"

"No. Never even seen it played."

"If we had time, I'd show you how to play it."

"I'd love to. Maybe later. If I had time I'd show you how to shoot. Have you had any experience with firearms?"

"No, but I would like to learn skeet shooting. That's popular among the parents of many of my classmates at Oxford."

"I could show you that. Shotguns are my specialty. I used to practice an improvised method of skeet shooting using old jar lids."

"Fascinating. Perhaps you could come for a visit later on. Have you ever been to Saudi Arabia?"

"Never have," Bill replied.

"What are you doing after you leave Egypt?"

"Nothing firm yet."

"Come for a visit," said Faisal.

"Are you serious? How would I get in there?"

"If you have me as a sponsor, it would be quite simple."

"Could you think up some business to take you there?" Khalisah asked.

"Since you have plenty of oil there, I'm sure I could."

"Call us after you're finished in Egypt."

"If you want me to. I'd love to come. Ever been to Birmingham?"

"England?"

"No. The city in the U.S. in the State of Alabama. That's my hometown. Maybe you could come visit me sometime."

"Would your wife mind?" Khalisah asked.

"I'm not married."

"Then come to Riyadh," Faisal said. "We'll take good care of you. I'll show you how to play cricket and you can teach me about skeet shooting." He excused himself and wandered off to the magazine stand next door.

"How about you? Are you married, Khalisah?"

"No. I'm not married."

"Any prospects?"

"Why do you ask?"

"I suppose it's none of my business, but you asked if I had a wife."

"It's not as though I'm veiled and hidden away from any males except family members as I am back home. Ask me what you like."

"All right. Have you made friends with any of the young men at Oxford?"

"Not really."

"Why not?"

"Oh, you know how it is. They're all part of the elitist class system that makes them think they're special—too special to bother with anyone who's not just like them. It seems that most of them develop a rather large ego."

"And you're not used to a system like that?"

"On the contrary, it's too much like our society back home. That's why I don't like it. It's very elitist at home, and women are virtually invisible."

"I suspect you've never said that to anyone before."

"You're correct. Not even in any of my classes at the university. But it's true. We can't even mention this at home. Even though my family is part of the house of Saud, I've often wondered why our family should rule our country by decree without any restraints. We aren't any better than the other Arabs living there."

"Yes, but you won. Ibn Saud defeated the Rashidis."

"You know our history well, it seems."

"It makes for interesting reading."

"What else do you know about us?"

"Just that you have a closed society. Are you sure I can get in there even with Faisal's help?"

"Oh, you can get in, all right. If my brother invites you and serves as your sponsor, you won't have any trouble. We have two million foreign workers there. It would be good if you could find a reason to come that's connected to your work, however."

"I suppose I can. I'll put in a request to travel there."

"What exactly do you do for this oil company?"

"I look for opportunities where Compton Oil might be able to get access to new oil through leases or by purchasing existing wells."

Bill had carefully rehearsed what he would say when asked about his work. He knew the parlance of the oil business, but he had no practical experience in it. He hoped that he would sound convincing enough if he had to converse with someone who worked in the oil industry.

"Then it seems that it could be profitable for you to come and look around at some of the oil operations in our country."

"Sounds interesting. May I ask you another question?"

"Yes."

"Don't you already have someone picked out to be your husband?"

She hesitated. "Yes, but I'm not going to marry him."

"Why not?"

"Oh, he's nice enough. I just don't want to stay in Riyadh after I finish school."

"Any place in mind?"

"I like Europe and especially England—the Midlands, or the Lake District. Anywhere but London. I visited Bronte Country during break."

"Why doesn't your hair smell like heather?"

Khalisah laughed. "I don't think you'd make a very good Heathcliff, Charley. You seem much too nice."

"Will you be able to leave Saudi Arabia when you're ready to live somewhere else?"

"I inherit half of what my brothers do—typical for female family members. But that will be plenty. I'm leaving when I graduate, if not sooner."

After they had talked a while longer, Khalisah suddenly posed a question.

"How about coming to Riyadh now?"

"Are you serious?"

"Yes."

"I suppose I could put my trip to Egypt off for a while."

"Good."

"Do you think we're good enough friends now for me to come to Riyadh?"

"What do you think? I've never had a male as a close friend, outside my family."

"It's up to you."

"Do you have a girl?"

"Do you have a guy?"

"Don't you remember? I already have a husband picked out for me."

"I wouldn't be normal if I didn't have a girlfriend at my age, would I?"

"Are you saying that I'm not normal because I don't have a guy I'm interested in—except for the one who's been picked to be my husband?"

"Hardly. Your situation is quite different from mine."

"Let's agree to let our current status regarding our relationship with members of the opposite sex remain uninvestigated at present."

"Agreed."

"Then you'll come to Riyadh?"

"I think I'd like to. I may never have another chance to see it."

"It's settled then. You're coming to our home to visit my brother. It will be better if we keep it like that."

"That's fine with me."

Bill knew he would never get into Saudi Arabia without the help of someone like Khalisah and Faisal, so he couldn't let this opportunity be wasted. And as Itzhak Kahan had told him, it was necessary to deceive people to be able to get where you needed to go and gain access to the information you wanted.

CHAPTER TWO

A Meeting in Paraguay

Klaus Wilhelm von Kleinmann had added the "von" to his name a few years after the National Socialists had assumed power, even though his family had originally come from peasant stock. It was not appropriate since Kleinmann was merely a family name and not the designation of a great estate where a noble family lived. But no one had ever challenged him about it although he had occasionally noticed wrinkled brows that indicated there were questions about the validity of such a surname. He liked to be thought of as a member of the nobility, however, and kept the addition to his name, even going so far as to falsify his birth certificate with the help of a young female clerk at the records bureau.

He never joined the Hitler Youth since his father was strongly opposed to the group, but when he was old enough he enlisted in the *Wehrmacht*. Much to his delight, he was assigned to the *Abwehr*, the army's intelligence branch. The leaders of the *Abwehr* thought that young men who were not army officers would be more loyal to the *Abwehr* than to the army. Most of these young recruits proved to be ineffective, however, except for Klaus Wilhelm von Kleinmann. He became one of the best agents to ever serve in the *Abwehr*.

He was the youngest member of the organization, being only eighteen, although he reported his age as twenty-one. He was assigned to the *Abwehrstelle* in the military district where his hometown of Dresden was located, near the Polish border. All of the members of the *Abwehrstelles* were given a great deal of latitude in choosing and carrying out their assignments to gather intelligence. He was considered instrumental in aiding in the invasion of Poland in 1939 since he was able to move freely in the country because of his ability to speak Polish.

He was able to gather valuable information about the size and capability of the Polish army, which helped convince the Fuehrer that an invasion would succeed. He was decorated with the Iron Cross 2nd Class for his work in Poland, which almost everyone who knew him felt was undeserved. But because it was not safe to question the decision of those who awarded the medals since they might be connected to someone close to the Fuehrer, he became a virtual "untouchable." He had entered service as a *mannschaften* or enlisted man and rose to the rank of non-commissioned officer with the rank of *oberfeldwebel*.

After he received the Iron Cross, he began wearing civilian clothes with the tacit approval of his commanding officer. He never wore his uniform again and an occasional remark about his Iron Cross helped to allay any criticism and added to his already substantial reputation. When he was transferred to an area near the French border, no one knew what his rank was and assumed that he was a commissioned officer. He facilitated that idea by never divulging any pertinent information about himself.

He had been contacted recently by one of the few remaining members of the *Schutzstaffel* or *SS*, who had escaped from Germany after the war and fled to South America just as he had. A hand-written message from former *SS* officer, Dietrich Mittelstadt, in a code that Kleinmann had often used himself during the war was delivered to his home in Buenos Aires. In it, Mittelstadt stated that the *RSHA* had concluded that there was a matter that needed Kleinmann's immediate attention and had summoned him to come to Paraguay for a meeting.

The *Reichssicherheitshauptamt*, or *RSHA*, was a part of the *SS* that had been given the duties of the *Abwehr* when it was disbanded in 1944. Hitler had cashiered Admiral Wilhelm Franz Canaris, the head of the *Abwehr*, because he suspected him of disloyalty and gave all of the functions of the *Abwehr* to the *RSHA*, under the command of Heinrich Himmler who he deemed more trustworthy.

It is typical of the SS to think that they are still in control even after the war has been lost, Kleinmann scoffed. *They bear the imprint of Reinhard Heydrich and Himmler even now. All of them must be old men by now since I was the youngest member of the Abwehr to escape.*

He did not care for the *SS*; in fact, he loathed them. Their arrogant behavior made it impossible to do more than merely tolerate them. They were the new organization that had not been a part of the armed forces in Germany until the rise of National Socialism. Henrich Himmler, the chicken farmer, had carefully carved out a fiefdom for himself in the National Socialist movement, and he had done it by gaining command of the *Schutzstaffel*. It had become his private army, fiercely loyal to him and dedicated to the service of the party and the protection of the *Fuehrer*.

They spied on the *Abwehr*, and everyone else, regularly, with a determination to root out anyone who showed the least bit of disloyalty to the *Fuehrer* or the movement. Kleinmann hated them because he did not like being spied on by a rival organization. Their arrogance, which he considered unnecessary and a weakness on their part made him detest them even more. Whenever they entered a room in their black uniforms, they demanded attention. If anyone in the room did not give them the respect they believed they deserved, one of their number would begin to converse with that person and make inquiries about their personal life.

And no one was completely free from actions that could be viewed with suspicion by the *SS*. Most of the members of the *SS* thought they were above questioning people in this manner but there seemed to be at least one of them in every group that relished the task of striking fear into the hearts of those who did not show them the proper respect. They had many derisive names applied to them, Kleinmann recalled, but they became a powerful and effective fighting force during the war. But they served with the approval of Himmler, however, fighting where he wanted them to fight and running the death camps.

Kleinmann was upset that Dietrich Mittelstadt and the three or four remaining members of the *RSHA* had learned where he was living now. Perhaps this remnant of the *SS* was more effective in their intelligence gathering than he gave them credit for. But no matter, Argentina was friendly to members of the Third Reich who had escaped and fled there after the war, and he was a respected, if reclusive, member of society in Buenos Aires. After a few days he resigned himself to meeting with Mittelstadt in Paraguay, even though he realized it could be a trap.

He was aware that there were several Jewish organizations engaged in hunting down former members of the *Wehrmacht* and especially those in the *Schutzstaffel*. Or perhaps someone in the *RSHA* wanted to take revenge on him. Since he had known Mittelstadt during the war he thought it would be safe to meet with him if he was alone. He had found him to be one of the less offensive members of the *SS*. So he packed a suitcase, kissed his common law wife, Margarita, goodbye, and told the foreman of his ranch and his housekeeper that he would be back in three days.

A Fear of Dying

"We need you to investigate why the *Mossad* were so successful before the Six Day War," Mittelstadt insisted. "They continue to be extremely well informed about everything, it seems. Those Jews have developed an intelligence gathering operation now that is much too good for us to ignore. We know how effective they have been and now, suddenly, we are confronted with an even greater ability than they have demonstrated before."

"Perhaps we only thought we knew how effective they were," said Kleinmann.

"The Israelis destroyed the Arabs in one week. How was that possible? And how do we know that they are not infiltrating our organization and preparing to take us one by one?"

"The Syrians found the traitor and executed him."

"We think there are more. There are bound to be more. We know they are looking for us."

"None of us have been taken yet."

"We will not know until it is too late, Klaus. We need to know before they locate any of us. They will have ways of breaking any one of us in order to find the rest of us. Most likely by promising to protect whoever they capture first. That is a very powerful incentive."

"And what do you expect me to do about your new found fears?"

"We want you to see what you can find out about their ability to locate those that they blame for their ill treatment. We want to know how likely it is that they could find us here in South America. We are their old enemies and they blame us for everything that happened to them during the war. We know that they have never stopped looking for us; particularly those of us who served in the...." He paused and looked around to see if anyone was listening.

"I can tell you that they have more important things to deal with now, Dietrich."

"You mean the Arabs?"

"Precisely."

"You don't think they are looking for us now?"

"I don't think they have a task force that is targeting us now. I'm sure if they stumbled upon one of us they would kidnap us and take us back to Tel Aviv to hang."

Kleinmann watched as Mittelstadt shuddered, rubbed his neck, and then sat quietly and listened.

"You don't have that many years left, Dietrich. Why don't you try to forget about the Jews and relax and enjoy life?"

"Somehow the thought of a Jewish noose around my neck seems to prevent me from enjoying my remaining years. After they captured Adolph Eichmann and hung him in 1962, none of us have been able to sleep very well."

"That was ten years ago."

"Yes, and that means they have had plenty of time to locate some of the rest of us. Is there anything you can do to find out whether or not we are in imminent danger here?"

"I will make some inquiries."

"Good. Thank you very much."

It was the first time Klaus had ever heard a *SS* officer show gratitude for anything.

"Who else is here in South America?"

"I shouldn't tell you that, Klaus, but I don't suppose it matters since you don't know where they are located. There may be as many as five thousand of us here."

Klaus did not answer; he stared at Dietricht and waited.

"All right. I will tell you about the ones you would know, who are not associated with us."

"Us being?"

"You know. We are the *SS* Officers who control what is done here. Other than us, the ones who came here are Eduard Roschmann. You know him, of course. And then there is Aribert Heim, and Erich Priebke, and then you also know *Bibi*, Ludolf Alvensleben."

"Is that all?"

Dietrich reluctantly replied that "Alois Hennemann and Hans Dusenberg came to South America also."

"Surely there are more here that I know."

"The Doctor, Josef Mengele, came here as well," he mumbled reluctantly. "After they captured Eichmann, I think he fled here to Paraguay and then went on to Brazil. We were all afraid that we were going to be next."

A fine group of murderers, Klaus thought. *To kill an armed man in battle was different, quite different, than sending people to the gas chambers or starving them to death.*

They paused in their discussion of the business at hand, ordered another round of drinks, and began to reminisce about the old days.

"If only the *Fuehrer* had concentrated on Egypt and breaking the life line of the British at the Suez Canal. We could have starved them into submission in a few years. Think what Rommel would have been able to do with the millions of men the *Fuehrer* sent into the Soviet Union. Stalin would not have attacked us. He was too afraid," Mittelstadt asserted.

"That's true, but the *Fuehrer* always acted on ideological grounds. He hated the Bolsheviks much more than he hated the British. The British were just a nuisance to be dealt with so that he could annihilate Bolshevism," Kleinmann countered.

"Yes, you always had things figured out, didn't you Klaus? I always admired you for that. Now I, we; we need you to find out for us how the Jews are able to know so much more about their enemies than they did before. And we are their enemies, their sworn enemies, even more so than the Arabs. A Jewish state. Who would have believed it? We are in hiding now while they are the ones who are carrying out the brilliant military campaigns, like they did in the Arab War."

"Perhaps they don't know any more now than they did before. Perhaps they were just fortunate in having one informant located in a crucial position. That would be all it would take."

"Klaus, Klaus. You know the *Mossad* better than that! They are becoming more and more efficient at rooting out their enemies!"

"I do not want to give them more credit than they are due. I think that their capabilities are about the same as they've always been. They have always been very effective at finding their opponent's weaknesses."

"Yes, well, you were the epitome of efficiency, weren't you? No one else even came close to you. I was never good at spying; I wasn't trained to be a spy. Oh, yes, traitors that I knew personally, I would have uncovered and turned them over for prosecution without delay."

Klaus was silent. He didn't want to hear any more from Mittelstadt. If he did, he knew what he would have to do about it.

"I think that's enough, Dietrich. We've both had too much to drink. Let's sleep on it and discuss this again soberly in the morning."

"All right. But one question before we go. Did you know that your boss was a traitor? Or I should say when did you find out?"

Klaus was afraid this was going to happen if Dietrich kept talking long enough. He tried to get Mittelstadt up and help him to his room before he said any more.

"Our boss, Himmler, was loyal to the end, to the very end," Mittelstadt mumbled as he moved along on unsteady legs. That was why Klaus never had more than three drinks. If the situation demanded that he keep drinking, he always drank vodka or kirsch and cut it with water.

"Your boss, on the other hand, was disloyal the entire time. Admiral Wilhelm Canaris, the head of the *Abwehr*, was plotting against the *Fuehrer* and the Party the whole time. That's why he was executed just before the war ended. He was guilty of the worst kind of treason...."

Klaus pretended not to hear what Mittelstadt was saying.

"But you know what? Our boss uncovered him. That he did. And I was glad that he did. I would have helped him too. But he didn't need my help. He had people watching Canaris and they eventually caught him."

Mittelstadt was too intoxicated to realize how close he had come to sealing his own death warrant. If he had claimed any responsibility for the death of Admiral Wilhelm Franz Canaris, then Kleinmann would have killed him within the next quarter hour; just as soon as he could get him to an isolated place. Klaus had a grudging respect for Admiral Canaris, who had worked against Hitler and the Nazi Party. As he had matured, Kleinmann realized how destructive the ideology of National Socialism was. It was a dead end street of nihilism.

Hitler wanted to kill everyone in the east, the Poles and all of the other Slavs, to create *Lebensraum*, or living room, for the expanding German population. He hated the Russians, not only because they were Slavs, but especially because they were Bolsheviks. There was nothing else for them to do except fight and try to keep the Third Reich from killing all of them. *You are fortunate, my old comrade and rival*, Kleinmann thought as he helped Mittelstadt onto the bed. *Fortunate that you were not smart enough or brave enough to turn Admiral Canaris in. Otherwise you would be going to sleep permanently now.*

A Quiet Demise

The next morning Kleinmann went up to Mittelstadt's room and knocked gently on the door. When there was no answer, he tried the door and found that it was unlocked. He opened it cautiously and looked across the room and saw Mittelstadt lying on the bed. He knew without examining him that he was dead. His lips were purple, a tell-tale sign that he had been given poison. Mittelstadt was already dressed so he must have taken a little of the cognac, the "hair of the dog that bit him," to stop his pounding headache.

Mittelstadt would have slept soundly last night and the cognac sitting on the bedside table could have been poisoned by anyone who found a way to gain entrance to his room. He closed the door softly and made his way down to the desk and left his key with the clerk, notifying him that he was checking out. When the clerk asked about his luggage, he said that he had sent it on ahead. It was still in his room but there was nothing of value in it or anything that would identify him beyond his assumed name. He moved quickly through the front door of the hotel and walked rapidly down the street.

He headed to the train station but when he came to a small park on the side of the street, two men stepped out from the trees to confront him. *They are probably Jews*, he thought. No one else would behave in this manner unless they were trying to apprehend him in violation of the laws of the country they were in. He assumed a submissive demeanor and when they asked him who he was and what he was doing in Paraguay, he moved to a table just inside the park that was sheltered by trees and sat down. This surprised them since that was they wanted him to do.

He began speaking rapidly, protesting his innocence and asking them if they were police officers. Their hands were close to their weapons, so he had to time his move carefully. The train behind them was preparing to pull out of the station and the engineer gave a blast on the horn. The man standing the nearest to the station jerked his head around to see what had happened. That was the opening Klaus needed. He leaped off the bench and pounded his knuckles into the temple of the first and then kicked the other one in the groin.

This dazed them long enough for him to render them both unconscious with the small leather sap that he carried in his hip pocket. He did not want another murder, a double murder, for the local authorities to have to solve, so he dragged them into the thick underbrush and tied them up with their belts and neck ties. They would eventually work their way loose but he would be far away by then. He removed their handguns and threw them into the brush. He was sure that they would not report anything to the police; after all there was a dead man in the hotel that they were probably responsible for.

The body would not be discovered for another hour or two when the maids came to clean the room. He walked rapidly down to the station and boarded the next train that was pulling out. Fortunately, it was going in the right direction. He hadn't had time to place the two men yet but they were young and not very accomplished, so they were not *Mossad*. Most of the Jewish organizations that hunted Nazis wanted them apprehended and brought to justice in a court of law. These two apparently just wanted to avenge the deaths of the Jews who died in the Holocaust; some of whom were their relatives, no doubt.

Yes, he thought, *they were most likely members of some shadowy group that referred to their organization as the Sword of Gideon, or something similar.* He had other things to do now, more important than killing young Jews. There had been enough of that during the war. He had not taken part in it, but because Dietrich Mittelstadt had been a member of the *Schutzstaffel*, he would have been high on their list. *I wonder how they located him?*

CHAPTER THREE

Mayo Clinic, Rochester, Minnesota

On the transatlantic flight from Tel Aviv to the United States, Rebecca Lundstrom's mind was filled with thoughts of Bill Smith and what their life would be like once they were married. But she was concerned about how much she was going to miss her young daughter, Olivia. She had left Olivia behind in Tel Aviv with Linda McIntyre, the baby's grandmother, who would hear of nothing else. It would be too difficult for Rebecca's mother to take care of Olivia the whole time that Rebecca was working, so she left Olivia with Linda. That was going to be the most difficult thing she had to endure, not seeing Olivia for the next three months.

Linda promised to bring Olivia to Rochester, Minnesota in three months—that was the only way Rebecca would agree to leave her. When she arrived at the Mayo Clinic in Rochester the weather was good. It was the middle of summer and as warm as it ever got in Minnesota. She was shown into the small room where she would live for the next year. She had brought only a few clothes since she would be wearing uniforms most of the time. Linda McIntyre had already sent her several sets of the most expensive designer clothes available.

When they brought them to her the next morning there was nowhere to put them. She would not have time to wear them so she pushed several garment bags full of designer clothes under the bed from both sides. She hung as many in the closet as she could; this left only enough room to hang her uniforms. The rest she piled on the bed. She would have to pile them on the floor to sleep and then put them back on the bed in the morning so she would have room to walk.

After a brief period of orientation the first day, she arose at 6:30 a.m. the next day with a full schedule ahead of her. She did a variety of tasks from making coffee and running errands to working with patients. The staff regularly supervised many new employees every year but Rebecca sensed that she was being treated differently. She wasn't sure why at first, thinking it was because of the clothes Linda had sent. Later one of the nurses told her everyone agreed she was the most attractive girl they had ever employed.

Rebecca met Dr. Matthew Avery at coffee break at the end of the week. He was a specialist in Internal Medicine and a friend of Dr. Jeffrey Caine, a psychiatrist at the Mayo Clinic. Matthew Avery was going through a difficult period and came to see his friend regularly. His wife had died of cancer a few months earlier and he could not reconcile himself to her loss. Rebecca overheard him tell Dr. Caine that they had decided to adopt children just before she became ill. When everyone left, she and Dr. Avery were the only ones in the cafeteria. She had come late but rose to leave and had to pass by his table near the door.

"Excuse me," he said.

"Yes?"

"You're new here, aren't you?"

"Yes."

"Where are you from?"

"Minnesota."

"Where at?"

"Blue Earth."

"How do you like Rochester?"

"Fine. It's much bigger than Blue Earth though."

"Where are you working?"

"Well, I'm filing records right now."

"Well, the next step is that they will actually let you read the records. After all, this place can't run without records. And they have to be put in order so they can be located," he said with a smile.

She smiled and excused herself and went back to work. She did not want to seem rude since he was a physician even though he didn't work at the Mayo Clinic. The next day at break time, he was there again, dressed casually. He seemed to be off duty and she heard someone mention that he was on vacation but had nowhere to go since he had no one to share his vacation with. As she was leaving the cafeteria, Dr. Caine, stopped her and introduced her to Matthew Avery. Then he left and she had no choice but to sit down and talk to him for a few minutes.

"I hear you're a psych major. Do you like that kind of work?"

"Yes, I am, and I really enjoy it," she said.

"Everyone here is very dedicated."

"Yes, they are."

"Do you have family in Minnesota still?"

"My mother."

"In Blue Earth?"

"Yes."

"Are you single? Or is that too personal?"

"No, not at all."

"Except that men ask you that all the time?"

"I was going to say that I'm engaged."

"You're not wearing a ring."

Bill had not had time to buy her a ring but she thought of Linda's huge engagement ring that her first husband had given her. Linda insisted that she was going to give it to her but Rebecca wanted Bill to have a chance to buy her one first.

"I don't wear it," she said.

"Oh? Any particular reason?"

"It's too large and too expensive."

"Well, congratulations. I wish you and him the best. What's his name?"

"Bill. William Smith," she said.

"Any family other than your mother?"

Rebecca started to answer and then tears began to form in her eyes. "I have a daughter. And I'm missing her terribly."

"Can't you see her on weekends?"

"No. She's not here."

"Too far away?"

"Yes," Rebecca said through her tears.

"May I ask where?"

"In Tel Aviv."

"Israel?"

"Yes," she said, and excused herself and started for her room.

Dr. Matt Avery followed her and tried to apologize. When she arrived at her apartment, she fumbled for her key. She was crying now and told him he didn't need to apologize. It was because she had to leave her daughter behind that she was upset. Now she was afraid that everyone would think she wasn't up to the work here because she had become so upset. He was trying to reassure her that no one would think that when she turned and asked him a question.

"Do you want to know why I have a child and I'm not married yet?"

"No. Not at all."

"Well, I'll tell you why."

"Rebecca, you don't need to do that."

"No. You asked me all these questions, so now I'll tell you why. I had my child in a home for unwed girls. And her father was killed in a car wreck later. But I would have never married him. So now you know," she said through her tears.

"I didn't mean to upset you."

"You didn't. It was when I started thinking about Olivia."

"I'm sorry."

"It's all right, Doctor. I didn't mean to be so cross."

"You weren't. I didn't know you were missing your daughter so much."

He left without saying anything else. She finally found her keys and went in and pulled the clothes off the bed and lay down and cried herself to sleep and did not go back to work. The next day after lunch Dr. Jeffrey Caine came by to see her and asked if Dr. Avery had upset her. No, she said. He explained that Dr. Avery's wife had just died of cancer and he had introduced her to him thinking she was not married or engaged. It was my fault, he explained. Rebecca assured him that it was because she was missing her daughter and that it wouldn't happen again.

Dr. Caine said he regretted that she had become upset because of what he did and that he and everyone else would do their best to make her feel welcome and a part of the team. Dr. Avery did not come around again and after a week Rebecca asked Dr. Caine if she could call him up and apologize to him. He said he thought it would be fine and gave her his number. When she called he was back at work and busy seeing patients.

"Hello."

"Dr. Avery, this is Rebecca."

"Rebecca? Listen, I'm behind now. Could I call you back after work?"

"Yes. Of course."

"Good. I'll call you back as soon as I can."

"That will be fine."

"Thank you."

"Goodbye."

He did not call that evening and she thought that he must have been too busy. After all, he'd been gone from his practice for a week. The next day was Saturday and Dr. Matthew Avery showed up for lunch at the cafeteria. He came to Rebecca's table and asked if he could join her. The two nurses sitting there left as soon as he sat down even though they weren't finished eating. He and Rebecca began to apologize at the same time and then they both laughed. He asked her to go first. She apologized, and when she had finished, he did the same.

"Well, now that we've gotten that out of the way, let's be on friendly terms again. I promise not to ask you any more questions."

"It's all right if you do. I've gotten over missing my daughter quite as much as I did when I first came here, although if I begin talking about her too much I may start missing her again."

"I'm sorry that I caused that. I know how it is to miss someone...."

"Dr. Caine told me about your wife. I'm really sorry."

"Let's not talk about that either. I just came here to apologize for being too inquisitive."

"That's kind of you, Doctor, but you weren't too inquisitive."

"Matt."

"All right, Matt. But you don't need to be so careful around me anymore. I'm sorry I behaved so badly. I was just homesick and lonesome, I suppose."

"But you're from Minnesota."

"Oh, I suppose this will always be my home, but I live over there now."

"Over there being Tel Aviv?"

"Yes.

"I suppose it is a lot warmer over there."

"It is. But it's more than just the warmer weather. Linda and Jim call it home now and I suppose I'll stay there with them when I go back until Bill and me are married."

When he didn't respond, she explained. "Linda is the mother of Olivia's father and Jim is her husband."

He didn't answer and she said, "I don't think we can carry on a conversion without you asking any questions. So please, go ahead."

"Well, if you insist."

"I do."

"Your fiancé, is he from over there?"

"No. He's from here; from the South. He was born in Kentucky."

"Does he work over there then?"

"Yes. Some of the time."

"Does he travel a lot?"

"Yes. Quite a bit."

"I suppose he must enjoy his work if he likes to travel."

"He does. But we didn't want to be separated Except for that, I think he enjoys it most of the time."

Dr. Matthew Avery decided to leave it there and after a few more exchanges, he apologized again and excused himself. He wished he could stay there with her longer, much longer, but he had to reconcile himself to the fact that she was already taken. It would do him no good to try and take her away from someone else, although he felt that it would be worth it if there was any chance of success.

CHAPTER FOUR

Moscow, Russia

Nicolai Olvestovsky, the assistant to the Deputy Foreign Minister, moved slowly down the hall toward the Office of the Foreign Minister, Andrei Gromyko. When he arrived, he paused, and then knocked softly on the door. The Foreign Minister's secretary opened the door and waved him in and then went to the door of the Foreign Minister's office and knocked on it. Andrei Gromyko was the head of the Foreign Ministry in the USSR and had served since 1939 in the diplomatic corps. He had entered the Foreign Service after the Great Purges of 1936-38, which opened up numerous positions and he had survived working for Josef Stalin.

He was the consummate socialist bureaucrat and viewed the interests of the state and party as his own. He had used the veto 79 times in his first ten years at the United Nations, compared to two vetoes for the next most active nation, which was China. For this, he was known as Mr. *Nyet*, by the other delegates. In spite of his reputation for intransigence, he was a pragmatic negotiator who believed that disarmament should be one of the major goals of socialism.

He was convinced that the USSR was a superpower and as such must be involved in any major settlement that took place anywhere in the world. At the present time he was trying to pacify Egypt, one of the USSR's client states in the Middle East. The President, Anwar Al-Sadat wanted to purchase the latest jet fighters from the Soviet Union and had been denied, due to the fear that he would immediately attack the state of Israel in an effort to retake the Sinai Peninsula.

"He is not well disposed this morning," she whispered to Nicolai.

Nicolai nodded and stood in a posture similar to parade rest.

"This matter with the spy master from Israel has interfered with his ability to concentrate on his other work which he considers more important," she said softly.

Nicolai nodded again and lowered his eyes. It was a question that he often found himself caught up in, much to his dismay; which official should come to the office of another official? Schedules were tight and a significant amount of time could be wasted sitting in someone else's office waiting for them to find time to deal with the problem that involved them both. Ordinarily it was the lower bureaucrat that reported to their superior without questioning how much time it might take to meet with them.

But Nicolai's superior, Deputy Foreign Minister, Vassily Vostorev, often chose to engage in a battle of wills with higher ranking members of the bureaucracy including his own boss, Andrei Gromyko. And as the assistant to the Deputy Foreign Minister, he, Nicolai Olvestovsky, was inevitably caught in the middle.

"Where is he?"

"Comrade Olvestovsky is here, sir."

"I don't mean him," Gromyko responded angrily. "Where is Vostorev? Go and get him, Olvestovsky. No, don't bother to call him. I want him here now."

Nicolai sped out of Gromyko's office and ran down the hall, dodging people adeptly as he had many times before. He bounded down the stairs two at a time and arrived at the Office of the Deputy Foreign Minister and informed him that the Foreign Minister wanted him in his office right away. Vassily Vostorev arose and began walking slowly towards the Foreign Minister's office, stuffing his pipe with tobacco as he went. *He is too young to smoke a pipe*, Nicolai thought. *It makes him look as though he is trying to appear more mature than he really is. But he would not listen to me. He is too young to take advice on matters like that, so I will not take the risk of trying to tell him.*

"Where have you been, Vassily?"

"I thought you were too busy to meet on this subject now, Comrade."

Andrei Gromyko bristled at being called Comrade instead of being addressed as Foreign Minister, but he ignored it. *Just as I have ignored many things from this pup*, he thought. Vostorev rankled him because Gromyko was sure that Vostorev harbored thoughts about being more intelligent than his boss. *A university degree, such as a doctorate, does not make you more intelligent*, Gromyko thought, gritting his teeth. *I am as well educated as him even though I attended technical schools. I also ran some of them later. And he has none of my experience. There were only a few universities where you could study for a doctorate in my day, and during the war most of them had been burned by the Germans.*

"This spy master from Israel—what has the surveillance of his contacts revealed about him?"

"The KGB reports that nothing more of substance has been uncovered yet, so we are no closer to learning what his recruits are after now, Andrei."

There he goes again; this time addressing me by my first name in front of these minions. But I will not correct him now. That would make me look petty. There will be a proper time to take care of him later on, he thought.

"What do we know about him?"

"We have evidence that he has been schooled extensively by the Israeli Intelligence Service to uncover activities that we are engaged in that would be of interest to them."

"Such as?"

"The most important thing as far as the Israelis are concerned is what type of access the Arab nations have to certain strategic military equipment."

"You say there is evidence that he has been trained by them to spy on us. What sort of evidence?"

"Indirect evidence."

"What do you mean, indirect?"

"Just that, indirect evidence."

"Don't tell me that! Don't say that word again! Now tell me how you know that he is here to undertake illegal acts of spying on us. The Israelis have been careful in the past not to send anyone over here unless they have the best of cover."

When Vostorev did not answer immediately, Gromyko dismissed his secretary and Nicolai, Vostorev's assistant. He confiscated the notes his secretary had taken and tore them up in front of the four of them.

"We don't want any record of this conversation. You are not to divulge anything you have heard to anyone, do you understand?"

They both nodded and scurried away. Gromyko then invited Vostorev into his office and closed the door. *Start slowly*, he reminded himself. *You can always shout at him when you have finished dressing him down. Too much shouting, especially at first, makes it less effective.*

"Now, Vassily, tell me how you know that about Isaac Ben-Chaim."

"I'm afraid I cannot, Comrade."

"What do you mean, you cannot? Do you realize who you are talking to?"

"Yes, Comrade, but…."

"Don't call me Comrade! I am not your Comrade! I am the Foreign Minister and your direct superior! You are only a Deputy Minister. And if you ever address me by my first name again I will have you sent to one of the prison camps in Siberia! I am the highest authority in the Union of Soviet Socialist Republics on foreign policy and you are merely my subordinate and if you don't tell me what I want to know immediately, you will be opening envelopes tomorrow morning."

A thoroughly chastened Vassily Vostorev stood before him with his head bowed. He nodded slowly during Gromyko's tirade.

"I have a friend in the military who is a Jew and he has a contact in the Israeli military. His contact is a loyal Zionist but secretly he is also a dedicated Marxist. He drops a few important bits of information to my friend on an intermittent basis. My friend's name is Major Vladimir Kerensky."

"What is the Israeli's name?"

"I do not know, Foreign Minister."

"Does the KGB know about your friend's contact?"

"I don't know if he has told anyone else or not."

"Get your friend over here, within the hour. And if you are lying about not knowing the Israeli's name…to say that you will regret it would be a gross understatement."

"Yes, Minister."

Gromyko smiled when the door closed behind Vostorev. A reckoning with the young pup had come sooner than expected and without any thought about what he would say to him. It had worked better that way. *Perhaps I will make him take down his doctoral degree from the university that he has framed and hung on his office wall and have him put it in his desk drawer. Better yet, I should make him take it back to his apartment and keep it hidden there,* he thought.

It occurred to him that if the KGB had not learned about the Israeli in the IDF who was passing on information it would be good to keep it that way. An exclusive source could prove to be extremely valuable to the Foreign Service. *Now what am I going to do about this Israeli? He should already know that we have refused to sell Anwar Al-Sadat and the Egyptians any of our newest jet fighters. What else does he want to know? He knows that we sell arms to Syria and many countries in the Middle East.*

One thing about this imbroglio is certain. We cannot afford to be viewed as anti-Semitic to any degree if we are going to continue to be accepted as an international movement. Other ethnic groups will begin to question our integrity. That's why we have laws that prescribe the death penalty for anti-Semitism. Even though that Stalin was one of the biggest anti-Semites of them all; publicly spouting the party line about how strictly we oppose anti-Semitism while raging against Jews in private.

But the current members of the Politburo would not care about whether we are viewed as being anti-Semitic or not, especially Leonid Ilyich Breznev, the General Secretary of the Communist Party. I am the one saddled with the responsibility of presenting the USSR to the world as a peace-loving nation. There must be a way to find this Israeli spy and deal with him, he thought. *It is not a question of stopping him from gathering information because he does not gather information himself. It is a question of stopping the people he recruits from stealing information and selling it to the Israelis.*

They have someone ready for him to recruit when he comes here and he must be very persuasive since is he is so successful, Gromyko thought. *I think it is the money he is able to offer that convinces them. He seems to have an endless supply of money. His network is difficult to penetrate. Another war is coming in the Middle East; Sadat is determined to have revenge for 1967. I need a source to find out how the Israelis are planning to defend themselves and prosecute this next war.*

I wonder if Dmitri Sheshanoff would be willing to help me. I have not spoken with him in years but surely he would be able to give me some assistance with this. He wants to sell the Egyptians surface to air missiles since he cannot sell them the latest jet fighters. He will need my help to do that. I could take care of both issues this way. This would be a means of making a great deal of money for the state by selling SAMS to Egypt. Then perhaps Dmitri would use his sources to find out more about what the Israelis are planning.

I'll contact Dmitri and met him somewhere. Sevastopol would be a good place. It would be nice to go there and relax on the beach for a few days. If he will leave Monaco and come back to Russia for any reason, it would be to spend a few days in the Crimea. My wife will be pleased if I take her to the Crimea. Our anniversary is coming soon and we can go there to celebrate and I'll talk to Dmitri about SAMS and mention this spy that needs to be dealt with. He may know something about him that we don't.

The Sniper

Grigori Morostev paused after shaving and put two pills in his mouth; then he took another large drink of vodka and threw his head back while he swallowed them. They did not stop the pain but they made it less severe and thus more bearable. He stared at himself in the mirror and came to the same conclusion as he always did. At fifty, he looked much older. When he turned away from the mirror, his body reminded him that it felt even older. His joints ached continuously and his shoulder throbbed day and night and the only thing that relieved it was ice, applied directly to it.

But with something to dull the pain, he could make it through the day. The worst torment he suffered came because of the memories that constantly flooded his mind. He relived the events they brought back during the day and at night they invaded his sleep and could not be stopped by thinking about something else. The memories that came at night were in charge and there was nothing he could do about it. As a result, he slept fitfully and wished for daybreak when he woke up at night. During the day and all night long, he relived the events of the Great Patriotic War, moment by moment.

In vivid detail he saw every battle, each man that he shot, the comrades that he saw dying, the times that he was wounded. It all came back to him just as though it was happening for the first time. He asked the physicians that treated him if it would ever stop. Not completely, they said, but the memories would diminish with time. For him, they never did. He knew that the anguish was caused by what he had done in the war. He had killed 417 Germans during the Great Patriotic War, most of them from over 300 meters away.

He had been designated as a *Hero of the Soviet Union,* but his papers had been lost in transit during the fighting, and he was never accorded the title. He knew there had been other snipers who had as many kills as him—Vladimir Pchelintsev, who fought with him at Leningrad, had accounted for over 400 enemy losses. He had heard of a German sniper with over 500 kills who had been killed by the famous Russian woman sniper, Lyudmila Pavlichenko. She had over 300 confirmed kills herself. *Women made the best snipers,* he thought. *They were more patient.*

After the war was over, he decided that all of the awards that had been given were meaningless and brought no advancement. There was only the occasional recognition a few times a year, the most notable being on May Day. He had only one means of keeping himself off the assembly line in some factory; that was his ability to shoot straight. He disappeared into the small, rural communities like the one that he was raised in. After a determined search, he finally made contact with a leader of one of the criminal organizations known as *vorovstoy mir,* the "thieves' world," who wanted to use his services.

After he eliminated the first target successfully, he was able to attract work from other members of the *vorovstoy mir*. He saved most of what he made by shooting members of the "thieves world." The remainder of the compensation was enough to keep him in a state akin to prosperity. There was a strict code of conduct among the "thieves-in-law" and the most important rule was that no one who had served in the army or worked for the state bureaucracy could ever be a member of any of the syndicates. This changed after the death of Stalin in 1953 when cooperation with corrupt officials became necessary for the members of the syndicates to continue their criminal activities.

Since he was a *Hero of the Soviet Union* on paper, the *vory v zakone*, the elite members of the "thieves-in-law" who ran the crime syndicates, would not allow anyone like him to join their organizations. He never wanted to join any of these groups of criminals because assassinating their members was best done by someone outside the syndicates. When he eliminated several members of two rival gangs, the leaders did not know who killed their members; only that they had paid him to kill the members of the rival gang.

He had carried out 46 assassinations since the war, most of them members of various syndicates that were a part of the *vorovstoy mir*. For him, it was much less disturbing than living in the muddy bunkers during the war had been; especially since he did not have to listen to his comrades cry out as they died. Even so, he frequently tired of shooting members of the thieves' world and determined not to do it again. He would go to Sevastopol in the Crimea and relax on the beaches, but after a while he would need money and be forced to go back and resume killing again.

At least tracking a new target consumed him so much that the pain from his memories was forced to the background while he was carrying out the assignment. Now he was traveling to Leningrad to find out about a new assignment; one that he knew would test his skill. He would do this job and then push it into the back of his mind to join the other ghosts that lived there.

CHAPTER FIVE

Chop-Chop Square

The flight to Riyadh was uneventful and as Bill gazed out over the barren landscape all he could see was sand. Saudi Arabia was a desert and it was at the peak of summer when the heat was the most oppressive, moderated only by the lack of humidity in the interior. The next plane that Faisal and Khalisah could catch had no other seats available so Bill had to wait for a later flight. When his plane touched down at the Riyadh Airport, he claimed his luggage and headed outside to find a cab. He chose one and decided to go with the meter rather than haggling about a set price.

He needed to change a portion of his dollars into Saudi riyads somewhere other than the airport, so he asked his driver, a Pakistani, to stop at the first bank they encountered. As they drove through the crowded downtown, they passed As-Suffaat, Deira Square, next to the Great Mosque, where there were many people assembled.

"What's that all about?"

"Oh, that is *Chop-Chop Square* and this is Friday."

"And what does that mean?"

"A beheading."

"A beheading? When?"

"Right after noon prayers."

"Who's it going to be?"

"A criminal."

"What's the crime?"

"It could be a number of things."

"Such as?"

"Apostasy, armed robbery, drug trafficking, witchcraft, adultery, rape, trying to overthrow the al-Saud, and murder, of course."

"Isn't that a bank on the left?"

"We can stop there if you want, but Westerners are sometimes dragged to the front row to watch."

"Why is that?"

"To shame the prisoner."

"Seems like losing your head would be shame enough. Go on to the next one then. You're right. I don't want to watch a beheading. Especially not from the front row."

"Are you hungry?"

"Yes, come to think of it, I am."

"Do you like curry and rice? My brother has a restaurant that has some of the best food in Riyadh. Better than the fancy restaurants that will charge you much, much more."

Patel's restaurant turned out to be housed in a rather dilapidated building, but the Pakistani and Indian cuisine was delicious. It was as good as Bill could have gotten in any of the best restaurants. He thought of the barbeque place in Tel Aviv and Grebel's maxim: "...the more rustic the building, the better the barbeque." The food was good at Patel's; he could eat it three times a day. When the owner asked him where he was going to stay, he answered that he would stay at a hotel. It turned out that the owner had a room "to let" behind the restaurant.

It was not large or particularly well-furnished, but it was clean. He decided to take it. Then Bill noticed a well-worn automobile parked behind the restaurant and asked about renting it. He struck a deal with Sinta Patel for a little less than he could have rented a new vehicle from a rental agency. Now he was as unobtrusive as it was possible to be, he thought. *Except for the fact that I'm a Westerner who doesn't speak Arabic.* Khalisah had told him that there were numerous people from many countries working in Saudi Arabia because of the oil boom.

Huge deposits of oil and gas had been discovered in the 1930s and the need for workers in every occupation had swelled the population by almost two million, she said. Bill knew that Friday was the holy day for Muslims and many businesses in Riyadh began observing it by closing on Thursday as well. The faithful fasted all day on Friday and then broke their fast with a meal after dark. Bill spent the weekend studying the language book he had brought and practiced using Arabic by conversing with Patel's young sons.

On Monday, he called the number Faisal had given him and when he came to the phone he asked Bill if he had eaten. When Bill said yes, Faisal invited him for the evening meal which did not begin until after eight o'clock. He agreed and then went to his room, laid down and fell asleep immediately. When he awoke, he showered and changed clothes and started for the address they had given him. The traffic was a nightmare as many of the drivers on the road were workers from parts of the world where there were no large cities.

They tended to drive by using their horn and weaving in and out of traffic ignoring the signal lights and signs posted along the road. The older vehicle he had rented from Patel now seemed to be a better choice for this type of driving. He arrived without a mishap although he had numerous encounters that could have easily turned into an accident. When he turned into the drive that led up to the address he had been given, he was amazed at the size of the residence. It was more like a palace than a home. Bill supposed that it housed an extended family, one that might include as many as three dozen members.

He parked his car in the circular drive next to two Mercedes and a Rolls Royce and rang the doorbell and was shown inside by a well coiffured major domo. He was ushered into a huge room with a vaulted ceiling full of family members waiting to begin the evening meal. Faisal came to meet him and that seemed to be all of the endorsement that was needed and no one paid any attention to him after that. No one spoke to him during the meal except Faisal, and Bill was relieved that he seemed to be relegated to the role of a student who was a friend of the youngest member of the family.

When he asked Faisal about Khalisah, he said that her and all of the other women ate in separate quarters and did not come where the men were dining. After a lengthy meal consisting of many courses, everyone adjourned to various parts of the house. Bill strolled over to the large set of French doors leading to the patio and gazed out. After a few minutes he looked up and saw

Khalisah descending the staircase, dressed in the traditional garb of an *abaya* in the form of a *caftan*. It had gold embroidery on the sleeves, across the chest, and around the bottom.

Her face was covered with a *niqab*, a veil covering all but her eyes. When she came to the bottom of the stairs she turned, lowered the *niqab* and smiled at him. The man coming after her observed them and then grimaced as a look of discernment appeared on his face. He recognized immediately that Faisal's friend had not come to see him at all; he had come to see Khalisah. Bill realized that he must be a close relative, most likely her father. Now the question was, what would he do about it? He did not hesitate but walked directly over to Bill and addressed him in impeccable English with an Oxford accent.

"How are you? I hope you are enjoying your visit. Is there anything we can do to make your stay more pleasant?"

"Thank you, sir. I am doing well. Everything has been very pleasant. This is my first visit to your country and I am enjoying it very much."

"Excuse me for not introducing myself first. I am Faisal Abdul Aziz Ibn Abd al-Saud."

"It is a pleasure to meet you, sir. I am Charles Harper."

"Are you attending Oxford then with my son, Faisal?"

"Oh, no sir. We met in London. We started discussing sports and struck up a friendship," Bill said, trying to head off any more questions.

"Yes. Faisal is fond of sports. He participated in soccer and crew this year, I believe."

"Yes. And he promised to teach me how to play cricket at some point," Bill said with a laugh.

That seemed to allay any suspicions that Prince Faisal might have had about Bill. He didn't bother to ask him where he was attending school. To him, he was just another friend of his son and if he was here to see Khalisah that could be dealt with quite easily later on. He assured Bill that every courtesy would be extended to him and took his leave to greet his other guests. Bill was greatly relieved that he had avoided giving himself away to the head of the family. He had no educational credentials and decided that he needed to ask Grebel about getting Itzhak Kahan to produce a more impressive resume for him. He was going to need more documentation if he was going to convince people like Prince Faisal Abdul Aziz Ibn Abd al-Saud that he was genuine.

An Assault on the al-Saud

Bill visited Faisal again on Tuesday and received the cricket lesson that he had been promised and gave young Faisal instruction about using a shotgun to hit the clay pigeons used as targets. Faisal invited Bill for the evening meal on Wednesday and asked him to be there at 7:45 pm. When he arrived and entered the great room there were many familiar faces. He ventured to ask Faisal about Khalisah again but he was noncommittal. She stays with the women, he said. Bill understood why she wanted to leave Arabia; women were virtually invisible in the Kingdom of al-Saud.

After the meal Bill went through the French doors and out on to the huge patio, which was surrounded by native vegetation. There were only a few men there and they were talking quietly. Bill occasionally recognized a word but could not understand what they were talking about. He listened for the sounds of the night but everything was quiet. He felt more comfortable here than inside so he took a seat and stretched out and relaxed. After a while he felt sleepy so he stood up and walked away from the house. It would be rude to fall asleep and have your host find out.

The night was quiet and whenever he encountered silence like this his mind was drawn back to Vietnam. It had been quiet like this when the massacre had occurred there and all three dozen workers of the Boucher Construction Company except him were killed. He needed some noise at night to feel comfortable now. He found himself scouring the horizon anytime he went out at night and there was no moon. In Vietnam it had been the lack of animal and bird sounds that had first aroused his fears. He listened and it seemed to be too quiet just as it had been that night in Vietnam.

He had become accustomed to the sounds of Riyadh by now and he searched his mind for what was missing now. It wasn't animal sounds. It was the sound that defined how most of the foreign workers drove in Riyadh. The sound of automobile horns was missing. That meant that there was no traffic on the road in front of the home of Prince Faisal. There had been traffic at this time of night when he was there last night and there should be traffic now. Why? Was the street blocked? Was there an accident? He did not have much time to decide.

As he moved back toward the house he caught a glimpse of something moving along the horizon. There was little vegetation to conceal movement out there where there should be nothing moving. Then he saw another shadow shift; and then another. He turned and moved quickly toward the house. There was no time to hesitate now. He had to get to Prince Faisal and get him out of the house even if he had to drag him. He entered the French doors and asked the first man he saw where Faisal was. Not young Faisal; his father, he shouted. The elderly man pointed towards the corner. Bill ran to Prince Faisal and grabbed his arm and pulled him toward the door.

"What are you doing?" Prince Faisal demanded.

"Men are coming to enter your house; at least three of them."

"How do you know that?" Faisal shouted. He was obviously very angry now.

"Come with me. We have to run now." He grabbed Faisal by the front of his robe and dragged him through the front door. Then he shoved him as hard as he could. Faisal lost his balance and staggered forward trying to keep from falling. Bill grabbed him again and pulled him along as he ran to the side of the house.

"Why are you doing this?" Faisal asked.

"Quiet! Don't talk. Whisper if you have to say something."

"Why are we doing this?" Faisal whispered.

"It's too quiet. There are no sounds."

"What sounds?"

"Traffic sounds. Your street has been blocked.

"Why?"

"I don't know. I just know that I saw men coming toward your house."

Bill froze when he heard noise on the other side of the wadi.

"Wait. Stop! Get down on the ground," he whispered. They lay motionless and could hear voices a few meters away. They were speaking in Arabic but Bill could not catch any of the words. When they could no longer hear them, Bill motioned for Faisal to follow him and they ran, crouching low to avoid detection.

"Now we have to run for it!" They ran parallel to the main road in front of the house. Faisal showed surprising endurance and when they had to stop he gasped for breath and asked Bill what he thought was happening.

"They were coming for you. Any idea why?"

They heard gunfire in the distance in the direction of Faisal's house and Bill insisted that they start running again.

"But I have to go see what is happening to my family!"

"It's too dangerous for you to go back. Start running!"

They continued running as fast as they could until they had to slow down and then jogged until they finally slowed to a fast walk.

"Where's the safest place for you?"

"We need to go right here."

"Listen! I think I heard something just now—back there behind us. Someone may be following us. You go ahead and I'll wait here to try and stop them if I can. Go! Start running again!"

Faisal obeyed this time without hesitation and began running as fast as he could through the wadi. Bill saw a figure closing rapidly and he crouched behind a bush until a man in camouflage came running through the wadi. He stopped momentarily as he delivered a burst from his automatic weapon at Faisal. He started running again but Bill jumped him from behind and the fall knocked his weapon away.

Bill kept him pinned to the ground and searched frantically for the pistol he knew he was carrying. *The small of the back; that's where they carry them,* he thought. He fumbled until he found it but as he ripped it from the belt the man reached back with his hand and grabbed it. They struggled and the gun flew out of their hands and clattered on the rocks. His opponent lay still and Bill knew he was gathering his strength to throw him off. He was smaller than Bill but he had no doubt that this man could easily kill him with his bare hands.

When he arched his back and came up Bill whirled and moved away before he could get his hands on him. If he let this man get him in his grasp, Bill knew it would mean a sudden and violent death for him. The wiry man circled seeking to land a blow on him and Bill threw up his hands as if he was practiced in martial arts. He had to have a knife, Bill knew, and when he got close enough he would pull it and finish him off quickly. Bill let him get closer but when his assailant reached for his knife it had shifted on his belt and it took him a few seconds longer to find it and draw it.

That was enough time for Bill to act. He reached down to the ground and when the attacker lunged at him with his knife, Bill threw two handfuls of dirt in his eyes. Then he turned and ran. The attacker chased Bill, trying to brush the dirt from his eyes but he ran into a small bush and fell. Bill ran down the hill towards the street and after a quarter of a mile he turned quickly and looked back. He could not see him but he was sure he hadn't given up. He felt certain that he had gone back to retrieve his automatic weapon. He saw a police car in the distance and ran toward it. He saw Faisal bent over and out of breath explaining what had happened to the policeman.

"Get down!" he shouted. "Get behind the police car!"

They both leaped behind the car as a hail of bullets riddled it. The assailant did not even bother to fire at Bill. He had seen Faisal and was determined to kill him. He ran toward them, reloading as he ran. One of the policemen began firing at him with his hand gun so he moved behind an embankment. Then he rose up and unloaded another volley at the policeman He had them outgunned and he was going to keep firing until he could get close enough to Faisal to shoot him.

"Run Faisal, run!" Bill shouted from his cover.

He could see Faisal start running, keeping the police car between him and the gunman. The gunman became furious now and sprayed the police car trying to shoot over it at Faisal. Two other police cars pulled up and they began firing in the direction of the gunman. They were not foolish enough to charge him but one of them fired a tear gas canister at his position. It fell behind the embankment but there was no movement. He had already left. One of the policemen was wounded and they rushed him to the hospital.

"I was with Faisal," Bill told the police. "Someone was trying to shoot both of us."

They took him to the station with them and he began to give them a deposition about what had happened when he was interrupted by another officer. Prince Faisal had called and ordered them to release him; he would give them a statement himself tomorrow. Bill learned from the officer that three people had been killed at Faisal's home: two bodyguards and one other man who resembled Prince Faisal.

CHAPTER SIX

A Meeting in Moscow

Isaac Ben-Chaim, ("son of life") began his day with morning prayers followed by the recitation of psalms. He always concluded with the passage that read:

By the rivers of Babylon, we sat down, yea, we wept when we remembered Zion. We hanged our harps on a willow in the midst thereof. For there they that carried us away captive required of us a song, saying, 'Sing us one of the songs of Zion.' But how can we sing the Lord's song in a strange land?

How indeed? He pondered the history of the Jews who had been scattered among many nations for generations, disliked, always viewed with suspicion, and often despised. Now that they were back in their own land, Isaac Ben-Chaim, born Iosef Storchov in Leningrad, was determined to do whatever it took to see that the Jewish people remained there. As a young boy, he had done everything from carrying water and ammunition to tending to the wounded during the war in 1948. He had progressed beyond that and now oversaw the largest intelligence gathering system ever assembled in the Soviet Union.

It was comprised almost entirely of civilians and although the majority of them were "sleepers," the ones who were active had achieved notable successes. During the Six Day War his informants had relayed information almost moment by moment regarding the disposition of the members of the Politburo about aiding the coalition of Arab states attacking Israel. The unanimous assessment was that the Soviets would not intervene in the war under any circumstances, no matter how successful the IDF was or how much territory they took.

Instead the Soviets desired an end to the war, especially after the Egyptian Army was routed. It was not because they wanted to see the Arab nations lose or to preserve the nation of Israel; they had their own reasons for wanting to keep the region inflamed. If one side won an overwhelming victory it would reduce Soviet influence in the area. It was imperative that Tel Aviv knew what the Soviet position was and Ben-Chaim's spies had reported the conversations of some of meetings of the Politburo almost word for word.

This was the work of the most valuable mole of all, Nicolai Olvestovsky, the assistant to Vassily Vostorev, the Deputy Foreign Minister under Andrei Gromyko. Neither Gromyko nor Vostorev were members of the Politburo, but Vostorev was often drafted to stand by during a crisis in case the members needed information quickly about the situation in question. Vostorev possessed a vast reservoir of information about the Middle East. Vostorev also took Nicolai Olvestovsky to every meeting he attended. In the meetings where he was present, Olvestovsky was able to pass on every conversation that the members of the Politburo had about the Six Day War.

The American shipping magnate, Jacob Messner, an Armenian Jew whose operational headquarters were in London, was the millionaire who funded Isaac Ben-Chaim's organization. *Mossad* reluctantly provided some secret funding out of a discretionary account but it was just enough for a bare bones operation. It was Messner's money that did the trick. All of those people that they located with *Mossad's* money had to be bought and that was where Messner's millions came in. He seemed to have an endless supply of money that he was willing to inject into Ben-Chaim's operation.

Most of the people they bought weren't interested in the preservation of the state of Israel; they just wanted to see the Soviet Union damaged and get paid for it. Passing along information was the safest way to do it. If they were caught actively attempting to do harm to the USSR, it would mean torture and death. The information they passed on ranged from useless and mildly interesting, to valuable, and in some cases, invaluable. Far above anything that was available to the other informants was the information that came through Nicolai Olvestovsky. In times past that information had been the salvation of the nation.

No one knew that Olvestovsky was a Jew. He had not been circumcised and he did not learn of his Jewish origins until he was an adult. Ben-Chaim recounted in his mind the story that Olvestovsky had told him. At his birth he had been taken away from his mother with her family's consent. She was only sixteen at the time and she had become pregnant by a Russian boy. Nicolai was raised by his father's family and never told anything about his mother or her family. Once he was grown, he spent two years looking for her and when he discovered where she was, he went to pay her a visit, Nicolai told him.

Her husband was at work and he pretended to be a family friend from her hometown. He had decided not to reveal who he was. He just wanted to see her. Her life was here now; she had other children still at home and he felt sure that her husband had not been informed about him. They talked for a while about news from Leningrad and other things of little importance and when he finally excused himself to leave she looked at him and said, "I had a son that I lost when he was born. He would be about your age now."

Has she recognized me so quickly? What gave me away? Surely not anything I said, he thought.

"They took him away from me, I would not have given him up for anything, but they took him from me."

"I'm sorry. Do you think he had a good life even though he was taken away from you?"

She displayed a wry smile and said, "Yes, I believe he had a good life. That did not stop my pain though. I was very young and it seemed as though my life had ended when they took him away from me. I have ached for him all these years."

"I'm sure he missed you greatly also."

"I knew I could not find him myself, so my greatest desire was that he would search for me when he was grown."

"I'm certain that he felt the same."

"Thank you for coming. Must you go now?"

"Yes, I'm afraid so."

"Will you come back again?"

"If you wish."

"Next month?"

"Yes, I can come then if you like."

"I will look forward to seeing you again next month. Please don't disappoint me."

"I won't. Good bye."

She leaned over and kissed him on both cheeks and whispered, "Good bye." He could see tears in her eyes but she was smiling radiantly. *It was best this way*, he thought. Her family will not be disrupted and he could get acquainted with her gradually. He needed to think of a reason for coming to see her if someone became inquisitive about his visits. He might pass as a family member, a cousin perhaps.

Ben-Chaim was keenly aware that Nicolai Olvestovsky was their most valuable informant by far. Indeed the entire organization revolved around him. He could not imagine any other informant being in a better position than Olvestovsky. Ben-Chaim had met Nicolai Olvestovsky early in the formation of the network of informants when he had only recruited about a half dozen people. One of them called for Ben-Chaim to come to Moscow to recruit Olvestovsky. He flew there in disguise at considerable risk. He met Nicolai Olvestovsky in a dingy apartment in a dismal part of Moscow.

It was all dismal, he thought, *but this part of the city seemed more drab and dingy than the res*t. He asked Nicolai if he was willing to pass on information that he had access to and why he would risk doing so. Nicolai affirmed that he was willing and told Ben-Chaim that he had recently learned about his mother's family. Ben-Chaim responded by asking him, "but what motivated you to agree to spy on your country?"

Nicolai paused for a moment and then slowly articulated his reason for doing so.

"It is simple," he said, "the Soviets are responsible for all of the upheaval in the Middle East. The fighting there is a direct result of their policies."

"You're certain of that?"

"I know because I am able to observe it every day. Their goal is to create unrest among those who are disenfranchised and disrupt the established governments, giving the USSR a means of influencing their decision making. It is the same method they use everywhere."

Isaac asked him if he thought oil was the reason for Soviet attempts at intervention there.

"It is a big part of it," he said, "although there is an abundance of oil in the Soviet Union. I think the primary reason is that the leaders in the Soviet Union have always wanted to have greater influence in the Mediterranean and to exert more control over the Suez Canal. Another reason for doing this, which is more important to me personally, is because of the treatment of the Jews here. The official policy is that anti-Semitism is strictly forbidden according to the laws of the Soviet Union. But in reality, if someone is Jewish, they are discriminated against both socially and professionally. In many cases, harassment and persecution of Jews is ignored by the authorities and it is often encouraged by local officials and sometimes even carried out by their subordinates. I want to work against such a system."

"In that case," said Ben-Chaim, "we will give you a contact who will supply you with everything you need to pass information on to us. There will be only one contact, the safest one that we have. To keep your identity hidden, only the two of us will know about you. Her name is Oksana Belachev and she can pass as your love interest."

"How will I meet her?" Asked Nicolai.

"She will approach you," said Ben-Chaim. "She is descended from the Tatars and will identify herself by the comment, *Scratch a Russian and you will find a Tatar*. You will reply, *Yes, but it is peace that brings us together now*. She has never been used by us or anyone else before so she is as free from suspicion as it is possible to be in this paranoid police state. But both of you must be extremely discreet because if you are found out we can do nothing to help you. You must not get emotionally involved with her, nor she with you."

"I understand."

"It will cloud your judgment and make it more likely that you will be apprehended. Inform us immediately if you decide to marry someone here. I recommend against it but if you must, we need to know. Eventually suspicion may arise because you and her are together often and yet never become involved beyond friendship. We will need to change to another contact then. But that is in the future and we cannot make any decision about that now."

"I agree."

"Do you have anything to give us now? No? Go to St. Basil's Cathedral when you do. On Saturday night at 1900 hours, stand in front of the statues of Dmitry Pozharsky and Kuzma Minin who led the counter attack against the Polish invasion in the seventeenth century. She will check there each week. Do you have any questions? Good. Then I must take my leave and I trust that the God of our fathers will give you wisdom and courage."

"*Do svidaniya*, Isaac."

"*Poka,* Nicolai."

Cairo, Egypt

In the chambers of the President of Egypt, Anwar Al-Sadat, a conversation took place between him and his Vice-President, Hosni Mubarak that fleshed out the plans for the long awaited attack on Israel.

"It is a brilliant plan, Anwar."

"Yes, I think so. Compliment the General Staff for their excellent work. I believe that we can retake the Sinai utilizing this concept if we execute it correctly."

"We will not overcommit with this plan. It will allow our troops to remain under the cover of the surface-to-air missiles that we have installed."

"How many more SAMS do we need for this, Hosni?"

"We have about half of the number we need."

"When can we expect to acquire the rest?"

"The arms dealer, Dmitri Sheshanoff, has promised the rest will be forthcoming shortly."

"Good. As soon as we have them I want us to be ready to put our plan of attack into operation."

"Excellent. What do you want me to do to expedite the execution of our plan?"

"It would be good if you paid our friend, Dmitri, a visit. Where is he staying now?"

"In Monaco, Anwar. He has been staying there for the last two years."

"Monaco, eh? That was never his style before."

"It's true, Anwar. He always kept a low profile. No one ever knew exactly where he was staying and he changed his location often. Now, it seems he does not worry about whether anyone knows his location or not."

"Well, as long as he can deliver the missiles. He has always been able to deliver what he has promised in the past. Who is he going to procure them from? The Soviet Union?"

"Undoubtedly. He has connections in the inner circle there. He has a good relationship with at least two members of the Politburo. Plus he is an old friend of Gromyko."

"Excellent. Go visit him then, Hosni, and see if you can speed things up."

"I'm not sure I can get him to go any faster. These things require time and patience. There is a very delicate balance involved when this much money and material are involved. Plus there is the need for secrecy and that is difficult to maintain under the best of conditions."

"Yes, that's true. But let him know that we need them as soon as possible so that the conditions don't change and affect the execution of our plan. You know that we are working on a schedule that requires that one thing follow closely after another once the plan is initiated. We must be able to set a start date first of all. Has the General Staff been able to come up with a possible date to initiate the plan on yet?"

"Anwar, they think that the Jewish holy day of *Yom Kippur* would be the best date to initiate the attack on."

"Uhm. That comes during the month of *Ramadan*. That will be of some concern to our own people. Does it seem that it would cost us a loss of support from any of the other nations because the date comes on *Yom Kippur*?"

"There would be some problems in that regard but they would be outweighed by the advantages of beginning the operation on this date."

"Then if that is the opinion of the planners let us proceed with that date as the time to launch the operation."

"Yes, Anwar. I will report that to the General Staff and then leave for Monte Carlo immediately."

"Good. Let me know as soon as you receive word of anything certain from Dmitri."

CHAPTER SEVEN

Charley Harper Uncovered

"Who are you, really, and what are you doing here?

Bill knew it would not do any good to try and evade the question. Prince Faisal already knew that Charley Harper was not who he said he was.

"I had you investigated. There was someone named Charles Harper at the Compton Oil Company but it is certainly not you since he left the company over a year ago. Yet you claim that you are him and are still working for them."

Since he knows my identity is false, Bill thought, *I am about to be expelled, or put into confinement and there will be no one to help me.*

"Why did you falsify your identity to come here? Just to see my daughter?"

"No."

"Then why?"

Bill stalled, trying to come up with a good story. *Why not tell the truth? It might work better than anything else. Just change who I am working for.*

"I was going to come here at some point. I happened to meet Faisal and Khalisah in the airport and things developed between us and I came at their invitation."

"Why were you going to come here?"

"It would compromise the reason I came here for if I tell you."

"Believe me; you're not leaving here until I know everything I want to know about you."

"If you insist. I was coming here to investigate the people who tried to assassinate you, and other groups like them."

"That seems unlikely. You don't even speak Arabic."

"There are enough English speakers here for me to find out what I want to know."

"I don't believe you. What other lies will you tell me?"

"I believe I saved your life a short while ago. If I had not done so, you would not be standing here now interrogating me like this. If I was here to do you or your family harm, would I have done that?"

"Who do you work for then?"

"I'm an American."

"And?"

"I work for them."

"Their government? I can easily find out if that is true."

"I work in an unofficial capacity."

"Who do you work for? What is his name?"

"He's retired."

"How is he able to send you here then, if he's retired?"

"He works through someone who is still in active service."

"I can find out who he is."

"No. You won't be able to. Look, if you try to check up on me, you won't find anything because I don't exist as far as anyone in our government is aware. You can look for me under the name Charles Harper or any other name and you won't find anyone. It has been set up that way so no one will be able to uncover me. I'm telling you this because I have to trust you now. You can do whatever you want to with me, but there is no way to connect me to anyone who works for the U. S. government."

Faisal paused briefly, shook his head and replied, "It sounds bizarre—completely ludicrous."

"Does it matter since you would be dead now if it hadn't been for me?"

"Yes. It matters. Everything like this matters. Who do you think was responsible for this?"

"I can't say. I can only report what I learn here."

"And you can't tell me?"

"I'm afraid not."

"Why not?"

"Because I don't know yet. But also because I don't work for you. If I find out anything about these assassins and tell you or anyone else that could compromise what I am trying to do here."

"I still don't believe you. I know who works for the CIA in this country."

"I don't work for them. There is no agency. There is only myself and two other men involved in this."

"Where does your information wind up then?"

"I'm not privy to that. I only get paid to find out what they want to know."

"Unbelievable."

"If you wish. What are you going to do then? About me?"

"I'm not sure now. But I don't want you to leave until I find out more about you."

"It won't do you any good to investigate me further. You can stop me but that would mean I won't be able to find out anything about these people."

Prince Faisal looked disgusted and waved Bill away with his hand. He had other priorities that were more pressing and he turned his attention to them now.

The Onset of Infatuation

Khalisah came running and jumped into Bill's arms and he held on to her to keep from falling backwards. There were two or three young men, members of the al-Saud, who were present but she seemed not to notice them.

"I want to thank you so much for saving my father's life!"

"I did it as much to save my life as his."

"You're just being modest. But that doesn't matter. You saved him and I want you to know how grateful we all are; even if he doesn't seem to feel that way. At least not yet. We know what you did and we love you for it. You are wonderful!"

"I'm sorry that the others couldn't be saved."

"They were all fine men; the bodyguards and my cousin. It is horrible what those murderers did!"

"I'm glad you're all right. Where were you when it happened?"

"With the other women. One of the killers looked into the room but didn't come in since there were no men present."

"I'm glad you weren't harmed."

Khalisah continued to hold on to him and he thought about how frightening an experience it must have been for her. She didn't see the murders taking place but she heard the gunshots and the screams. He needed to ask her if she knew why something like this would occur. He slowly unraveled her arms from around his neck on the pretense of wanting to sit down on the couch nearby.

He wanted to keep her trust without allowing anything serious to develop between them if it was possible. He felt he had struck the mother lode here in Riyadh by developing this friendship with the family of Prince Faisal. He only hoped that Prince Faisal would not be able to find out anything about him.

"Why would they want to kill your father?"

"He is a wealthy and powerful man and one of the top dozen or so leaders in the state."

"What does he do in his leadership role?"

"He is Minister of Finance."

"And who would want to kill him because of that?"

"I don't know. There could be many reasons but right now I don't know who it could be."

"Do you think anyone will take credit for the attack?"

"I don't know. I don't think that it is likely though."

"Why not?"

"It could be dangerous for them to do so."

"Why is that?"

"Our police and security forces know who all of these groups are and they know most of the members in them."

"So they could arrest them right away?"

"Yes. Most of them. I have heard my father and others say that there are a few of these groups that have cells that do not know about the existence of the other cells in their organization. That way, they cannot betray the other members."

He talked with Khalisah for almost an hour and then left to return to his room at Patel's. She had clamored to go with him but he did not want to do anything to make his position in Riyadh even more precarious. He was looking over his phrase book when he heard a knock on the door. When he opened it, Khalisah and Faisal were standing there and she burst into the room without asking. She looked dismayed when she gazed around the room.

"This is where you are staying?"

"This is it," Bill answered.

"I thought you were staying at a hotel!"

"I was planning to, but the cab driver brought me here to his brother's restaurant to eat and he showed me this room. I was too tired to go look for a hotel so I took it."

"But this is….it's terrible, even for an American."

"Thanks, Khalisah. I need some encouragement."

"But you can't stay here!"

"Oh, the food makes up for it," answered Bill.

"Oh, no. This is terrible. You should….you should be somewhere much nicer and more comfortable than here," Khalisah said.

"I'm sorry, Charley. She nagged me until I agreed to follow you here. She threatened to tell about some things that happened at the university if I didn't drive her here," Faisal said apologetically.

"Must have really been something," Bill responded.

"Oh, only a little incident with a girl," Faisal said.

"Little incident, hah! He went home with her and met her parents and wants to…." Khalisah said.

"Enough!" said Faisal.

"He has someone picked out for him also," Khalisah explained. "He has done everything he can to postpone it. It seems that she is not as pretty as me—or the English girl he fancies. He will be cut off if he refuses to fulfill his obligation and marry here."

"Can't you have more than one wife?" asked Bill.

"He must marry here first. Can you imagine a British girl agreeing to come here and move in as wife number two?"

"Not really," said Bill.

"I'm leaving now, Khalisah. Now that you've told Charley what you promised not to tell anyone."

"Don't worry, Faisal. Your secret's safe with me," Bill said.

"I have to go, Charley. You are coming to dine with us tonight, aren't you?"

"Yes, Khalisah. I'm coming. Even though it means missing Patel's curry and rice."

"You can't mean that. You could have stayed in a better place than here, couldn't you?"

"Yes. My expense account would have covered a hotel. I just like it here," Bill replied.

"Come early," Khalisah said. With that, she and Faisal left and Bill returned to his phrase book.

An Ulterior Motive

After the meal, Khalisah came looking for him and addressed him in a tone that he knew was not suitable for an Arab woman to address a man—even if the woman was a member of the al-Saud.

"You are going to leave that dismal place where you are living and move into our home."

"What?"

"I'll send someone for your things, so you can't run and hide somewhere. My father has agreed."

"How did you get him to agree to that?"

"I ran and jumped up on his lap like I did when I was a little girl. I asked him to let you move in here, since you saved his life. I told him that he needed you here to help protect him." *That would allow him to watch me closely and prevent me from leaving until he has learned everything he wants to know about me*, thought Bill.

"I don't even carry a handgun."

"He has bodyguards for that. You won't need a gun."

Bill realized that he had no choice. He had to move into Prince Faisal's home for now. But for how long?

"I have a special relationship with my father as his only daughter. I try not to take advantage of it very often, but in your case, I will use all of the leverage I have to get him to agree to keep you here."

She doesn't know that he was already planning to keep me here in Riyadh, but certainly not in his home. She must have a lot of influence with him, he thought.

"And not only that, he agreed to let me and Faisal take you to see the oil fields. So you will move in here and get rid of that dilapidated vehicle you have been driving. You and I and Faisal will have a Range Rover to drive and the two of you can take me shopping. I shopped regularly in Oxford and I miss it."

"Uhm." *Prince Faisal must be humoring her*, he thought, *since he knows I am not in the oil business.*

"What does *uhm*, mean?"

"I'm not sure."

"Don't think I am doing all of this just for you. I have an ulterior motive for doing this."

"I'm almost afraid to ask what it is."

"You are going to teach me to drive."

"You don't know how to drive? No. You wouldn't, would you?"

"And you are going to teach me. We will have to do it out of sight of everyone, but I think we can manage it. I will need to be able to drive when I move to England; although they do drive on the left side of the road there. Have you driven there? How difficult is it?"

"I've never driven there, but the Brits don't seem to have any difficulty. I don't think it would be too hard to master once you learn how to drive."

"You know, my father told me that he didn't have you figured out yet. That's strange."

"Why?"

"Because my father has everyone figured out. Usually right after meeting them. I wonder why you are different."

The Roots of Terrorism

Bill felt that now was the best time to find out as much as he could about the terrorist groups that might have been responsible for such an attack. It was still on everyone's mind and he felt that it would be easier now to get them to discuss it since it would not seem out of place for him to ask about it. He applied himself to the study of the Arabic language and in a little more than six weeks he was able to communicate with anyone who was patient enough to listen to him and prompt him when he needed help with a word. He decided that he had a facility for languages; French had come rather easily to him after some initial setbacks.

Once again he began using the immersion method and attempted to speak only Arabic. It was much more difficult this time and he often had to ask for help with a forlorn look on his face. He conversed mostly with the old men of the household. They were patient and enjoyed having someone spend time with them and talk to them. They also knew more about the extremists in the country than anyone else, except perhaps the security force.

He began to build a file containing the description of terrorist cells operating in the Arab world. Yitzhak Kahan had told him not to write anything down but keep it all in his head instead. He felt that it would be safe to record information here since he was working to insure the safety of Prince Faisal, even though Faisal didn't trust him. He formed a friendship with one of the older men, Muhammed Bin Ali Hussein al-Saud. He was Khalisah's great-uncle and was approaching ninety. Most of the information about the extremists came from him.

Much of it was outdated, Bill was sure, and some of the groups he told him about might not even exist anymore but it gave him a clearer understanding of the situation. He found Bin Ali to be sympathetic with the goals of many of the groups. He was a supporter of the Wahhabis, but he did not approve of slaughtering innocents to achieve results, as many of the extremists advocated now. He had seen a great deal of bloodshed in his youth and did not think that much had been accomplished after the fighting was over.

It soon became apparent to Bill that most of the money that financed the activities of Arab terrorist groups came from the al-Saud themselves. They would deny it, of course, but large sums of money in the form of charitable contributions from Saudi Arabia went around the world to develop mosques and schools devoted to the teachings of Muhammed Ibn Abd al-Wahhab. The al-Saud thus financed the education of individuals determined to see Sharia law spread across the world.

The al-Saud was paying for these radical organizations to flourish and carry out their violent plans. This meant that the al-Saud was paying for their followers to be taught to destroy those who stood in their way. The problem for the al-Saud was that many of these groups now thought that their patrons had become a part of the problem. They were too wealthy and had become too westernized and decadent and should be removed first. These groups were more than willing to bite the hand that fed them.

CHAPTER EIGHT

Rochester, Minnesota

Rebecca Lundstrom was so excited she was almost giddy. Linda and Jim McIntyre were coming for a visit and bringing Rebecca's daughter, Olivia. Jim was going to drive down to Blue Earth to pick up Rebecca's mother the day after they arrived. Rebecca had not taken any time off so she was allowed to miss Friday and have a long weekend when they came. After they arrived and checked into a hotel close to the clinic, Rebecca went there to greet them. She tried not to cry as she took Olivia into her arms after three months separation.

The next morning, Jim drove to Blue Earth and picked up Rebecca's mother, Mrs. Annike Sofia Solvang Lundstrom. She was packed and waiting for him, but as they drove back to Rochester he noticed that she seemed tired and listless. When they arrived she said that she needed a nap and let Rebecca put her to bed. She was tired, she said, and hadn't been sleeping well.

"Do you know a doctor here?" Jim asked.

"Yes. There are a number of them at the clinic," Rebecca responded.

"I think it would be good if you would call someone. She isn't well, Rebecca," said Linda.

Rebecca dialed the number to the clinic but hung up before it rang. "They are all have a full schedule and more patients than they can take care of," she said.

"I'll call my doctor in Riverside and get him to call someone here," Linda said.

"It will take a while to do that. I think she needs help right away. Do you know another physician here, Rebecca?" Jim asked.

"Yes. I do know one; a specialist in internal medicine."

"Then call him right away," Jim said.

She dialed Matthew Avery's office using the number that Dr. Caine had given her. When the receptionist answered she asked for him and in a few minutes he was on the phone.

"Hello, Matt. This is Rebecca."

"How are you? It's good to hear from you. Is something wrong or is this a social call?"

"It's my mother, Matt. I'm afraid she's very ill."

"What has she complained of?"

"She says she is very tired and she hasn't been able to sleep well lately."

"Has she complained of indigestion?"

"Yes."

"Does she have shortness of breath?"

"Yes."

"Does she have angina?"

"She said her arm had just begun to hurt."

"Go and give her two aspirin right now. I'll wait."

"Two aspirin? Linda is getting them for her right now."

"It sounds as though she has symptoms consistent with coronary heart disease, Rebecca. She certainly needs to be examined and have some tests run. She may be having a heart attack right now though. Has she ever had a heart attack before?"

"No."

"She needs to be taken to the hospital right now. I'll call an ambulance myself. I can get them there more quickly than you can. I'm a little further away from the hospital than they are but I'll meet them at the hospital. Just make her comfortable until the ambulance comes. Do you have any digitalis there by chance?"

"No."

"What hotel are you at and what's your room number?"

The Hilton. Room 224."

"I'm not far from there. I can beat the ambulance there. I'll bring some digitalis and other medication. As soon as we hang up, you call the ambulance so I can get there as soon as possible."

"Yes. I will. Goodbye."

When Matthew Avery arrived, he went straight into the bedroom and gave Annike Lundstrom an injection of digitalis.

"We need to run for it. Fifteen minutes can mean the difference between life and death." He gathered her up in his arms and moved quickly out of the door and down the stairs, not bothering to take the elevator. Jim followed him, running to keep up. They stretched her out in the back seat of Jim's car and he sped away following Matt's directions.

"I've called my friend, Henry Cosgrove, who is a heart surgeon and he is already at the hospital waiting for us," said Matthew Avery.

When they arrived, Henry Cosgrove was standing at the emergency entrance with some of the members of his surgery team. They took Annike Lundstrom directly to surgery and Matt called Rebecca to let her know what was being done. She asked if there was anything she could do. He told her no and offered to return with Jim and drive her back to the hospital. She agreed and waited for them to return. After Matt Avery was introduced properly to Jim and Linda McIntyre, he and Rebecca left in his Porsche and headed to the hospital.

He had the top down and didn't want to take the time to put it back up. Rebecca glanced at him as he drove and thought, *how handsome he is*. She had heard a rumor that he was a member of MENSA, the organization for those whose IQ scores ranked them in the top one percent of the population. To make conversation she asked him if he found it interesting to be a member of that group.

"Oh, no. I'm not a member anymore."

"Why not?"

"Well, those folks take it way too seriously."

And he is humble, reasonable, and personable. And very hurt and lonely. And much too interested in me, she thought.

"Matt, do you have some close friends who could help you during this time?" she asked.

"I've been so busy I've neglected to keep in touch with most of my good friends. I've heard from all of them but they're spread around the country. I still get phone calls from many of them though."

"Are all of the women married?"

"No. There are a few ladies that are either widowed, divorced, or have never married. I could have married someone else by now, I suppose."

"You just haven't found the right one yet?"

"I just haven't been able to think about starting over with someone else."

"I'm sorry, Matt. I know that must be painful."

"I don't plan on marrying anyone else now though. I enjoy talking with you but I know you're already taken so I won't bother you."

"Oh, Matt. You don't bother me. You aren't ever going to bother me."

"I hope not."

"I enjoy talking to you too. I think we can make some time to talk. Would you like to do that?"

"Only if you want to."

"I do. We'll talk some every day."

"Are you sure?"

"Yes. I'm sure. You are far too nice for me not to talk to you. And I think you have saved my mother's life."

"I only did what needed to be done."

"Yes, and if you hadn't come as soon as you did, she might have died."

CHAPTER NINE

Berlin, Germany

When the plane landed at Tegel Airport in Berlin, Klaus Wilhelm von Kleinmann was surprised by how strong the old feelings were that surfaced. The land of his birth, where he fought in a great war, had a stronger hold on him than he thought. It was pleasant here now with the city completely rebuilt. Berlin now had more wooded areas and parks than any other city its size. He remembered it the way he had seen it the last time, with only a few buildings standing and great piles of debris everywhere and people begging for food and water.

It was so pleasant here now that he found himself thinking about how good it would be to live here again. But that would be too dangerous. It was not safe for him to be in Germany now but he had deemed it necessary to return. There was the gold to consider, after all. He was the only one left who knew where it was hidden. He would not be able to carry much of it out of the country but it wouldn't take much to make it worthwhile. He had considered not disturbing its resting place for a small amount. Things tended to get complicated when such places were compromised.

People learn about its existence somehow. He could never understand how it happened but concluded it was usually the result of a sloppy job. Disturbing a secure site always left telltale signs no matter how carefully it was done. But he was getting older and wanted to make use of the gold. It had been hidden by four young German officers who planned to surrender to the Americans at the end of the war. They wanted Kleinmann to join their scheme since they thought an *Abwehr* agent would have the best information on how close the Russians were.

Kleinmann had observed that army officers were not only suspicious of *Abwehr* agents, they often feared them even more than the *Gestapo* or the *SD*, the *Sicherheitsdienst*, the intelligence organization for both the State and the Party. He had assured them that there was enough time to move the gold to a safe hiding place, since the Soviet Army led by Marshal Zhukov was slogging along in the inclement weather on the eastern front.

The leader of the group of officers had chosen the crypt of a World War One hero in a nearby cemetery as a safe place to bury the gold. They had rounded up four enlisted men to drive the two trucks and unload the gold at the site. Since the officers could not be bothered with getting their hands dirty by digging, they directed the four young soldiers to dig a large hole along side the crypt. Then they had them hollow out an area underneath the crypt that was large enough to store the gold bars.

As they dug, they supported the crypt with a framework of wooden beams and then covered the bottom of the hole with tarpaulins. Then they unloaded the gold from the crates and stacked it near the hole. Next they moved the crates into the hole underneath the crypt and loaded the gold back into the crates again and replaced the dirt. It took the entire night to dig the hole and store the gold, but the officers were pleased with the result. The site looked as though it had not been disturbed. Kleinmann watched as the gold was being hidden. He was certain he knew what was coming next.

The officers gave 6 bars of gold to each of the four enlisted men who had done the work. While the young soldiers were celebrating their good fortune and thinking secretly about how they could come back and retrieve the rest of the gold, the four officers shot them with their pistols. Then they buried them in shallow, freshly dug graves nearby. This time there was no way for the officers to keep from getting their uniforms dirty. They offered the gold bars to Kleinmann since they did not want to be found with them. When they laid them at his feet, he took out his Mauser pistol, cocked it, and held it with the barrel pointed toward the sky.

"I can kill three of you before you are able to shoot me," he said.

They assured him that they were not going to do him any harm, but he kept his pistol out where he could get off several shots quickly if he needed to. Then the officers all took a solemn oath to return in three years, on the same day, and divide the gold.

Klaus had returned to Berlin near the end of the war to look for Ericka, the girl he planned to marry and their daughter, Elise. When it was evident that the war was lost, he left France and hurried to Berlin to get them out before all of the escape routes were closed. He had wasted valuable hours waiting for the officers to bury the gold and when he had arrived where Ericka and his daughter were staying, no one was there. He panicked and frantically began searching house to house for them. When he could not find them he became despondent and determined to die there since he was sure they were already dead.

Why had he allowed himself to be pulled into a scheme to steal gold? He should have gone immediately to 23 *Hasselbach Straye* where they were staying. Now they were lost. He sat on the floor of the apartment all night with his head in his hands. In the morning he searched again and asked everyone he could find about them. He promised them gold if they could tell him anything about their whereabouts. While they wanted the gold they could not eat it and no one would trade food or water for it. Worst of all no one seemed to know where Ericka and the baby were.

He lay on the floor for three days in the apartment at 23 *Hasselbach Straye* despairing of life. When he heard shells from the Soviet artillery pieces begin to crash into the buildings near the apartment, he walked outside hoping that he would be killed. Kleinmann felt sure that all four of the officers were either dead or captured since the few remaining escape routes out of Berlin were closed. *The ones who died were the fortunate ones*, he thought. *Much better than dying years later in a prison camp in Siberia.*

He was experienced at surviving in situations like this and had already planned how he was going to escape. But to what end? He would rather die here looking for Ericka and Elise. But he did not want to die fighting for Hitler and the Third Reich. He decided he would die later on his own terms. He donned a uniform that he took off of a dead Soviet soldier and made his way out of the city by stealing a motorcycle and pretending to be a messenger. When he reached the American front lines, he exchanged his Soviet uniform for a Polish one he had brought along and then started for France. Once there, he became a French citizen from Marseilles returning home.

Next he crossed to North Africa and spent a few weeks in Tunis, Tunisia before traveling on to South America. He had pilfered enough of the gold from the main cache to buy his way to South America. He filled his ruck sack with one kilo gold bars while Captain Rolfe Wittenbaum stood by and watched him. He did not protest since Klaus took it from the main shipment. It would have been different if he had tried to take it from the cache of gold bars the four officers had stolen. It made for a heavy load but it allowed him to escape.

He made his way out of Europe before either of the two major "ratlines" through Spain or Italy were established by those who were sympathetic to the Nazis. Over 10,000 Nazis were ferried safely out of Germany and Austria through these two routes. He arrived in Argentina before any of them and posed as an escapee from Soviet controlled Poland. He wondered where the main shipment of gold was headed but was unable to find out. No matter, he thought, the smaller stash of gold was enough to allow all four of the officers who had stolen it to live in luxury for the rest of their days, had they survived long enough to retrieve it. He began to formulate a plan to return for the gold even before he left Germany.

Reunion

She wasn't difficult to find. Not if you had been in the business of finding people during the war and insuring that the wrong people didn't find you.

"I need a job and would like to apply here," Kleinmann said.

"We do not have any positions available at this time. Do you have any experience in banking?" she asked.

"Some," he lied. "Is it possible for me to fill out an application anyway if something should come open?"

"I suppose. But it is unlikely. It will be an exercise in futility, but you can do it if you insist," she said.

When she returned with the application a few minutes later, he turned his gaze away. He did not want to betray the fact that he was only interested in her. He scribbled on the form for several minutes, pretending to fill it out. He just wanted to have as much time as he could to look at her. *She is so beautiful*, he thought. *She looks so much like her mother*.

When she came and collected the application, she glanced at it and started to walk toward the file cabinet. Then she turned and looked at him with piercing green eyes.

"23 *Hasselbach Straye*? How do you know this address, Herr…Herr Kruger?"

When he did not answer, she asked him again.

"This address, how do you know it? You don't live there. It does not exist anymore."

He watched as the other employees began to depart, tipping their head in her direction as they walked out to go home. He had timed it so that it would be closing time shortly after he arrived. She stared at him, obviously annoyed, until the last member of the bank staff had left.

"Now, Herr Kruger, will you please tell me what you meant by putting this as your address?"

"It is a place that we are both connected to."

"How are we connected? This is where I lived as a child during the war. It doesn't exist anymore. If you think you will somehow get me to hire you by putting it down on the application…."

Then a look of understanding came into her eyes. He did not want to be hired. He was staring at her too intensely. He would not do that if he wanted to be hired.

"Why are you looking at me like that?"

"I'm sorry. I did not intend to be impolite."

"Why then? Do you know me?"

"Yes."

"How do you know me?"

"We are related."

"How?" She was interested now. Perhaps he could tell her about her family.

"I knew your mother well."

"I thought you said we were related. How are we related? On my father's side?"

"Yes."

"How were you related to him?"

"We had the same mother."

"I see. Well, perhaps you would tell me what you know about him."

"I will be happy to tell you all that I know."

"What should I call you then? Uncle?"

"If you wish."

"Well, I'm famished. Can we do this over *Nachtessen*?"

"Certainly."

She took the application with her and as they walked around the corner to a restaurant, she glanced at it again. When they were seated she mentioned that he did not complete the application but had listed another address.

"Is it a house address also?"

"Hardly. It's a *friedhyfe*."

"Really? Why did you put it down then?"

"It is a bequest to you."

"For me? From whom? What does the number mean?"

"It is the number of a *krypta*."

"A *krypta*?"

"Yes."

"And who has bequeathed me this *krypta*?"

"Your father."

"Why would he bequeath me a *krypta*? This is all very confusing. Perhaps you'd better explain to me what this all means. Tell me about my father. I know very little about him. I know some things about my mother but not him."

"Your father was a member of the *Abwehr*, army intelligence, and he was working near the American front lines when the Russians began closing in on Berlin. So he left his post, deserted, because he knew the war was lost and came to get you and your mother. By the time he arrived, the Russians had moved into Berlin quicker than anyone thought and he was not able to locate you. Since he did not find either of you at 23 *Hasselbach*

Straye, he always blamed himself for not coming to get you sooner, but he did not know where else to look."

"And how do you know this?"

"I am very close to your father."

"Is he alive then? Where is he? I would like to meet him."

"He lives in South America now."

"Does he ever come back to Germany?"

"It is dangerous for him to do so."

"Why?"

"He was never repatriated. He was not captured and investigated by the Allies and his status is questionable. He feels it is better to remain where he is for now."

"Why? It's been over thirty years. Was he guilty of war crimes?"

"No."

"You would say that whether he was or not. Tell me, Herr Kruger, where did he meet my mother?"

"They met in Munich during *Oktoberfest* in 1939."

"When did they get married?"

"They never married."

"What? Why not?"

"War broke out and he had to leave suddenly."

"Where did he go?"

"First to Poland and then to France."

"Did he ever come back to see her."

"Oh, yes. He wanted to see you and her more often but it was difficult for him to get away."

"So he did care about me then?"

"Oh, very much. You were very precious to him. You were almost three when he saw you the last time."

"What I remember most about him is that he was tall and blond and always carried me on his hip everywhere we went. He must look a lot like you."

"Yes."

"Could you get me to him? If I went with you to South America, would he want to see me?"

"He wanted to see you so much that he came here at considerable risk."

"Where is he? When can I see him?"

Then she realized that he must be her father.

"Is it you? You've been talking to me in riddles the whole time. Why didn't you tell me you were him?"

"I was afraid to. I thought you might hate me for not coming back for you sooner. I have regretted it my whole life. I was afraid both of you had died when I could not find you."

"My mother did die. And I laid there curled up on her body all day and all night because I didn't know what else to do."

"Elise, I am so sorry."

"It's not your fault. You did what you could, I suppose."

"I have suffered from guilt every day and night since then because I was not in time."

"The neighbors found me the second day and I survived— but just barely. You wouldn't have been able to get me and my mother out anyway, and if you had tried you would had been caught and killed."

"I would have tried, and I would have gladly died if I could have gotten you both to safety."

"So, it was better that you didn't find me. We would have both died if you had tried to get me out."

He could not deny her logic and said nothing.

"What is this about a *krypta*? Why would you leave me something like that?"

"It is not about the *krypta* but what is buried underneath it."

"What is buried there?"

"Gold."

"How much?"

"Enough to allow the four German officers who stole it to live like kings for the rest of their lives."

"They didn't survive?"

"No. They were all captured or killed by the Russians."

"And why do you leave it to me?"

"Because I hope that in some way you may find it in your heart to forgive me for not saving your mother."

"I forgive you, but I wish that my mother could have lived and that we could have all been together while I was growing up. Nothing can make up for that."

CHAPTER TEN

Lord Acton's Dictum

Khalisah was amazed at how well Bill was learning to speak Arabic and they did all of their conversing in it now. When they left to find a deserted area for her to take driving lessons, her brother, Faisal, had to come along. He already knew how to drive so he would go off and leave them alone when Khalisah was practicing her driving. Bill was allowed a great deal of latitude in being with her now; almost as if he was a member of the family. He could not decide if that was by design or not. He did not think that Prince Faisal would use his own daughter to try and find out what he was up to.

Maybe it was something that Khalisah had insisted on. If that was true, he decided, she did have a great deal of influence with her father. He was sure that they were being watched closely by members of Faisal's bodyguard, however. He caught a glimpse of a man with binoculars once when Khalisah was kicking up a small sand storm while driving. He hoped that when Prince Faisal learned that he was teaching her to drive, he would be amused by it.

Bill had met the new bodyguards that Faisal had hired and they seemed to defer to him. The older ones seemed jealous of him. The head of the bodyguard detail had been killed in the attack and Bill wasn't sure who had replaced him. The previous methods that were used to protect Faisal had not worked at all and Bill suspected that security had become lax long before the attack occurred. The thought that someone on the inside had aided the attackers came to mind, but he did not know enough about the household to be sure—not yet.

He wondered if he should even think about staying here any longer. Prince Faisal could decide to throw him out of the country at any time, despite Khalisah's protests, or even worse, have him detained indefinitely. He was certain that his connection to the Israelis would not come to light; he was the only one who knew and he wasn't about to inform on himself. Thoughts of Chop-Chop Square came to mind; but if he was uncovered or even suspected of working for the Israelis, being drawn and quartered seemed more likely.

Bill and Khalisah had plenty of time to talk while she practiced driving and the subject of what she was studying at the university came up.

"Science. I'm a chemistry and biology major, actually."

"I thought you would be majoring in sociology or something like that. Maybe even English literature or the Golden Age of Greece."

"Hah! You would think that, wouldn't you? Although the last two sound interesting."

"What do you plan to do when you graduate?"

"Go to medical school."

"That's very interesting. Have you always been good at math and science?"

"Always at the top of my class. I actually did advanced studies on my own while the rest of the class was trying to master the basics."

"That's amazing."

"Why? Because you think like all the rest of the men that we cloistered women aren't capable of anything like that?"

"No. Uh, just a bit of advice."

"Yes?"

"We men are the way we are and you aren't going to change us. It's the same here or in the UK, or the United States, or anywhere else in the world."

"And your point is?"

"My point is that you sound a little bitter."

"Why should I be bitter?"

"Actually, I don't think that you are. Even though you would have good reason to be bitter, living here."

"What are you trying to say, Charley?"

"It's just that men never stay around bitter sounding women any longer than they have to."

"Oh?"

"And if you leave here, at some point you will want to attract a man of your own."

"And I would have trouble doing that if I sounded bitter?"

"Exactly."

"I'll keep that in mind. It's not the most profound thing I've ever heard but it might be useful someday."

Bill shrugged his shoulders and asked her to slow down a bit. The more rapidly she talked, the faster she drove.

Khalisah renewed the discussion and asked, "How do you know that I won't decide to be married to my work?"

"Do you plan on doing that?"

"No."

"Game, set, match."

"Oh, you think you are so smart! I may need to take your advice, but only because it might be useful when I leave here. Actually, I think that you would be the ideal one to take me out of this country. See how sweet I am, and how I submit, and cater to your every whim."

"Cut it out. I know better. You don't need any help to leave here. You will be able to do whatever you want to do. I'm not making light of your offer either. It's an excellent one. Maybe the best one I've ever had. Except that I'm…."

"Already committed to someone?"

Bill nodded his head.

"I thought as much. A fellow like you wouldn't get this far in life without some beautiful girl latching on to him. Especially someone as handsome and intelligent and likeable as you. She must be very beautiful."

Bill nodded again.

"Oh, don't worry. You aren't going to hurt my feelings or make me think any less of you. I'll just go home and cry myself to sleep tonight…and every night for the rest of my life….Poor little me! Spurned by a cruel, cold-hearted American."

"You really are quite something, you know. I have greatly underestimated you."

"Thanks for that ringing affirmation. How about you, Charley? What are you after?"

"Let's talk about you instead. When did you decide you wanted to become a physician?"

"When they noticed how good I was in math and science and wanted me to become a physicist."

"Oh, why was that?"

"They wanted to encourage youth like me to become knowledgeable enough to be able to help start a nuclear program for our country."

"And you didn't want to?"

"No. I didn't. Even at that age I knew that our country didn't need such a program. It would eventually lead to trying to build an atomic weapon. The government of this country, such as it is, cannot be trusted with something like that."

"I'm sure they have mentioned Lord Acton's dictum to you at Oxford, since he was one of their own."

"You mean, 'power corrupts?'"

"Yes."

"And absolute power corrupts absolutely," they both recited at the same time.

"Hey, watch out! You almost hit that dune head on. You'd better slow down and be more careful when you turn that sharply."

After she had corrected her course, Khalisah spoke in a more serious tone.

"You know, Charley, Lord Acton was right. Our power here, our economic power, has corrupted us."

"How so?"

"Oh, you haven't been here long enough to encounter any of the seamier side of life here in Saudi Arabia. Hopefully you won't ever see any of it."

"It's pretty bad, I take it."

"Yes. And that's why I want to get away from it. Attending medical school will keep me away from here a few more years and then I'm going to find a place to practice medicine somewhere else. Somewhere in Europe, perhaps."

"What exactly does this seamy side of life consist of? A lack of concern about poverty or something like that?"

"No. Although many of the guest workers here are exploited. It's about the wealthy and what they wind up doing when they become bored."

"Oh. I think I'm getting the picture."

"Yes. It's the same thing that dissipated playboys and their playthings do everywhere in the world. Alcohol, drugs, promiscuity, pornography, gambling, consulting psychics, whatever else takes their fancy, all of which is forbidden to Muslims."

"Strange. I thought that it would be unlikely for that kind of behavior to flourish here."

"Well, it does go on here. Among the ultra-rich, who have so much money they don't concern themselves with anything except seeking pleasure."

"Hedonists in the truest sense of the word."

"Exactly. That's why I'm leaving here and the sooner the better."

"I have a great deal of admiration for you, kiddo; even more than before. I would take you out of here myself if I could."

"Which raises another point. I'm curious about your work. What kind of work are you really doing here, Charley?"

"Oh, you know. Looking for opportunities for Compton Oil."

"I know what you told us. But are you sure that's what you're doing?"

"I don't know what you are referring to exactly."

"It's just that you seem more interested in terrorist cells than how we pump oil."

Bill didn't respond and became apprehensive about what she had concluded about him.

"So I asked myself, 'why hasn't my father figured you out by now?'"

Bill sat quietly and waited for her to continue. It was not going to be very pleasant to see how much she had figured out. She was a very clever girl and he had greatly underestimated her, he realized.

"Did he tell you anything about me?"

"No. Does he know more about you than anyone else?"

"You'll have to ask him about that."

"I plan to. But I am curious enough about you that I began to analyze your actions. More interested in terrorist groups than drilling oil. Does that mean that you are interested in protecting the al-Saud? Or the U. S., since you are an American? It must be the al-Saud since these groups are not close enough to the U. S. to be a threat. But why would you want to protect the al-Saud? You weren't even coming here until you met me and Faisal. You jumped at the chance to come here but I don't believe you think that Saudi Arabia is a society worth preserving any more than I do."

"You have a very analytical mind. I don't think I want to hear anymore though."

"But I'm not finished."

"I'm afraid you're going to get me in serious trouble."

He waited for her to resume since she seemed determined to continue.

"I was only going to say that since you were headed to Egypt and came here instead, it seems that you might be interested in something that concerns both Egypt and Saudi Arabia. What do these countries have in common? And why would knowing about terrorist groups be important if it was not to protect the al-Saud? Could it be to protect some other country than Saudi Arabia? It doesn't seem likely that protecting Egypt would be the goal. Who then? What country is the most vulnerable when it comes to terrorists?"

Bill swallowed hard and slumped down in his seat. How had she come up with this? She had him squirming around now trying to think of a way out.

"Do you want to hear the conclusion? I think you are here gathering information about terrorists that will help protect the nation of...."

"Wait! Before you say anything else, you are moving me swiftly in the direction of 'Chop-Chop Square.'"

"I'm not trying to get you sent there or anywhere else. But is what I am saying true?"

"Who are you going to tell about this?"

"No one. I just want to know if I'm correct in my assumptions."

Bill did not answer. His mind was churning with ideas about how to get out of the country before someone else came up with the same conclusion.

"I think that all of the countries in the Middle East should be able to live together in peace. Everyone should have a place they can call home," Khalisah said,

"You may believe that, but no one else in the Arab world does."

"Then I am correct. You are working for…."

"Don't say any more. With every word you say, I can feel my neck being stretched tighter and tighter."

"Oh, don't worry. I'm not going to say anything to anyone else."

"I wish I could be certain of that."

"I give you my word that I won't say anything about this to anyone else."

"My biggest worry now is that someone else may have come to the same conclusion as you."

Khalisah frowned but said nothing. It had not occurred to her that anyone else could have come up with the same analysis of him as she had. No one else thought about Charley Harper as often as she did.

CHAPTER ELEVEN

The Shining Sword

The day began with the coolness of the night still lingering but Jamal Al-Gashey, also called Samir, knew it would not be long until the searing heat would arrive and hold the land in its grip. He was accustomed to the heat. It was the unrelenting enemy but it was also the giver of life in this barren land. He moved slowly as he prepared for a journey that would take him out of the refugee camps along the Syrian border where he had spent his youth.

He had heard of the sophisticated society of the ultra-wealthy where oil had created a paradise for those fortunate enough to be a part of it, but he knew it was a world that he would never belong to. The world that he had grown up in consisted of shacks perched precariously on slivers of land between nations that the Palestinians did not belong to. Those who lived there were refugees who had remained perpetually stateless since 1948. They belonged to no one and no one wanted them. The militants among the Palestinians saw to that.

For a nation to accept them into its boundaries was to invite anarchy. All of the Arab states stoutly proclaimed their support of the Palestinians and clamored loudly for them to be given a homeland, as long as it did not involve giving up any of their own territory. That territory must come from the Jewish state which had taken it from the Palestinians in the first place, they insisted.

Jamal Al-Gashey had been raised as a Shiite in one of the strictest sects under the influence of one of its most devoted followers, Sahel Iskrit al-Husseini. Sahel was one of the few Shiites among the Palestinians, the majority of whom were members of the Sunni sect. Jamal Al-Gashey had lost his parents in a bombing raid and would have perished if it had not been for the mercy of Sahel Iskrit al-Husseini who had found him wandering around the craters, crying and starving. Sahel said he looked to be about three or four when he found him.

Jamal's nearest relatives were his uncle's family but they could not afford to take care of another hungry child so Sahel and his wife took him into their home and raised him along with their six children. Now that Jamal had come of age, he could not inherit with their children. There was not enough for another male to share. So when a member of the Martyrs Brigade had approached Sahel, he reluctantly agreed to let him attend one of their camps for training. When Jamal Al-Gashey finished at the training camp, he came back for a brief visit with Sahel and his wife and children— the only family he had ever known.

Sahel took him aside and warned him about the people who would be directing him.

"My son, do not let these people make you waste your life so that you cannot continue to serve Allah."

"How can I avoid that, my Father?"

"Do not let them use you as one of those whose life is to be thrown away so that the ones who send them may receive credit. Refuse to do such a thing and wait until you can prove yourself as someone whose life is too valuable to be spent just to kill a few of the enemy. Only if you live a long life can you fulfill the work that must be done. Promise me that you will heed my words."

"I promise, my Father. Only in that manner can I bring praise to you rather than blame. No one shall take my life from me to further their earthly plans. Only Allah shall take my life when it pleases him according to his heavenly plans."

"Good, my son. You will please me greatly if you do that and live a long life. Watch closely those who lead you so that you do not become a cast off whose life has meant nothing. Now go in peace and may you be protected from all harm. *Insha'Allah*, my son."

"*Insha'Allah*, my Father."

Jamal Al-Gashey, or Samir, had learned to read in the mosque, which would prove to be of great benefit to him. Many of those he was acquainted with did not know how to read. He enjoyed reading and spent much of his time reading the Qur'an and the writings of the great scholars who had commented on it. He had spent his life learning the tenets of Islam like all Muslims. But he had not learned much about the life of the Prophet until a wise man of great age named Muhammad Ashrat al-Enbededi took the time to teach him.

In the mosque the faithful were given the precepts of the Islamic faith and told that they were indisputable and that they must believe and practice them. Only when he learned about the life of Muhammad did Samir begin to understand the message of the Prophet. He learned of Muhammed's early life and his visions in the cave and how he doubted at first. Then as his resolve hardened, Muhammad began to spread the message of the revelation he had received and Samir learned how he met with fierce resistance.

He had to flee from Mecca to Medina to escape persecution from those who would not accept him. His escape became known as the *Hegira* and the Muslim calendar was based on this flight of the Prophet. Samir learned that the Prophet returned to Mecca and conquered it, and he learned of the *Ka'aba*, the holy stone in Mecca, that once was white but had been turned black by the sins of those touching it. He learned of the Prophet's ascent into heaven from the mountain in Jerusalem. Samir understood the true meaning of Islam much better after his sessions with Muhammad Ashrat al-Enbededi When he was ready to leave, he thanked him, and the old man smiled and commissioned him.

"Be a shining sword that displays the brilliance of true service by your obedience as a pure and devoted servant. Now go, and fulfill your destiny. Let your name become an example that shall show others how to serve well."

"I thank you, and esteem your counsel. May your good deeds be returned to you many times."

"*Insha'Allah*, Samir. Be a shining star of this land."

He pondered the words of the old man as he prepared to leave the only home he had ever known. Samir had carefully practiced the teachings of the Qur'an and observed the Five Pillars of Faith. He had not taken a pilgrimage to Mecca yet but determined to travel to Saudi Arabia as soon as it was possible for him to do so. He did not have a wife as he could not support one, but he wanted one who was as devout as he was in the observance of the holy faith. He knew that the old man did not possess any titles or have any rank among the faithful in the city. But he had discerned that the old man who taught him did not wish to have any titles and would have refused any honors if they had been offered to him.

Samir realized that there were those who had great gifts and who served Allah in ways that those in an official capacity would not bother to do. The old man had told him to let his faith remain pristine and allow his devotion to Allah become the very essence of his being. Since he was an orphan who had been rescued, the old man said, he had nothing else to cling to except his faith. This would make him the perfect instrument for those who wished to retake Palestine. Samir packed his belongings and departed for a new training camp where he would learn more about how to fight the enemies of *Allah*.

Journey to Jordan

"What is your name?" demanded the man who was instructing the group in martial arts.

Samir paused before answering, trying to decide which name he would give: Samir or Jamal Al-Gashey.

"What is your name?" he demanded again. "Tell me or I will punish you for your disobedience."

Samir lifted his head slowly and started to answer when the man grabbed him and pulled him into the middle of the circle of men sitting on the ground. Samir lay there in the dirt, looking at the man who stood over him. The man had told them he was Abdul Baraq al-Querida and that he was going to teach them to kill their enemies with their bare hands. Samir did not move and the man kicked him as hard as he could and then stepped back. Samir rose to his feet slowly and faced the man who was about his size.

"Why did you kick me?" he asked. "You are supposed to teach us." Abdul seemed to be caught off guard by what Samir said, but then he began circling him, answering him angrily.

"You did not answer me quickly enough. You must obey me instantly when I speak."

"My name is Samir."

"That is not your name. What is your real name?"

"Jamal Al-Gashey."

"I am your enemy, Jamal Al-Gashey," Abdul spat out his name in derision. "Now see if you can keep me from killing you."

Abdul circled him and then lunged at him. Samir grabbed his tunic and pulled him toward him. *He is trying to throw me over his hip*, Abdul thought, and resisted him, pulling Samir toward himself and setting his body to flip him instead. When Samir felt the pressure from Abdul he allowed himself to be pulled toward him. Before Abdul could throw him, Samir thrust his right leg behind Abdul's right leg and let the pressure of Abdul's pull take them both to the ground. Abdul realized what Samir was doing and tried to reverse the downward motion but it was too late.

Abdul hit the ground hard and when he tried to rise, Samir slipped his right arm around his neck with his wrist on the side where the main artery was. He held his wrist tightly with his left hand for five seconds and then began to look for signs that Abdul had become unconscious. *No more than ten seconds when you are practicing with a partner*, he remembered his instructor saying. Samir held for fifteen seconds and felt Abdul go limp. Then he released the pressure, keeping his wrist in place. After another five seconds he felt of Abdul's artery. It was pumping blood again. *Perfect timing*, he thought. He would recover. If he had held longer than twenty seconds, Abdul would be near death and could suffer damage that he might not recover from.

Samir noticed one of the men arising slowly and looking in the direction of the tents where the other instructors were. With a flip of his fingers Samir motioned for him to sit down again. He allowed Abdul to slip from his grasp and lay unconscious on the ground. In a few seconds he began to stir but he would not be demonstrating martial arts again today. A few minutes later, two men came running with a stretcher and took him into one of the tents. The men sitting in the circle looked at each other, unsure as to what to do. Samir motioned with his hand for them to go and they all arose and went to their tents.

"Why did you do this to Abdul?"

"He kicked me and dragged me in the dirt."

"Don't you know he is your instructor? You almost killed him."

"He told me to see if I could stop him from killing me."

"That does not mean you should have almost killed him."

"He was trying to kill me."

No one on the council could dispute Samir's answers. He was only doing what Abdul had told him to do. Abdul should be more careful about what he told the students from now on, they decided. Samir was sent back to his tent until they could arrange for him to be moved to another phase of the training.

When Abdul approached him the next day, Samir was sitting on the ground and he shifted his legs so that he could spring up quickly if Abdul attacked him. Abdul was rubbing his neck but did not seem to be interested in getting even with Samir.

"You did well in your defense against me. My neck is still sore today."

Samir did not immediately answer him, so Abdul continued.

"Let us be friends and forget what happened yesterday. I am not angry at you. You were just doing what I told you to do."

"I would like to be friends with you."

"Good. Where do you come from?"

"Palestine. And may I ask about you? Where are you from?"

"I have been in many places but I am a Palestinian also, displaced from my home by the Zionists."

"How did you come here to instruct us?"

"I must tell you truthfully that I was sent here for failing to assassinate someone in Saudi Arabia," said Abdul.

"I would like to go there," Samir said.

"No. You will not be sent there," said Abdul.

"No? Why not?"

"Because it is not a place for someone like you. It is a place where someone like me goes in and performs a sudden strike and leaves quickly. You would not be successful there. You would not fit in well, even with the Arabs who are foreign workers there.

Most of the foreign workers are not Arabs. They come from many other countries."

"Where will you go next?"

"I am going to Jordan to help the Palestinians there who are trying to overthrow King Hussein. You should come with me. There are many things that you need to learn and I can teach them to you."

"What if I am sent somewhere else?"

"I will see that you are not sent anywhere else. You need me to show you how to fight. Have you ever been in battle before?"

"No."

"You will need a new name where we are going."

"I would like to keep my name. I am the last of my family. Everyone else was killed in an airstrike."

"This is only for a short time. What family did you live with before coming here?"

"I do not wish to name them. They are no longer my family. But the man who took me into his family is a good man. I do not wish to involve him and his family in what I am doing now."

"How did you get the name, Samir?"

"It means *entertaining companion.* My friends call me that."

"What else should I know about you?"

"A wise man who taught me said I would be a shining sword, a warrior who would give light to those who fought the enemies of Allah."

Abdul was perplexed at his answer. Only someone who was guileless would give such an answer. What sort of person sat here in front of him? Surely such a person did not exist.

"Do you believe that you have been chosen to do some great deed then?"

"No."

"What then?"

"I am merely a fighter seeking to follow the will of Allah."

Abdul sat quietly and considered what Samir had said. Now he wanted to have Samir come with him so he could see if what he had been told about himself was true.

"You will still need a new name. What would you like to be called?"

"Samir."

"You will need another name also. I think I will call you, Ali. You shall be Ali Khaleel al-Barrida. Don't worry. We will call you Samir. But you need a name for your passport. Your name will be changed again when we go to fight in another place."

"Am I going with you then?"

"Yes. We leave as soon as they can get our papers ready."

CHAPTER TWELVE

Faisal's Dilemma

"Faisal has a new woman that he is interested in. So interested that he may marry her."

"Which family is she from?"

"None of them."

"None of them? Who is she?"

"An American."

"It can't be!"

"And that's not the worst part."

"No? Then what is the worst part?"

"She's a movie actress."

"What is she doing here? Surely she did not come here to act in a movie."

"No. She will certainly not be doing any acting here."

"What is her name?"

"Rhonda Gialetti. I heard that she started as a "bit part" player and has had mostly supporting roles since then. She played what is referred to as a "vamp" in the two films she starred in. I saw the last one. She is very beautiful."

"And Faisal is interested enough to want to marry her?"

"He is said to be. Who knows if he is serious enough to follow through?"

Bill slipped silently away after overhearing the conversion. *So the Prince does have a weak spot after all*, he thought.

"Khalisah and I are just friends."

"Don't tell me that. I've seen the way she looks at you."

Bill hung his head. It would do no good to try and deny what Prince Faisal had seen. He debated whether to tell him that he had a fiancée. He would probably think that he was lying. Even worse, if he believed him, he would want to know all about her and where she was so he could have some of his legion of subordinates investigate her. No. That would not be advisable.

"I did not intend for that to happen."

"So you admit it. And you will try to take advantage of her at some point."

"No. I won't. I don't want to end up at Chop-Chop Square."

"That's for our people who break the law. No. It wouldn't be your neck that I would be interested in cutting off. I think I would keep you around here as one of my eunuchs."

"My reward for saving your life?"

"That's the only reason that I'm keeping you around."

"May I give you some advice then?"

"What possible reason would there be for me to want advice from you?"

"In the interest of preserving my life, I give you the following advice so that you may use it to preserve your life."

Bill could see an almost imperceptible change in Faisal's demeanor. Good. His statement had hit Faisal with enough impact to change his attitude from an exclamation point into a question mark.

"Let's say that I put enough credence in your supposed ability to rescue me again that I gave you another opportunity to deceive me. What are you going to say this time?"

"When we were running for our lives, you seemed a bit more willing to listen to me."

Faisal grabbed him by his shirt and pulled him toward him until they were almost nose to nose.

He is surprisingly strong, Bill thought.

"I still haven't decided exactly what you are up to yet, but I am certain that I don't like it." With that he released his grip and pushed Bill away.

"If you don't want to hear it, that's fine with me," Bill said and started for the door.

"Tell me what you have to say so I can get rid of you and get back to other things that I need to be doing."

"I have only one thing to say. You should fire your security force, all of them, and replace them with someone more trustworthy."

"And why should I do that?"

"Because I'm pretty sure that the attack was aided by someone on the inside. Someone who knew enough to let those fellows get in so easily."

Faisal said nothing. *That's strange*, Bill thought.

"Find some security provider that is not connected in anyway with the Kingdom of Saudi Arabia. I suggest German nationals. You have two million foreign workers here already. A few more won't matter."

When Prince Faisal gazed at him, his eyes suddenly looked tired, and he had a defeated look on his countenance.

He asked, "Why would someone in my household help those assassins?"

"Do you really want to know?"

Faisal nodded his assent.

"Because there are many dissidents here who want to do away with the al-Saud. They are everywhere—your society is shot through with them—even at the highest levels, except for the al-Saud themselves."

Bill thought about telling him that the al-Saud was paying for the training of radicals in the Wahhabi mosques and schools they were financing around the world, and that it was these radicals that were being financed by them that wanted to eliminate the al-Saud. But he thought better of it and said nothing. He had unsettled Prince Faisal enough for one day. He turned and walked out before Faisal could say anything else.

Honeywell H632

"My father has not been himself recently. It seems he has a new love interest—an American actress. It is humiliating to my mother, even though she is happy here. This is all she has ever known," Khalisah lamented.

Bill sat quietly and let her talk. She needed to vent.

"They ruined me when they hired an English governess for me. She told me about the outside world and I realized how different it was. I wanted to go there," Khalisah said. "I hate this place where I have to cover myself completely and will have to walk 20 paces behind my husband—when I get one."

"Do you know why women have to walk behind their husbands?"

"To show that they are submissive to them, of course."

"Actually, that is not the reason."

"Why then? You seem to know more about us than we do."

"In the medieval period, one of the learned doctors of the law was walking behind his wife when she stepped up on the curb and her abaya rose up enough for her ankle to show. He said that caused him to lust after her and to keep that from happening to other men he wrote that it would be good for wives to walk behind their husbands. And that is how it has been since then; not so that wives will show submission but so that their husbands will not be tempted."

"It is still all about the man."

"I suppose."

"Where did you learn something like that?"

"I read a lot."

"I don't even know which university you attended."

"I didn't."

"You couldn't be as knowledgeable as you are by attending public school."

"I didn't go there either."

"You never attended school at all?"

"I'm afraid not."

Khalisah looked incredulous so Bill recited what had transpired in his life up to this point, leaving out the fact that no records existed about him and who he was working for, although it was apparent that she already knew.

"Well, that is incredible," she said. "I thought that you were a normal middle class American. But you're far from normal, aren't you?"

"Yes, I guess I am."

"And now you want to learn about terrorist groups."

"Let's not discuss that."

"Why not? I'm opposed to them also. In fact, I hate them. One of them just tried to kill my father. Let me help you expose them."

"I don't want to expose them."

"Well, whatever you want to do with them; let me help you."

"Look, Khalisah. I can't try and turn you against your father. He dislikes me a great deal already, even though I saved his life. If I let you get involved in something like that, it would be dangerous for you, too dangerous."

"I'm already upset at him for getting involved with that American actress and making my mother look like a woman scorned. Besides, these groups are trying to kill him. That's good enough reason for me. It really doesn't matter to me what your reasons are for wanting to uncover them."

"Khalisah, listen. I'm going to tell you this because I trust you, and because I don't think that you are aware of it. It is clear to me now that the al-Saud, your family, is distributing large sums of money around the Arab world to help educate Muslims and spread the teachings of Islam across the globe."

"I assumed that everyone knew that. Why is there a problem with that?"

"Because every mosque and school that they finance is dedicated to the extremist teachings of the Wahhabis who want to use violence to further their aims."

A look of understanding appeared on Khalisah's face.

"Which means that…." She did not finish her statement.

"Yes. Unfortunately, the al-Saud is financing the development of the very groups that want to destroy them. They think the al-Saud have become too westernized and corrupted by their wealth. That's the irony of it."

"It's already happened here. And it's because of what I told you about the ugly, hidden side of life among the ultra-wealthy."

"Maybe it's not as well hidden as they think."

"Somehow I had not made the connection between the attempt on my father's life and the financing of radical groups by our own family."

"Possibly because you were too close to it."

Khalisah paused and sat quietly for a moment and then turned to Bill and said, "Now let me tell you something that you will need to know to uncover these groups. I am telling you this because I also trust you and because I want to see them stopped. With all his faults he is still my father and I don't want to see him killed if another group makes an attempt on his life."

Bill did not think that she would have anything of real importance to tell him, but he tried to appear interested.

"Are you familiar with computers?"

"No. I've heard about what they can do but not much else."

"Well, neither am I, except that they may have some use in the field of medicine in the future, according to one of my professors."

"Oh? And how would that be?"

"Because they can handle large amounts of data: words, figures, and such."

"Which means?"

"Which means that a computer can process large numbers. It can handle large numbers of things that would be difficult to track otherwise, such as great sums of money."

Bill's interest was suddenly aroused.

"My father has one. A large, new one that he recently purchased in the U. S. when he took a trip to Framington, Massachusetts. Actually he has always had one but they were too large and he was always dissatisfied with their performance. This one will fit in a small room. It's from a company called Honeywell and I heard him say he paid less than $100,000 for it. He also said it is the first one to be mass marketed."

Khalisah appeared proud of herself since Bill was now listening to her with rapt attention.

"It was while he was on this trip to America that he met the actress. It would have been much better if he had stayed home."

"What else have you heard him say about computers?"

"Well, let's see. The old ones were very large. The last one he had was called a mainframe, I believe, and it used a language known as COBOL."

"Which means?"

"I think it means Common Business Oriented Language."

"Have you seen the new one?"

"As a matter of fact, I have."

"Anything interesting about it?"

"Well, I liked the color. It was yellow."

"Anything else?"

"It had the name, HONEYWELL, on it and the model was H632. But before I tell you anything else, I want something in return."

"And what would that be?"

"More driving lessons, of course."

"We've already established that. What else?"

"I want you to pay some attention to me."

"What do you mean?"

"You are only interested in me when I am talking about something that you want to know about like we are doing right now. When we talk about anything else, you have this distant, detached, far-away look in your eye, as though you were thinking deeply about something else. Perhaps the real reason you are here…."

"Don't….I thought we agreed not to mention anything like that."

"I only agreed not to say anything to anyone else."

"Well, I need you to agree to not mention anything about it again. Someone might be listening to us. Your father may even have this whole house bugged."

"Fair enough. If you will agree to pay attention to me when we are talking about other things than what you seem to want to know about."

When he did not answer immediately, Khalisah smiled wryly.

"You know, Charley, I think I might even consider psychiatry; it would be quite interesting, I think, especially when some individuals are so easy to read."

CHAPTER THIRTEEN

Deutsche Reichsbank Feingold

Klaus Wilhelm von Kleinmann had concluded long ago that he did not regret his actions during the war. He had simply done what every male in Germany had done; follow those who wanted to avenge the humiliating defeat in WWI and restore the honor of the Fatherland. The Treaty of Versailles containing Article 231, the "war guilt clause," forced Germany to bear the sole responsibility for the war. The huge reparations that the nation was forced to pay to England and France wrecked the nation's economy and brought ruinous inflation wiping out the savings of the middle class.

But when the time came for revenge, no one could foresee how far the death and destruction would reach under a megalomaniac like Hitler, he thought. They were all just doing their duty to the country by helping restore a sense of pride in being German. They could not know that the result would be even worse than the first war and that the thought of Germany being a world power would forever be shattered. *How ironic*, he thought, *that Germany should achieve the status of a prosperous nation once again by peaceful means after being completely disarmed.*

The greatest regret of Germans now was that the hated Bolsheviks held half of the country in their deadly grip. He had not fought on the eastern front but his hatred of the Soviets was no less than those who had. It was the Soviets who destroyed Berlin, and laid waste to the country. No one could lift a finger against the Soviets now and that was what angered every German to their core. Now that he had found his daughter, Elise, he would be glad to leave Germany and return to his home in Argentina.

He was known as Franciszyk Wojciechowski there, a Polish immigrant who was a successful rancher. He was well respected, raising pure bred cattle on his ranch, which kept him busy and fulfilled. Wild cattle had roamed the Pampas for centuries and were scrawny and disease-ridden until pedigreed breeds from Europe had been introduced. He had chosen Aberdeen Angus or Black Angus as his breed. They were naturally polled, smaller, and calved easily without the services of a veterinarian and their meat produced some of the best steaks imaginable.

The Pampas, thousands of kilometers of grasslands in the interior of the country, had produced the gaucho culture, the life of the wild, untamed Argentine cowboy. Opposing the gauchos were the *Porteños*, the inhabitants of Buenos Aires, the capital and chief port city, where roughly one third of the population resided. They represented the civilized element of society in Argentina. One of Argentina's own Presidents, Domingo Sarmiento, had written that the clash of cultures between the *Porteños* and gauchos represented the struggle of civilization against barbarism. Sarmiento felt that the *Porteños* had to win in order for civilization to survive.

Klaus had taken up the life of the gaucho and had become a type of *caudillo*, a strongman, with a large ranch occupying hundreds of kilometers with many gauchos working for him. He enjoyed the company of the *Porteños*, however, since almost all of them were Europeans who had immigrated to Argentina from Spain, Italy, France, Germany, and many other countries in Europe. He visited Buenos Aires often to attend the theatre, enjoy the opera, and play bridge with the friends he had there. He could enjoy the best of both cultures living among the barbarian gauchos and socializing with the civilized *Porteños*.

He never married after losing Ericka in Germany at the end of the war. He had courted several of the young society ladies in Buenos Aires when he first arrived, but they were all determined to get married and the sooner the better. He had settled on the daughter of his foreman, Alejandro Rodriguez. Her family had come from Barcelona and spoke Catalan instead of Castilian. She was a beautiful girl, named Margarita, with red hair and skin so white that it immediately identified her as a member of the class designated as *peninsulares* by the Spanish crown in the Sixteenth

Century. *Peninsulare* meant someone from the Iberian Peninsula and they were the only ones that the Spanish king felt could be trusted.

But after Margarita's family had stayed in South America for a generation, they were referred to as *creoles*, meaning they had become permanent residents in South America and did not plan on returning to Spain. She was happy just being the consort of the lord of the manor and had never tried to get him to marry her although he had heard her mother urging her to do so on more than one occasion. He would have married Margarita but there was always the chance that he might be uncovered someday and he did not want her to be involved if it happened.

Tonight he was going to the *krypta* and he brought along a few tools to get into the bunker where the gold was buried. Two shovels, a rake, a sledge hammer, wire cutters, burlap sacks, flashlights, an axe, a hammer and nails, a hand saw, and fence posts to reinforce the rotting timbers with. He rented a small Mercedes truck to carry the gold. He would need to work most of the night just to extract part of the gold and then he would need at least two hours to store it in the cave he had in mind. He had originally planned to only take a fourth of the gold but now he had decided to take as much as he could carry out.

He did not believe he could move all of the gold in one night by himself but he could not trust anyone else. He knew that he dared not use any sort of power tools. Digging under the crypt would leave telltale signs but he had no choice. He was counting on the rain that was forecast to cover the area where he dug. He left as soon as it was dark enough and drove slowly through the cemetery to the crypt of Colonel General Ernst von Zimmer, one of the heroes of the Battle of Verdun.

He dug furiously for the first hour and slowed only when he was too tired to continue. He rested briefly and started again and after another hour he reached the timbers that supported the crypt. He noticed immediately that the timbers were not in their original position. He had watched them being put in place twenty-five years earlier and knew that someone had already come back for the gold. The three posts in the middle were missing so he squeezed through the opening and turned on a flashlight and shined it around the bunker. The gold was gone.

He found about two dozen gold bars that were still stacked in the back corner of the bunker surrounded by the wooden slats that remained from the case it was in. These bars would be worth about 135,000 marks, he calculated. When he shone his light against the back wall he noticed a skeletal body clad in a German uniform. When he turned it over he recognized the epaulets and the insignia. The uniform was that of Captain Rolfe Wittenbaum. *So he was the one who had returned for the gold*, Klaus thought. No doubt he had been killed by those that he had brought with him to move the gold.

It appeared that they had departed immediately after killing him and in their haste had left the two dozen gold bars behind. *Rest in peace, Rolfe. I bear you no ill will. I just came a quarter of a century too late; but then I would not have wanted to share your fate*, he thought. It occurred to him to look through Rolfe's clothes and he searched the pockets and found a small packet of papers wrapped in a waterproof pouch. He tucked it in his pants pocket and loaded the gold bars into his vehicle. He decided not to move the dirt back. He was too exhausted to do it. That would insure that Rolfe's skeleton would be found and given a proper burial.

There was no need to conceal the bunker any longer. The need for secrecy was gone now that all of the gold had been removed. He looked up as the lightening began to flash across the sky. The wind smelled moist and fresh. The rain would cover his tire tracks and now he began thinking of how to exchange the gold for currency. He could do it much easier in Argentina, but it would extremely difficult here. He had no contacts and all of the bars bore the insignia of the Reichsbank, which had been stamped into them when they were recast.

He would sell the bars and give the money to Elise if he could manage to smuggle them back to Argentina. They were worth the equivalent of about $25,000 U. S. dollars. *Maybe I should see if Elise would go back to Argentina with me. If she did not approve of my living arrangements, however, that might not be a good idea*, he thought. He stared at the large eagle on the bars, then extinguished his light, loaded his tools and wound his way out of the cemetery and back toward Berlin.

As he drove, he recalled that near the end of the war, General Patton's Third Army had found 100 tons of gold hidden in the Kaiseroda potassium mine near Merkers, Bad Salzungen, a small community southwest of Gotha in the state of Thuringia. The American Army had to use a demolition crew to blow the vaults open so they could get inside. The Nazis had stolen the gold from the state banks of other countries and had tried to hide it there from the Allies when the war was lost. He remembered every detail that he had read in the French newspapers. The distance was approximately 288 kilometers southwest of Berlin.

He was certain that was the main shipment the four officers had stolen the gold from. When he arrived back at his hotel room, he undressed to shower and pulled the waterproof pouch out of his pocket and laid it on the table. He had forgotten about it and thought now that he should have left it in Rolfe's uniform pocket. It was likely some personal items that should be interred with him. The light had been poor in the bunker so he did not open it there. He decided to look at what was in the pouch and then destroy the contents.

When he opened the pouch he could see that the papers were official documents bearing the imprimatur of Albert Speer, Reichsminister of Armaments and War Production. Speer had ordered all of the gold remaining in the Reichsbank in Berlin be shipped south by truck to Oberbayern in Bavaria under guard of the *SS*. Members of Organization *Todt*, the Reich's slave labor force, were to be sent there also to build a bunker to contain the gold. The orders were dated 12 April, 1944. He wondered if it ever got to Bavaria or if it was diverted to another location.

Gold did strange things to people and that much gold would tempt an angel, he thought. He had also heard rumors that there was a large shipment of gold buried in a bunker somewhere in the Leinawald Forest near Leipzig. Other rumors had placed the location of the bunker that was constructed to hold the Reichsbank gold in the Ore Mountains near the small community of Deutschneudorf. Near the bottom of the orders and barely legible were scrawled these coordinates:

50 degrees, 58 minutes, 48 seconds N
12 degrees, 26 minutes, 24 seconds E

He recognized the location; it was near Altenburg, in the Leinawald Forest, where a prisoner of war camp was located during the war. *SS Gruppenfeuhrer* Baron Erich von Kessler had been the commandant and was rumored to have acquired a sizeable fortune for himself not only in gold but also in art. No doubt he would have eagerly welcomed the gold from the Reichsbank into his jurisdiction with plans to "rescue" part of it from the American Army that was rapidly approaching.

Klaus knew that wherever this last shipment of gold from the Reichsbank had been sent, it would be difficult to find. Speer had ordered the area around it to be bombed to cover up the location. This was despite the fact that late in the war German aircraft could hardly get off the ground before being attacked by Allied war planes. Klaus was satisfied that all of the Reichsbank gold that had been moved to Merkers in the first shipment in 1944 had been found. The rest of the Reichsbank gold that Albert Speer ordered to be moved to Oberbayern in Bavaria was unaccounted for, however.

He had searched for any information about the Reichsbank gold he could find while in Argentina. Had it been moved to Merkers as well? He had thought so until he read an article in the *Argentinisches Tageblatt*, the German daily newspaper in Buenos Aires. An important part of military intelligence was to determine if the nation had enough money to fight the war all the way to the end. In the *Abwehr* it was well known that there had been sufficient gold remaining in the Reichsbank for Germany to keep on fighting long after the Allies had invaded. So where had it all gone?

He had a German cook who worked for him pick up all of the copies of the *Argentinisches Tageblatt* when he went into Buenos Aires once a week. No one knew that Klaus could speak or read German and he wanted to insure that no one ever found out. If he ever used another language beside Spanish, it was Polish; but there were not many people to converse with in Polish, so he rarely used it. The article in the *Argentinisches Tageblatt* stated that about $750 million in gold had been confiscated by the Reich from the other countries of Europe during the war.

Of that amount, about $450 million in gold had gone unaccounted for at the end of the war. The Allies knew about the existence of this gold and most of them were certain that the bulk of it had been deposited in many of the banks in Switzerland, including the Swiss National Bank. That was the only logical place for the rest of it to be; where the leaders of the Reich had put it for safe keeping. After the Reich fell there was no one left to claim the gold, a windfall for the Swiss bankers. For the Jewish community, the biggest insult of all had been the $14 million of the infamous *Schutzstaffel* gold that was deposited in the Swiss National Bank, which the *SS* had taken from their relatives in the death camps, part of it extracted from their teeth.

After the war, Switzerland had reluctantly turned over a token amount to be divided among the nations whose gold had been looted. Nothing had gone to the relatives of those who died in the death camps. According to the Reich's own records, the article stated, the remaining $350 million in gold had been transferred to Berne by the Nazis and it was still sitting in the Swiss National Bank. *There was no need to look for Reichsbank gold anywhere in Germany*, he realized. *All of it was in the hands of Swiss bankers, especially those of the Swiss National Bank, and the national banks of the neutral countries that traded with the Reich during the war.*

Numerous groups had searched across Germany for the Reichsbank gold after the war and found nothing. *They could have saved themselves the effort. There would be no way to retrieve it from the Swiss National Bank in Berne, Switzerland*, Klaus thought. He also learned from the article in the *Argentinisches Tageblatt* that the French and Polish governments had been the shrewdest of all the European nations in keeping their gold from the Nazis. The French shipped their gold, the equivalent of 2 billion U. S. dollars, to England, Canada, and the United States before the Nazis could get to it.

The Poles shipped their gold through Rumania, Turkey, and Lebanon by train and trucks and were able to get it to the "Old Lady of Threadneedle Street," the Bank of England, where it resided until the end of the war. It did the nation little good, however, since after the war Stalin made Poland and the rest of Eastern Europe part of the Soviet Bloc known as the Warsaw Pact Alliance and lowered an "Iron Curtain" across their borders. Then the Soviets ruled with an iron fist, controlling all of the wealth of the Polish people.

He sighed, and thought that it was best for those who wanted the gold to have it disappear, since it had only brought death to those who possessed it. *It was too powerful an incentive, for it made people willing to destroy anyone who could keep them from obtaining it. It was better for it to remain where no could be tempted to kill for it again. And the Swiss National Bank would make sure of that. It seemed destined to remain in its vaults forever. Even the gold that he had now was covered with the blood of innocent people*, he realized.

All of the gold was stolen and millions of people had been murdered by the Nazis for the *Schutzstaffel* gold. *I should not give this to Elise*, he thought. *It will only bring her tragedy. I should not have retrieved it. I do not need the gold; I have everything I need in Argentina. But the desire for what the gold could buy was too great even for me*, he thought. *Now I am caught in the trap that possessing such blood-stained wealth brings. I must think of someway to dispose of it before it brings death to me.*

I wonder what my daughter will think about the loss of the gold that was buried under the crypt. She will want to know what happened to it. I will tell her the truth, that all of it had already been taken. She can read the account about the empty crypt in the newspaper in a day or two. Surely she will not think that I took it for myself. I would not have told her about it if that was what I was planning to do. I will hide this gold and find a way to dispose of it before I leave, he decided. *I do not think that it has a curse on it except for the hideous greed that it engenders. That is curse enough.*

CHAPTER FOURTEEN

An Audience with the Actress

Bill received a note in a woman's handwriting and when he opened it, there was a light rose fragrance that wafted up into the air. *Beautiful*, he thought. It was an invitation to join Rhonda Gialetti for lunch at the Al-Arabi hotel downtown. *What could it hurt to speak to her?* When he arrived at her table she looked up and gave him a beautiful smile. He could understand how even someone as serious as Prince Faisal could be attracted to her. She seemed to be everything she was touted to be. Not as flamboyant as Bill thought she would be, but just as beautiful. His first impression was that she looked a bit shy and withdrawn and he thought she would not have the persona of a brash actress. Perhaps that was what Prince Faisal found interesting about her.

"Hello," she said. "I am Rhonda Gialetti. Please join me."

Bill introduced himself as Charley Harper and sat down and she replied, "Yes. I know who you are."

"May I ask how you know that?"

"I made some inquiries."

"And what did you learn about me?"

"You're the young American who helped Faisal when he escaped from the attempt on his life."

So that's the way he tells it, Bill thought.

"Yes, he's a brave man," he said.

"I also found out that a more accurate version is that you saved his life despite having to drag him along with you."

"You may believe either one."

"You won't tell me what really happened?"

"I don't think I want to dispute anything Prince Faisal said."

"I see. Well, I don't suppose it matters except to you and him, but I choose to believe the latter version."

"May I ask you a question?"

"Yes, of course," she replied.

"Where are you from in the U. S.?"

"Well, I was born in Tifton, Georgia."

"I thought you were from the South."

"And you sound Southern to me as well."

"You're right."

"Where?"

"Kentucky. A little place that's so far away from everything else it doesn't even have a name. Closest town is a little burg called Wild Horse Canyon. The name is almost as big as the town."

"Have you been back there recently?"

"Never been back. How about you? Do you ever go back to Tifton?"

"Never. I don't ever want to go back there. It reminds me of my childhood."

"It must not have been very pleasant."

"Pleasant? Huh! We went to California every year during the growing season and tried to make enough to live on back in Georgia for the other half of the year."

"Not an easy life."

"That doesn't even begin to describe how hard it was. When your name is Mavis Travertine and everyone in your family is the next thing to a migrant worker, you are at the bottom and there is no way out. My clothes were flour sacks that were made into dresses, and that lasted until I ran away and got married," she said.

"And in case you're wondering, I've only been married twice. The first time, we were both too young and it didn't last and the second time I was married to the agent who gave me my first break and he was much older than me and drank too much. Any other questions?"

"No. That pretty much explains everything."

"You take me to be pretty shallow, don't you?"

"No. Not at all. In fact, you are a very impressive lady. My first impression of you was that you were innocent looking and shy, even bashful, and sort of a shrinking violet. That just went out the window. You have had to be one tough lady just to survive."

"Hah! You don't think about trying to survive. You just scratch and claw your way out of the hard times until you can get enough to eat and have something to put on your back. But you wouldn't know anything about that, would you? I still have to scratch and claw but in a different sort of way."

"My opinion of you has gone up considerably in just these few minutes we've been talking."

"That's nice of you to say."

"What about now?"

"Well, I realize that I have a limited amount of time to establish myself in a position where I won't ever have to go back to the kind of life I had as a child. In ten years, I will not be as beautiful and men will not be interested in me then. That's why I'm here with Faisal. I thought you could tell me more about him and what living in Saudi Arabia would be like."

"Let's see. Where should I begin?"

She listened carefully as Bill gave her his candid evaluation of Prince Faisal and Arab society and culture. When he finished, she seemed impressed but disillusioned since she realized that she would not be able to survive in Saudi Arabian society.

"What about you? Are you wealthy too since you're over here 'hobnobbing' with these rich Arabs?"

"I'm afraid not."

"What exactly are you doing over here then?"

"I'm a guest of Prince Faisal's family."

"And?"

"And I'll probably be leaving soon."

"That's not what I've heard. I heard that he's going to keep you here until he's satisfied about whom you really are and what you're doing here."

"Did he tell you that?"

"He didn't have to. I have made a few sympathetic acquaintances among Faisal's staff, so I can find out things that I really want to know about."

"Since you asked about my financial situation, it seems fair that I should ask about yours."

"What do you want to know? Do I have any money? Would I be here if I did? Most of what I earned, I squandered, along with the help of some of my 'friends.' When the money was gone, so were they. I didn't have anyone to advise me on how to keep from spending everything I made. Now I need to find a husband who will take care of me when I can't earn anything myself. The IRS claims that I owe them a considerable sum of money, which I don't have. All of this makes me seem like a gold digger, doesn't it?"

"No. Just a girl who is trying to survive and needs a helping hand."

"You're a few years younger than me, but it would be nice if you were wealthy and needed a wife...." She seemed to be thinking aloud.

"What now?"

"I suppose I'll go back to the U. S. and keep looking for someone who wants me enough to help me get out of this mess I'm in."

"I think Faisal is still your best hope."

"But from what you told me, it's obvious that I can't live here, and now that I know, I don't even want to live here."

"He has enough money to pay off your back taxes and never miss it or even blink an eye about spending that much money."

"How would I get him to do that?"

"Ask him."

"Just like that?"

"Add a few tears to the request. I think he likes you enough to take care of something like that for you. How much do you owe?"

"I don't know for sure. About two hundred thousand dollars, I think."

"Just pocket change to him."

"I could go back and work in the U. S. if I could settle up with the IRS."

"Don't underestimate yourself. He is still very much taken with you."

"How could we even be together here?"

"If he wants you to be here, he'll take care of it. Do you like this hotel you're staying in?"

"Yes, it's very nice."

"He will probably keep you here. At least until he finds a suitable residence for you and you can be assured it will be luxurious."

"After what you said, I was ready to leave tomorrow. You had me convinced that it was impossible for me to stay."

"Difficult, but not impossible."

"Maybe I will wait and see what he will do for me."

"Just tell him how much money you need, and then let him take care of making the arrangements to keep you here. This place grows on you. You might even begin to like it a little bit. Who knows? He might even want to marry you."

Physician, Heal Thyself

Rebecca Lundstrom noticed that Matthew Avery appeared discouraged and even morose when they talked in the evenings. When she asked him about it, he said that he was having difficulty getting over his wife's illness and death but he had been able to cope with it until now.

At last he is willing to talk about it, she thought.

"She must have been a wonderful lady. Do you mind talking about her? What was she like?"

"My wife, Natalie? She was 19 when we married and I was 25. She was brilliant and became a well-regarded scientist in her own right. She earned a PhD in microbiology. As it turned out we were ideally suited for one another. We didn't realize how much we were suited for each other before we were married; but we really were. And we had nine wonderful years together until she was ripped from me. It hurt me so badly that I sometimes wish I had never found anyone like her, so perfect for me; and as she often told me, I was so perfect for her. If I had found someone who was just satisfactory, I could have grieved for her, gotten over it and gone on.

But I found someone who was so wonderful that it knocked me off course, and I'm still having trouble because of losing her. I believe that she was the only woman that I could have become so devastated about losing that I couldn't go on. Didn't want to go on. Saw no reason to go on. Life became meaningless without her. There is the supposition that everyone feels that way about their spouse if they lose them suddenly. But I've seen many cases where that was not true. In fact, I don't think that it is normative.

She was the only woman that could have made me suffer this way if I lost her, because I'm a strong man, emotionally and psychologically. Before this happened I took part in a study utilizing numerous psychological tests and they showed that I was as capable of withstanding emotional trauma as anyone that had ever been profiled. But I had a premonition, a couple of years before it happened, that she was the only woman that could knock me off my keel if I lost her. Ever have a premonition like that? I hope not. It isn't pretty when it happens."

"What about your parents, Matt. What were they like?"

"My parents were old when I was born. My father was forty-five and my mother was forty. Being an only child I was especially receptive to the way they behaved. They trained me by example mostly. They were both physicians and I noticed that they hardly ever became emotional about anything. It interfered with one's judgment my father once said. You should decide about everything in a rational manner. So I grew up acting like them and it worked well for me until I realized there were drawbacks to doing things that way.

While it's true that it may be best to make decisions that way, it keeps everything bottled up inside you and you never have any sort of emotional release—no catharsis. I was an adult long before my time when it came to making decisions based on reason. I had a childhood but it was tempered by the example of my parents. They worked such long hours that they stayed in the frame of mind where they could make sound decisions based on critical thinking. I learned about Aristotle's deductive method and how to utilize his syllogistic reasoning while I was still a precocious child.

You've heard the cliché, the child is the father of the man? For me it seemed to be accurate. But no matter what my conditioning had been as a child I suppose I would still have had difficulty getting over losing Natalie. What do you think, Rebecca? You seem to have some insight into things of this nature."

"Matt, maybe you should cut back on your work schedule for a while. Is there someone you could get to cover for you for a while? Would you be able to do that without having financial problems?"

"I wouldn't have any financial problems."

"Are you sure?"

"Yes."

"Do you have some money saved then? Enough to get you through for a while if you are not practicing medicine?"

"I'm wealthy, Rebecca. I don't ever need to work again. My parents left me millions."

"Oh, I'm sorry I asked. I was only trying to be helpful."

"I know you were and I'm grateful. Money is not the problem. But it's not the solution either. I suppose I will be more empathetic now with people who have gone through something like this."

"I still think you should take some time off."

"I guess you're right. I do need to take some time off."

Poor Matt, she thought. *It's like he's being punished for something terrible that he did. He's like all men—too proud and self-sufficient to admit that they need someone to help them, and they certainly wouldn't ask for any help. That would make them feel like something less than a man. He looks as though the last prop has been knocked out from under him*, she thought.

The next morning Dr. Jeffrey Caine came by and after a brief conversation, he suggested a regimen of exercise for Matthew Avery and made him an appointment with a grief counselor at the Mayo Clinic. He told Rebecca that she had done the stop gap work that was necessary to keep Matthew Avery from being in such deep despair that it incapacitated him. Now he needed to begin the next phase of his life. By the end of the week, he had begun seeing a counselor and started a program of cycling, weight lifting, and golf. *Jeffrey Caine was right*, he thought. *Physical activity is one of the best ways to relieve stress brought on by grief.* He found a colleague who would take over his practice. He began turning over in his mind the idea of writing about his experience and doing serious research on the subject of dealing with grief brought on by the death of a family member.

Rebecca took a leave of absence from Mayo Clinic and moved her mother back to Blue Earth to continue her recuperation. She wanted to hear from Bill but she knew that he couldn't communicate with her until he came back to the U. S. It could be a year or even two before he could get back and so she reconciled herself to a period of loneliness that might stretch on interminably. She signed up for a course at the branch campus of the university system in Mankato and hoped that Bill would finish his work sooner than expected.

CHAPTER FIFTEEN

Fighting for Fatah

Abdul moved ahead quickly and then motioned for Samir to follow him. They wore the uniforms of Fatah, a group founded by Yassar Arafat that was the military arm of the Palestine Liberation Organization. Fatah represented the violent, uncompromising element of the PLO. The name, Fatah, was a carefully crafted acronym using the first letters in Arabic of the name of the Palestinian National Liberation Movement and putting them in reverse order.

Abdul rehearsed in his mind the events of the fight for control that was going on in Jordan. The PLO had established control over numerous parts of Jordan by 1969 and although King Hussein had negotiated with the PLO to end their control, it continued despite the signing of two different agreements. The problem for King Hussein was that only one third of the population of Jordan was composed of indigenous inhabitants. The other two thirds of its people were displaced Palestinians who had fled from the West Bank after the 1967 Arab Israeli War.

The PLO claimed to represent all of the Palestinians, both refugees and the indigenous part of the population, and that threatened King Hussein's ability to govern. After negotiation with the PLO did not work, King Hussein finally declared martial law and determined to remove Fatah and the PLO from Jordan by force. The Palestinian paramilitary group known as the *Fedayeen*, or men of sacrifice, had already attempted to stage a coup d'état and remove the King from power. Fatah also hijacked 4 jets and landed them at Dawson Field, a remote air strip in Jordan, and then blew them up.

The King now felt he had no choice but to drive them out. The Jordanian Army began attacking the PLO on September 15, 1970. The attempt was complicated by the actions of Hafez al-Assad when he ordered 200 tanks from the Syrian Army to invade Jordan to aid the PLO. King Hussein panicked but kept fighting because he had no other choice, and after the Royal Jordanian Air Force attacked the Syrian forces and inflicted heavy losses, they turned their tanks around and headed home. Then on September 28, 1970, The President of Egypt, Gamal Abdel Nasser, died and the PLO lost its most powerful supporter.

Now Abdul and Samir and all of the other Palestinians were being driven completely out of Jordan by King Hussein's forces. The PLO was losing its main base of operations and most of them began moving to Lebanon. After six weeks of fighting in Jordan against the army of King Hussein, Abdul was convinced that this was a disaster that pitted Muslims against each other and wasted their lives in a fight for political control instead of uniting them against a common enemy. He had decided to leave instead of continuing to fight against other Muslims.

Abdul had concluded that the leader of Fatah, Yasser Arafat, was egotistical, blood-thirsty, and greedy; willing to sacrifice the lives of innocents in order to strengthen his own position. He did not seem to have a plan, except to create mayhem and destruction everywhere he went. His military strategy, if it could be called that, was short-sighted and wasteful of lives and material. He never seemed to lack money or weapons though, and Abdul learned that he was being supplied by several countries, including Egypt, Syria, the Soviet Union, and even China.

Now, when he and Samir looked back at the rolling hills behind them they could see the troops from the Jordanian Army pursuing them and closing fast.

"This is where we must part, my brother, Samir. You choose which way you will go and I will go the other way. Hurry! Or we will be captured. Our only chance at escape is to separate."

Without hesitation, Samir went right and Abdul hurried to the left. *Perhaps we will both be caught*, Abdul thought. When he rounded a small hill, he dropped his weapons and ammunition belt. Then he ran across a small clearing as bullets whistled around him. When he rounded the next hill, he continued running as fast as he could, knowing the Jordanian troops could not fire at him until they mounted the first small hill.

By then he would be behind another hill and safe from any one on foot. Only a vehicle could catch him now. He ran until he could not run anymore and slowed to a walk. After five minutes he started running again and when he could run no further, he slowed to a walk again. He repeated the pattern until he reached a stream of water. He plunged into it and struggled across and collapsed on the other side.

He tried to crawl into the bushes and hide but as he pulled himself up he saw that uniformed men had surrounded him. He felt the barrel of a gun on his back and when he looked around he saw that it was an Uzi. Then he was shackled and dragged away. When he heard their voices, he realized that he had been taken prisoner by the Israelis.

Blut Goldbarren

While he was in Germany, Klaus wanted to attend the Olympics in Munich. He remembered attending the last Olympic Games that were held in Germany in the capital city of Berlin in 1936. He was only a boy and it was the most exciting thing he had ever done. He could not have imagined anything better than for him to go to the Olympic Games with his father. They enjoyed themselves so much that he wished it could go on all summer. It was a short-lived triumph, however. His father died 18 months later from the wounds he suffered during WWI. His lungs had been severely injured when some of the nerve gas that the German High Command had ordered to be released blew back over their own lines. That left Klaus and his mother to try and eke out a meager existence.

After he had showered and ordered a meal to be brought to his room, he felt better about things. He began to formulate a plan in his mind about what to do with the gold. It would involve some risk but he had not done anything similar since the war and he wanted to see if he could still operate as he did when he was a member of the *Abwehr*. And he knew exactly which group he wanted to try out his plan on. First he would need to purchase a weapon.

"Can I look at a Walther PPK?" Jouls Prout scrutinized the clerk behind the counter at the gun shop carefully as he asked the question.

"I think I want a new one rather than a used one."

The Walther PPK was a 7.65 mm hand gun, and one of the most easily concealed weapons due to its short barrel; yet it was accurate and carried a considerable punch. Klaus had met Jouls at the *Steinadler Kaffeehaus*, where people from various discontented groups congregated at times. After Jouls had bought the Walther PPK for him, Klaus inquired about whether he knew anyone from those organizations. Jouls denied having any knowledge about them at first and then asked the man who had introduced himself as Herr Kruger why he wanted to know.

"I am interested in learning about a specific group here in Deutschland that is referred to by the colloquial term *neo-Nazis*."

Jouls' body tensed but he kept his face from betraying any emotion as he questioned Herr Kruger.

"Why?"

"I am interested in their work. I would like to meet with some of them."

Jouls proceeded to explain how difficult it would be to locate such a group, and ended by stating that, "Even the *polizei* can't locate them."

Then he turned and looked Herr Kruger in the eye and asked, "You are not from the *polizei* are you?"

He knew that Herr Kruger would not tell him if he was but he wanted to get a good look at him when he answered.

"Certainly not," Herr Kruger replied.

He seemed to pass the test and Jouls said, "It would be very difficult and dangerous to locate such a group, Herr Kruger. And you would need to have a very good reason for wanting to meet them. Do you?"

"Yes, I do."

"Do you mind if I ask what it is?"

Klaus ignored his question and said, "It would be expensive, I assume, to find such a group, and, as you say, there would be no small amount of danger involved."

"As I have already stated, that is correct."

"How expensive?"

"I would have to see how much expense I would incur and then there would be an amount commiserates with the risk involved."

"I see. Well, what do you say to a retainer in the amount of 2,500 marks?"

"And the amount that is to be paid at the successful completion of such a meeting?"

"Ten times that."

"Twenty."

"Without haggling about it, fifteen times."

"Done."

"Good. I will check here twice a week at this time."

"What if I just take your money and don't come back?"

"Then you will forfeit a sizeable sum of money."

"I will still need to tell them why you want to meet with them, Herr Kruger."

"*Blut goldbarren*. Tell them I want to speak to them about *blut goldbarren*."

Herr Kruger then took a package out of his briefcase, un-wrapped it and slid the bar of gold out of the paper so that the inscription showed. At the top of the gold bar was the national insignia, the *Reichsadler*, an eagle with its wings fully spread, holding a swastika surrounded by an oak wreath. Underneath was the inscription:

DEUTSCHE
REICHSBANK

1 KILO
FEINGOLD
999.9

DRO53487

Then he covered it up and quickly put it back in his
briefcase before anyone else in the coffee shop noticed it. Jouls
was noticeable affected by the sight of the gold bar; he tried to
react calmly but could not keep from panicking.

"They will think it is a trap; most certainly, they will think
it is a trap. I think it is a trap. I'm leaving."

"You've forgotten your retainer, Herr Prout."

Jouls did not stop or even look back.

The narrative was playing out just as he thought it would.
Klaus smiled, and finished his *Kaffee und Kuchen*, the elegant
sweet, taken in mid-afternoon that had become a national -
obsession. Then he went back to his hotel room and began devising
a plan for putting the gold in the hands of those he deemed most
worthy of it.

The Mission in Munich

The evening was cool and there was a full moon hanging
over the Winter Palace in St. Petersburg. The city had been built by
Czar Peter the Great and named for the Apostle Peter. It had been
renamed Leningrad by the Bolsheviks as was their custom. Tonight
the Palace Square was crowded with people enjoying the brief
summer respite and admiring the Palace's brilliant Baroque
architecture. There was a festive atmosphere despite the fact that
the Communist Party usually disapproved of such large
spontaneous gatherings since they reasoned that nothing good
would come from something that people enjoyed so much.

There were even a few *babushkas* present, elderly widows,
dressed all in black, who had lived through the Great War. Grigori
Morostev enjoyed watching them as they came ambling around the

Alexander Column in the center of the Square. He remembered when all of the buildings were burned out shells. He had clambered up almost all of them searching for targets during the war. He did not want to come back here and felt that he would be badly affected by it. He was doing better than he thought he would but he had not tried to sleep here yet. The nights he spent here would be the real test.

The city had been constructed in the middle of a marshland and there were more than 200 bridges over the canals and rivers that connected the land areas. Fyodor Dostoyevsky, the great nineteenth century author, had portrayed its dreary slum dwellers and the city's dark side in his novels. But now the attitude of the crowd at the Winter Palace seemed to belie his description, even though the Communists had done much to return the city to a level of dreariness similar to that of Dostoyevsky's time.

Grigori checked his watch against the Winter Palace Tower clock in the central pediment before leaving the Square. He was on time. He walked with the crowd along the Neva River until he came to a small illegal restaurant a few blocks from St. Isaacs Cathedral called the *Col Bleu*, meaning blue collar, a tribute to the proletariat. Because the food was so good it was one of the few unofficial restaurants allowed to stay open. Chef Antoine's mother was French and she had married a Russian sailor when his ship docked in Marseilles. She passed her knowledge of classic French cooking on to her son.

The excellent *haute cuisine* attracted mostly patrons who were part of the one percent of the population that belonged to the Communist Party. There was nowhere else in the city to dine on *hors d'oeuvres* such as *foie gras* and *escargot*, and a *plat principal* consisting of *filet de boeuf au poivre, confit de canard*, or basil salmon terrine, served with vegetables such as *sauteed haricots vert,* mushrooms and onions, and cauliflower *au gratin.* This was usually followed by several types of *fromage* and a salad. The meal was usually accompanied by a bottle of wine such as *Cabernet Sauvignon* or *Chardonnay*, and followed by desserts such as *crepes Suzette, crème brulee,* or *mousse au chocolat.* No one with the authority to do so had the heart to shut down *Col Bleu* and Antoine's culinary creations remained in demand by those who could afford them.

Grigori ordered one of the most popular dishes, *Salad Niçoise*, after he located his contact by the red scarf she wore. She was quite attractive and appeared to be about 15 years younger than him. When they finished dining they stepped outside the café and walked slowly away from the crowd of people coming from the Palace Square. He waited for her to describe the job before deciding whether to take it. The problem was if you turned down work, word got around and it could be more difficult to be hired. When he asked who she worked for, she said it was not important. He replied that it was important to him.

"Do you work for Dmitri?"

"No. Who I work for won't affect your assignment," she said. "If I told you I was KGB would it matter? Be satisfied that we know you are a *Hero of the Soviet Union*, and that you work exclusively in taking down members of the *vorovstoy mir*. That is why we have let you alone. You are doing part of our work for us. We take down about ten per cent of the *vorovstoy mir* every year. If we rounded all of them up and shot them, there would be others who would take their place; so we control them, like the pests they are. Your job has nothing to do with them, however."

"Who then?"

"You are to find and eliminate an Israeli named Isaac Ben-Chaim, born Josef Storchev in Leningrad sometime before the war. He immigrated to the state of Israel with his parents at age fifteen. He is an agent for professional athletes and he comes to Europe when international competition is scheduled here. He may have encouraged some of our athletes to defect in the past. But that is not why he has been targeted," she told him.

When he asked why, she answered by mumbling that he had angered the wrong people by spreading "western propaganda" and threatening the security of the state.

That sounds like code words for spying, he thought. He wondered why the KGB was not handling this. *They are internal security, foreign intelligence, and domestic police all in one, and they have their own assassins. Why wouldn't they take care of him? Surely Yuri Vladimirovich Andropov, the head of the KGB, could have someone handle this fellow. But it could be that someone is going to make a great deal of money when this person is eliminated. That is a good enough reason to hire me and keep it a secret. It is likely someone in the Communist Party who is offering this contract. This would be the first time I have ever received payment from anyone in the government. I'm not sure I want to do that*, he thought.

"We think he will be in Munich for the Olympics and you are to deal with him there, away from the games, in as quiet a manner as possible," she said. "If you can dispose of the body there will be extra compensation," she informed him.

"That is not how I work," he said. "To do it that way would involve getting close to him and using a pistol with a silencer. You need to get someone else if you want it done that way."

His refusal unnerved her and she became agitated and then told him to go ahead and do it however he wished. She reiterated that there would be extra compensation if he did it the way she had outlined. When he refused again she stood there, arms akimbo, looking exasperated.

"You realize what the consequences are if you do not accept, don't you?"

"Do you want to tell me what would happen if I don't take this job?"

"You will regret it. So you really don't have a choice. Either you do the job…or you will find yourself out of work— permanently."

Then she thrust a large envelope at him. He examined it and found that it was full of currency, mostly German marks and a smaller amount of Swiss francs. When she asked for the number of his Swiss account, he hesitated, and then handed her a small piece of paper with the number on it.

"One fifth now and four fifths upon completion," she stated, and handed him a dossier containing the most current information on the target. Then she turned and walked away, looking disconcerted.

He had the job now since he had taken the money; but he did not want to wind up in the hands of the KGB because he refused to do their work for them. He began to dislike this fellow Dmitri even more. *Dmitri will make a fortune while I will take all the risk. But I am going to do it my way or not all.* He had not been able to complete some of the jobs that the "thieves-in-law" had given him and it had not been a problem. But this was a much more complicated affair and he wondered what would happen if he did not finish the job.

Back at the office of Major Vladimir Ostrokovich, Captain Ana Shelepin explained to him why she had not attempted to persuade Grigori Morostev to do things the way she had outlined them. His medical records indicated that one of his four wounds from the war had left him impotent, she said. The Major looked surprised but did not attempt to counter her statement and she left without any further discussion about Morostev.

CHAPTER SIXTEEN

The Poet Jalaluddin Rumi

"What can we do to stop these terrorist groups?" Khalisah asked.

"There is only one way," Bill replied.

"What's that?"

"We have to get into your father's computer and find out where the money is going."

"That is going to be difficult. Do you have any idea about how to do that?"

"You have to convince him that your professor told you that computers were going to be important in the field of medicine and you want to learn as much about them as you can," Bill said.

"I'll see if he will agree to that," Khalisah replied.

"Wait until the *new* wears off of it a little bit. Then he will be more likely to let you get near it."

"How long do you think that will be?"

"About a month, but the sooner the better because my presence here makes me vulnerable. He hasn't bothered with me recently because he has other things on his mind."

"Meaning the movie actress?"

"Yes."

"Have you learned anything about her?" Khalisah inquired.

"Actually, I met her for lunch at the hotel where she was staying. She sent a note asking me to come talk to her."

"Oh? I suppose you couldn't wait to meet her," Khalisah said and frowned.

"She's older than me by a decade."

"I'm sure that wouldn't bother her one bit."

"Well, I can't be too hard on her. I found out that she was a dirt poor Southern girl who scratched her way out of the hovel she was raised in, sort of like me."

"If you think that I am going to have any sympathy for her, Charles Harper, you're mistaken. I am fixing to give my father a good scolding for this! Oh, listen at me. I'm beginning to sound more and more like you—using your idioms from the South. My father even says that I'm beginning to pick up your accent."

"Maybe we should stick to Arabic."

"You can express yourself well enough in it now, but I don't want you corrupting my accent in my native tongue so that I wind up speaking Arabic with a Southern accent."

"That would sound rather peculiar."

"Back to her. What is she really like?"

"She's not so bad, actually. She does owe quite a bit in back taxes though."

"That's why she's after my father."

"True. But he could have done a lot worse. She's not a typical Hollywood actress. She just needs a wealthy man to help her now."

"Huh! Don't make her sound like one of your saints! I've seen enough of your American movies in England to know the difference between saints and actresses."

"You've done a lot of things female members of the al-Saud are not supposed to do."

"And I'm going to do a lot more. Now back to the computer. How would it be possible to find out what's in there if we could get access to it?"

"I don't know. That's why you'll have to depend on your father's favor to learn how to do it. You have an edge now since he knows that you disapprove of his latest antics. Just don't overdo it when you put pressure on him. Just see if he will let you use it to try and solve a few null hypotheses in medicine."

"You know, you really do have a very calculating, some would even say, a very devious mind."

"Maybe that's why you find me interesting."

"Huh! I really would like to see what psychoanalysis would reveal about your persona though."

"Ah, it would only reveal the simple nature of a country boy from the South."

"That's a laugh."

"Here's looking at you, kid."

"Don't try that bogus, tinsel town jargon on me."

"How's this then?"

"Shall I compare thee to a summer's day?"

"That's a little better."

"Or do you prefer this by Jalaluddin Rumi?

At every instant and from every side, resounds the call of Love...."

"How do you know about the poet we quote the most?"

"Oh, I read a lot."

"You really are something."

"I'm glad you think so."

She didn't answer and he turned his attention to the question of getting into Faisal's computer. He thought that it would take at least a month to get the data transferred to the new computer. He wasn't sure but that seemed reasonable. He was thinking about the problem and apparently had gotten that look in his eyes that Khalisah had said made him impervious to any communication from those around him. He suddenly remembered that she had insisted that he pay her more attention; not just when he wanted to know about something that she could help him with.

She began to cry softly and he joked, "What's this now?"

Then he realized that she was hurt and embarrassed. Not by what he had said but because she had been betrayed by her own emotions—her feelings for him. He had no way of knowing but Khalisah had just realized that she would never be able to be with him on a permanent basis, and that he was just using her to get what he wanted—information from her father's computer. Always before when they sparred verbally she had been his equal. He had never considered her feelings or that she might have become more emotionally attached to him than he realized.

He had concluded that she had a "school girl crush" on him, at most. But even a school girl, especially a twenty year old one, often fell in love with someone before they realized it. Now he had to figure out how to handle the situation—if he could.

"I'm going," she said and walked away quickly, leaving him standing there with a puzzled look on his face.

Let's see, he thought. *This makes number three; all in about two years. And I had nothing at all to do with girls in the previous twenty years.* He concluded that he was clearly not as capable of understanding them as he thought.

The *Blutfahnenweihe*

When Klaus von Kleinmann entered the *Steinadler Kaffeehaus* the next night, there was a young man waiting for him.

He walked up to Klaus and said, "Come with me."

Klaus squeezed his left arm against the side of his chest so he could feel the Walther PPK he had holstered there. Now it was time for him to play his part in the small drama that he had set in motion. He had rehearsed what he was going to say and thought that he could make it sound plausible. It would require him to assume the persona of a somewhat deranged, fanatical Nazi, however.

During the war, he had assumed the identity of a Polish laborer and a French partisan and he had successfully passed himself off as Polish cattle baron in Argentina. So this masquerade should not be too difficult. He thought that he could play the role of an unrepentant Nazi without too much difficulty. He followed the boy outside to a phone box where the receiver was lying on the shelf. He stepped inside and closed the door and spoke into the receiver.

"*Ja?*"

"Is this Herr Kruger?"

"*Ja, es ist.*"

"What do you want with us?" The voice was that of an older man.

"I am interested in what you are doing."

"Why?"

"I have a connection to the Third Reich. I am curious about you."

"You are from the *polizei*. I am in a phone box so it will not do you any good to try and trace this call."

"I have no intention of trying to locate you."

"Then why do you want to meet us?"

"I have gift for you."

"Then give it to the messenger that we will send."

"If you wish. Can you trust him not to abscond with it?"

"He will die if he does not obey."

"Then send him. If you will not meet with me, I have other things to do."

"Is it gold you are trying to give us?"

"Not just any gold."

"What kind of gold? And why do you want to give it to us?"

"Because it is *blut goldbarren*."

"What do you mean, *blut goldbarren*?"

"Do you not remember the *Blutfanhe*?"

"I am familiar with the *Blutfanhe*."

"The *Blutfanhe* has disappeared. This *blut goldbarren* can be used in place of the blood banner to consecrate new articles, including banners, which will be used by those that are engaged in the struggle now."

"You don't believe in that mysticism, do you?"

Klaus feigned anger and replied loudly with a tremor in his voice, "What do you mean mysticism? Without symbols and articles of faith, no movement can succeed. Perhaps you should consider how little success you have had and why you have so few members. You do not have any symbols to give a sense of authenticity to your beliefs. That's why you cringe in fear and hide from the *polizei* like rats in the dark!"

"We believe in the struggle. We have no need of objects to trust in."

"Then you are a fool! The rallies in Nuremberg were huge, attended by over 150,000 party members at the *Ehrenhalle* and the *Blutfahne* was the center of attention. When the Fuehrer touched the *Blutfahne* to the guidons of new *SA* and *SS* units during the *Blutfahnenweihe*, the blood of the martyrs from the *Putsch* consecrated their new *Standartens*."

"I know the history of the *Blutfahne* as well as you. How are the gold bars supposed to take the place of the blood flag?"

"They have the blood of many, many more on them than the blood of the few martyrs that was sprinkled on the *Blutfahne* during the *putsch* on 9 November 1923. The *blut goldbarren* represent the blood of all of the millions who died fighting for the Fatherland."

"And you believe this?"

"It does not matter whether I believe it or not. It does not matter whether you believe it or not. It does not matter whether anyone outside the struggle believes it or not. It is a means for those who see it to visualize the solemn nature of the struggle, and feel that they have become a part of the *kampf*. In the future, when flags are touched to the *blut goldbarren*, it will symbolize an acceptance of the dedication to the struggle just as the blood flag did. Are you incapable of understanding that?"

"Who are you then? And why should I accept what you say?"

"I am a member of the *Abwehr*, holder of the Iron Cross, 2nd Class, and an eye witness of the Nuremberg Rallies and how the *Blutfahnenweihe* made the members of the new units feel that they had become a part of the *kampf*. Now the *blut goldbarren* must replace the lost flag of the martyrs as an even more powerful symbol. A symbol of the transference of a feeling of belonging to the *kampf*.

There was silence for a while, then the voice on the phone said, "Then you honor us with your bequest. We shall arrange to pick them up whenever you say."

"Good. Send your messenger. I will be waiting here at the phone box and I will give him directions as to where he can pick them up."

"How many will there be? Should I send more than one messenger to carry them?"

"There will be 24 bars, each weighing 1 kilo, enough to form a swastika to be used in ceremonies involving the transference of the responsibilities of the National Socialist Party to new adherents. The blood of all who have died in that mission will be represented by these *blut goldbarren*."

Klaus could sense that the person on the phone was calculating the value of the bars.

"So you will need to send only one messenger. He will be able to carry all of them."

"He will be there shortly, Herr Kruger."

"One other thing."

"Yes?"

"You understand that these emblems are to be used only for ceremonial purposes. They are not to be sold under any circumstances."

"Yes, I understand."

"How can I be certain that you will not dispose of them in that manner?"

There was silence on the other end.

"I want you to take a brief oath. Are you willing to do that?"

"Yes, I will."

"Repeat after me: I solemnly swear…."

"I solemnly swear…."

"That I will hold these emblems in the highest regard…."

"That I will hold these emblems in the highest regard…."

"And use them only for the purposes for which they are intended…."

"And use them only for the purposes for which they are intended…."

"And never sell or otherwise desecrate them in any way."

"And never sell or otherwise desecrate them in any way."

"As God is my witness."

"As God is my witness."

"And now you may feel that you have only repeated a few meaningless words, but let me assure you that your words are witnesses of what you have sworn to do, and they will return back to you in vengeance if you do not honor your vow. Do you understand?"

"I understand."

"Then send your messenger."

"He is on his way. *Auf Wiedersehen.*"

"*Heil Hitler.*"

"Ah, yes. *Heil Hitler. Sieg Heil!*"

Good. He has decided to take them, if for no other reason than to purchase a few weapons, thought Klaus. *There will be many ways for the bars to do their work. Perhaps they will get caught trying to sell them, or be killed trying to use the new weapons they purchase from the sale of the bars. One of them may try and steal some of them, or they may keep them and allow the greed that they create to bear its fruit,* he thought. *The bars have only brought death and destruction to whoever has them and these misfits are the ideological heirs of the ones who stole them.*

It will be regrettable if anyone is killed by the weapons purchased from the sale of the bars, but it cannot be avoided. I have rid myself of them and put them in the hands of those who are the most deserving of them, and of the tragedy they bring to whoever possesses them. Then Klaus chuckled and thought, *I was more effective in portraying the half-crazed, incorrigible Nazi fanatic than I thought I would be. Maybe I should audition for a part in the next stage play in Buenos Aire*s.

It was not long before the messenger appeared. He was young and looked athletic and he took the map that Klaus gave to him and sprinted away.

They will have someone watching to make sure he is not followed and they will search the sky for helicopters to see if he is being watched from above, Klaus thought. *But if the polizei are capable they will be able to follow him with night vision binoculars and if they lose him they will be able to use the tracking device that I put in with the gold. The device that I mailed to them will allow them to follow him to the lair. Then all they need to do is surround the safe house he leads them to and pull the net in after a day or two.*

True to his plan, Klaus learned two days later that the *polizei* had detained one of the most prominent leaders of the neo-Nazis in Berlin, Bernhard Weiser, along with a number of other members of his group. They also reeled in the two leaders of the Red Army Faction, Andreas Baader and Ulrike Meinhof, who were meeting with them, apparently to plan a joint operation. *No one had ever accused the last two of being overly bright,* he thought, *and they proved it by their lack of caution.* It seemed that the gold had once again brought tragedy to its bearers without delay. Klaus was greatly relieved as he thought of what might have happened if he had kept the gold—something that had so much innocent blood on it.

CHAPTER SEVENTEEN

The Elusive American

"What do you have to tell me about him?" Prince Faisal demanded of Hans Kreiser, the German who headed up his new security detail.

"We cannot find any information about him. The fingerprints from the glasses he used here—we have all ten prints—have been of no help to us."

"Couldn't you come up with anything on him?"

"Only that his passport is a chop shop job; not as professional as most forged passports are. It is good enough to get him through airports, but it does not appear to have been done by an agency or bureaucracy of any country."

"Anything else?"

"He is clearly from the Southern part of the U. S. But that is of no help by itself."

"Where have you looked?"

"We have not been able to find any record of him in Europe."

"What about the Middle East?"

"So far, nothing."

"Where did the plane he came to London on originate from?"

"It came from New York."

"Where did he come from to catch the plane to New York?"

"Sir, there were almost 200 people on that plane; he could have come from many different places."

"Well, get busy tracing all of them."

"Sir, it may take some time to find that out. I am not a detective. My organization provides security and we do an excellent job. I can assure you that nothing will happen to you as it did before. However, if I spend my time trying to trace someone, I cannot devote myself to providing you with the best possible security."

"Then hire someone to do it. Hire a detective agency, or two, or three. However many it takes. Have them find out where all of the passengers came from. Have them show his picture to all of the airline personnel at Heathrow who were on duty that day. Have them interview all of the passengers and show them his picture. Someone had to see him. I want to know who he is working for! Have them report to you and then keep me informed with regular updates."

"Very good, sir. That would be the best way to do it. I should mention that such services are expensive."

"Money is no object. However, I want good value for what I pay to get this done."

"Perhaps we could save a great deal of time if you would allow us to 'interview' him."

"No. He did save my life. Besides, he has my daughter wrapped around his little finger. I don't want anything to happen to him. Not yet anyway."

"As you wish, sir. And may I say what a pleasure it is to work for you, Prince Faisal."

Faisal merely grunted and Hans Kreiser backed out of the room and began to formulate a plan on how to get the information the Prince wanted. *Perhaps we should go ahead and "interview" Charles Harper anyway without the knowledge of the Prince*, he thought. That would save a great deal of time, but it carried considerable risk if he turned out to not be a threat. *Faisal might not even pay us*, he decided. *That would not work at all.*

Kreiser did not want to risk upsetting Prince Faisal. He and his team were not working when Faisal contacted them and this was the best paying job they had ever had. Also, the situation seemed to be a permanent one, which warranted using the utmost caution to make sure the Prince did not get upset. *No, Saudi Arabia was not a bad place to live, especially when the pay was this good*, Kreiser decided.

The Blank Check

When Bill arrived back at the mansion of Prince Faisal, he found that a note had been put under his door. When he opened it, the same sweet smell of a classic tea rose wafted up and he knew it was from Rhonda Gialetti. She asked him to meet her at the restaurant in her hotel for tea that afternoon. As he drove there, he decided that he was going to need some help to get information out of Faisal's computer. But who could he get to do it? And how could they get into the country? It would need to be someone as inconspicuous as possible; someone who would not be connected to him.

He was sure that he was being watched closely now and there was no doubt that word of his meeting with Rhonda would be relayed on to Faisal. He was going to let her handle that. Bill was sure that she could explain it, or anything else, to Prince Faisal and he would accept it without hesitation. *Isn't love grand?* No. He wasn't going to think about love or he would start missing Rebecca too much. He needed to get word out to Simons Grebel about the computer and ask him to get Yitzhak Kahan to find someone who could get into Faisal's home and extract the information from it. If such a person existed.

This was the most important information that Tel Aviv could ever get—where the money was going. It simply could not be passed up. He had to be extremely careful in trying to contact Grebel though. He was certain that any letter he sent would be opened. He did not dare use the phone to relay word on to Grebel. He could only imagine what would happen if he were to call a number in Tel Aviv. When he arrived at the hotel, she was waiting for him, only this time she did not seem worried or agitated.

"Hello," she said with a smile. "I have some great news."

"That's always good. What has happened?"

"Oh, a great deal has happened. I received word from my lawyer that the IRS wanted to see me again, and I told him that's why I had hired him."

"It doesn't sound good so far."

"Ah, but here's the good part. When I told Faisal, he told me to go take care of it."

"Yes. It is beginning to sound interesting now."

"And that's not all. He gave me a check, a cashier's check."

"That does sound better—much better."

"And the best part is, Bill, it will cover all of the back taxes the IRS says that I owe! Isn't that great?"

"I couldn't be happier for you."

"And not only that, Faisal gave me another check from his personal account. And listen to this, it's a blank check!"

"A blank check?"

"Yes, to cover my legal expenses and any other debts that I need to settle. In fact, he gave me his check book! I can pay off everything I owe! Oh, Bill, I have you to thank for all of it! I was ready to pack up and go back to the States until you advised me to wait and see what he would do for me."

"That's great. When are you leaving?"

"In a few days. When I have had time to pack. We ladies need time to get everything together, you know."

"How long are you going to stay?"

"A couple of weeks at least. Maybe more. But I don't want to stay away from him too long."

"Let's go for a walk."

"All right."

They left the restaurant and walked down the street and stopped at a park bench.

She asked him, "Why is it necessary to do this?"

"It could be that someone Faisal hired is listening in on you in your apartment and perhaps even when you go out. You eat at the same table every time. I couldn't take a chance."

"You think he is bugging me? Why that low down...."

"Either on his orders or without his knowledge, I'm sure that someone is keeping a close watch on you," Bill said.

"What do you need to talk about?"

"I need your help. I have to get a message out. I won't have another chance to ask you before you leave."

"What message?"

"An extremely important one."

"And you need me to help you."

"Yes. Will you?"

"All right, kid. I'll take the message for you."

"Thanks. Here's a phone number. Commit it to memory and burn this note. When you get to New York, call it from a pay phone. It's long distance. Ask for Simons Grebel. Tell him Charley Harper needs a computer technician to come to Riyadh to get a list of extremists receiving money from the al-Saud. It's in a Honeywell computer, model H632. Tell him it's too important to let it get away."

"So you're after something from Faisal also."

"Yes. But not anything that will hurt him. In fact, it may help save his life again."

"How?"

"The groups that receive money from Saudi Arabia through Faisal follow the radical Wahhabi doctrine that directs them to kill their enemies who are subverting Islam. They consider the members of the al-Saud, who finance them, as being too westernized and so degenerate that they are a part of the problem. They want to rid Islam of them."

"So this is what I'm getting into."

"I'm afraid so."

"What about Faisal? What can I tell him about us taking a walk?"

"Take the offensive. Act like you're his wife. His western wife. He went to Oxford. He understands western women. If he asks why you went for a walk with me, ask him why he is spying on you. Tell him that you refuse to be spied on. Don't worry about me. I'm already in danger of something worse than Chop-Chop Square if he gets angry enough with me. It couldn't get any worse."

"Then what?"

"Then just throw the little checkbook at him, but not the cashier's check."

"Do you really think I should do that?"

"He's a man. He'll understand that. Anything less might not impress him enough."

"What should I do after that?"

"Skedaddle. Go back home and pay your taxes. He could stop payment on that cashier's check at any time."

"What if he does stop payment on the check?"

"He could, but there is an element of pride involved in the giving of gifts, so I don't think he will. It has to do with an Arab man's sense of honor."

"And what if he doesn't want me anymore?"

"Well, you know what they say; absence makes the heart grow fonder. I think you are underestimating yourself. If he still wants you, and I don't think there's any reason to doubt that, he'll do whatever it takes to get you back here."

"Oh, Bill, I hope you're right. Otherwise, I have lost everything when I had it right in the palm of my hand."

"And I would be responsible for making you lose it. I shouldn't have involved you. But I have to get a message out. Now I'm hoping that this will work and that it will make him even more anxious not to lose you. You are the only female in his life now."

"But he has three wives."

"Two of them are older than him and the third is not much younger, and you are...."

"Twenty-nine!"

"My point exactly."

CHAPTER EIGHTEEN

The Sniper Rifle

As he traveled to Leningrad to meet his contact for his assignment in Munich, Grigori thought of his comrades, the heroes, the snipers of the Great Patriotic War. Numerous Soviet snipers had more than 400 German kills during the war, but the most famous snipers were Anatoly Chekhov and Vassilli Zeitsev who fought in the Battle for Stalingrad, and Vladimir Pchelinstev, who fought with Grigori at Leningrad. Pchelinstev had relished the role of "hero" and loved being paraded before adoring crowds in an attempt to stir up patriotism.

Grigori never cared for it and rebuffed every attempt to get him to appear before audiences as Pchelinstev did. He did so if he was ordered to and only after asking to be excused because he was needed at the front. *Who knows? Perhaps I would have fared better if I had gone on more of those tours.* Like Grigori, Anatoly Chekhov had been born in the town of Kazan, the capital of the Republic of Taterstan, Russia. Grigori's small village was only fifty kilometers from Kazan. Like him, Anatoly Chekhov had joined the army and became a sniper because of his superior vision.

He excelled at every phase of his duty as a sniper: marksmanship, camouflage, forward positioning, and most importantly, patience. Grigori had met Chekhov during the war and because they were both from Kazan they became friends despite being together for only a short time in Moscow. After a few weeks, Chekhov was sent south to Stalingrad and Grigori was dispatched to the north to help defend Leningrad. Once the war was over Grigori never saw Chekhov again. He went to work dispatching members of the "thieves" world."

When Chekhov died in 1967, Grigori heard about his death but could not get there in time to attend his funeral. He made a pilgrimage to his resting place later, however, and spent hours standing over the grave. He bought a wreath and placed it on the grave site to honor his friend, the brave patriot from Kazan who had killed over 250 German invaders.

When Grigori was shown into the apartment, he was amazed at the luxurious furnishings. He had never seen one this nice before, although he assumed that they existed. The pantry and refrigerator were stocked with the finest quality food: meat, bread, wine, fresh vegetables, canned goods, and the best caviar. Most of these items were not available on a regular basis in Moscow. He began to suspect that a great deal was going to be required of him and thought of leaving before he started the job. But how could he get out of this contract now?

He did not like the first thought that came into his mind. The reason that he was being treated this well was because they planned to get rid of him after he did the job to cover their tracks. He was afraid he had been caught in a neatly laid trap. *So now I am going to have to go along until I can find a way out of this.* As he was about to sit down and get comfortable, he heard a knock on the door. When he opened it, an unkempt man with silver hair asked him if he could come in. He was carrying two silver cases and had a bundle wrapped in linen tucked under one arm.

He laid all three on the couch. He did not bother to introduce himself. Instead he asked, "What rifle do you prefer?"

Grigori asked him why he wanted to know something like that. He gave Grigori a quizzical look and asked again. Grigori replied that he preferred the standard issue Soviet sniper rifle, which was the gas operated Dragunov SVD (*Snayperskaya Vintovka Dragunova*) put into service in 1963. The man looked at him with sad, piercing blue eyes and began reciting the specifications of the SVD.

"Yes, I suppose that you would. With the open butt stock design it is very light, weighing only 4.3 kilograms unloaded," he noted. "It has a flash hider and a 4 power telescope and a maximum range of 1,300 meters," he continued. "It is chambered in 7.62 x 54R, a rimmed cartridge, and can fire 30 rounds per minute in the semiautomatic setting." And he concluded, "It is deadly at 400 meters and is accurate up to 600 meters if the wind is still."

Grigori merely nodded at his description. Anyone who dealt with sniper rifles would know that, he thought.

"The Dragunov is not considered a serious sniper rifle, however, among those who know about such weapons. I have here another piece for you to examine," he said.

Then he unfastened the larger of the two silver cases. In it lay a beautiful weapon that Grigori could tell was custom made. He had never seen one like it. When he opened the smaller case it contained a large scope and a smaller scope, a number of cartridges, and a cleaning kit.

"It is custom made, so I have another one just like it to practice with. It can also be used if this one is lost or it can be used to provide replacement parts for the primary weapon," said the man with the piercing blue eyes. "That is not ideal but it is necessary if speed is important."

"What did it cost to make it?"

"More than it would cost to make many SVDs."

"Just how good is it?"

"It is superior in every respect to any other sniper rifle, especially the Dragunov. In fact, it is one of the best sniper rifles ever built," he remarked.

"It looks light."

"It is light. The stock is made of a fiberglass and will not expand or shrink due to the weather and affect the use of the scope. Here, feel for yourself."

Grigori took the weapon and put it to his shoulder. It had a better feel than any that he had ever handled.

"What are the specifications?"

"It has a manually operated rotating bolt action, with a 600 mm barrel and it holds 5 rounds in an integral box magazine. It is built on the design of the German Mauser K98k and it is chambered in .300 Win Mag. Its overall length is 1250 mm and it weighs 4.09 kg loaded. It has a ten power telescopic sight made by Schmidt and Bender," he said with a noticeable degree of admiration in his voice.

"The flash is completely blocked from sight but there is no sound suppressor since that affects the accuracy, although some would disagree with that. Here is some ammunition, .300 Win Mag, which is designed to fit in a standard length action such as this weapon has. These are 7.62 mm cartridges also known as .30 caliber magnum rounds. They have been the world standard for shots of 1,000 meters or more for several years now. These Winchester Magnum rounds have all been hand loaded by the gunsmith," he stated.

"Here is an additional large scope in the other case that can be used by a spotter or the shooter and the smaller scope is a range finder. You are aware, of course, that the scope on the rifle and these two items are the most important part of your equipment. Also, you know much better than me, that there is a combination of factors that make for an accurate shot, especially at 1,000 yards or more."

Then he un-wrapped the bundle covered in linen, revealing an Uzi sub-machine gun and a pistol.

"And the Uzi is for when the sniper has to shoot his way out?"

"Yes. Since it is likely a sniper could encounter opposition after eliminating a target. The position for the shot may be close enough to the target that it would be necessary to neutralize that opposition to escape. The Uzi provides a means to do that."

"I have found that running along a predetermined escape route is much safer."

"You are no doubt correct."

"And the pistol?"

"It is the Stechkin APS, the *Automaticheskij Pistolet Stechkina*."

"I prefer the *Pistolet Besshumnyj*, the 'silenced' pistol, based on the Makarov design and issued to the KGB and other groups."

"It is a matter of personal preference. Since you are a sniper you will probably not need it. A handgun is useful primarily to keep a man with a knife from getting to you; when he is more than 10 meters away, that is. You would be able to get off one shot before he covered that distance, if you saw him first. At 25 meters you need to use a Stechkin in the full automatic mode, which neither the Makarov nor the PB/6P9 have. Beyond 50 meters a handgun cannot be relied on."

"Who paid for this?"

"His name is Dmitri."

"There are many people with the name Dmitri."

"True enough. But Dmitri has many names. It depends on where he is and what he is doing."

"Is he Russian?"

"No one seems to know for certain, or even care for that matter. One rumor is that he is a Ukrainian, from Kiev. I personally think he is from Vladivostok and not a Russian; but rather of European and Oriental stock. But it makes no difference really."

"What does he do?"

"Since you must know, I will tell you. But you're not KGB, are you? No. You don't look like it. Although you could be one of those they recruit to do work like this; they like to use harmless looking fellows like yourself."

"I am not KGB. I have served only in the army, in the infantry."

"Good. Then you won't turn me in. Besides it is certain that Dmitri would know all about you already. He is a merchant; he buys and sells things. What things? All sorts of things. Very expensive things. Like weapons. He is an arms dealer, although I have never heard of him turning down any transaction that would be profitable. Except drugs. He doesn't traffic in narcotics."

"Why not?"

"Because he believes it to be too dangerous. Those in the drug cartels believe it is best to kill first and ask questions later. Those who want to buy large amounts of arms are more reasonable. They know they will need more weapons later and that it would be foolish to do away with the middle man. They know that reliable arms dealers are scarce; very scarce."

"And who would Dmitri want me to use this weapon on?"

"There are always problems that arise in Dmitri's line of work. Someone who refuses to cooperate, or someone who goes too far, or someone who knows too much. Those are the people Dmitri has to deal with."

"Do you work for Dmitri?"

"Only indirectly. I'm a small arms dealer who sells him weapons from time to time, although he pays me well to deal with people like you."

"Why do you think Dmitri would give me such an expensive weapon?"

"To impress you I suppose. You are valuable to Dmitri because it is necessary for him to be rid of someone who is interfering with one of his transactions; and the only type of transactions he engages in are large ones, very large ones that are highly profitable."

Grigori did not respond. He was certain that this fellow did not know what his job was. He wondered how Dmitri fit in with the woman who had contacted him about the job. She was obviously KGB. He considered what his options might be, but at the moment he could not think of any way to get out of this contract.

"I have other rifles that are adequate for what you may need to do and they are accurate up to about 800 meters. You can requisition one from me if you prefer one of them. This one is not a show piece, however. It is to be used for distances of 1,000 meters or more," he said.

"And since you snipers like to practice with the same weapon that you use on a target, I will bring you the other model to practice with. I understand most of you shoot about 100 hours for every shot you take at a live target. So you can practice with one and shoot with the other. You can only get so many shots out of a barrel, you know."

"Did you make this piece?"

"No. But I know who did make it. I might be able to make one but it would be far inferior to this one. The maker of this piece also designed it. I helped him test it. Believe me, it will amaze you when you use it."

"I will need to test it myself."

"Do it secretly, in a safe spot. I can direct you to some locations that would be satisfactory."

"What is your name?"

"It is better that you do not know," answered the man with the silver hair and piercing blue eyes.

"I need a name to call you by even if it is a false one."

"Call me *Golos* then."

"The voice?"

"Yes."

"What now *Golos*? Am I supposed to wait until I am contacted?"

"Yes. It may be a while, so enjoy the wait, without attracting any attention. You will need someone who speaks German to go with you on this job. You will meet this person in Zurich and then cross over into Germany and go to Munich. I will return shortly. *Do svidaniya.*"

CHAPTER NINETEEN

The Lion of the Littoral

Bill felt sure that he would not receive any word back from Tel Aviv if they found someone who could get into Faisal's computer. He would have to be patient and trust that Rhonda Gialetti forwarded his message and that Yitzhak could find someone to do it. It seemed impossible for anyone from the outside to get into the country and penetrate the maze of security that Faisal had set up. He heard that Rhonda had left the country and that Faisal had become very irritable lately. Whether he would go after her or not remained to be seen; but if he did, then things were going according to plan.

Bill received a rose scented letter from Rhonda a few days later. He could tell that it had been opened. It had a cheerful greeting and a few sentences about how well things were going. He hoped that meant that his message had been sent. She closed by saying, *Well, honey, I hope that the little yellow flower you like so well doesn't wilt. It would need an expert to come see about it, wouldn't it? That's why I like roses better. See you later on. Your friend, Rhonda.*

He was confused by the last part; it didn't make sense until he read it several times. *...little yellow flower...that I like...hope it doesn't wilt...* She had started with, *Well, honey... She's talking about the computer, the Honeywell,* Bill suddenly realized. That made the last part clear. *If it wilts, it would need an expert to come see about it.* Clever girl. He hoped she was clever enough so that whoever opened the letter didn't get the meaning. This meant he needed to disable the computer somehow so that Tel Aviv could find a way to insert one of their technicians to come work on it. No small task.

Three days later he found out that Faisal had left for the United States. This would be the perfect time to disable it. He had to get Khalisah to use the computer so he could figure out how to disable it. It had been a week since they talked and she had cried and walked out. He sent word that he needed her help and she came the next day, but her mood was such that he was afraid she was not going to help him.

"Your father has gone to the United States, I understand."

"Yes. He claims that he is going to watch of one his latest two year olds run. But I know better. He's gone after her. She is leading him around as though he had a ring in his nose and she had the cord."

"Two year olds…run?"

"Horses. This one is an Arabian stallion, white and magnificent. He asked me to name it when it was born."

"And what name did you come up with?"

"Well, I thought about it for a long time and really stretched my knowledge of English. But I finally decided on, *Tantamount to Victory*. How do you like that name?"

"It is an excellent one. Did your father like it?"

"Yes. He liked it a great deal. But that's not what he named it."

"Why not?"

"I don't know. I think because he decided it was too flippant and did not sound noble enough for an Arabian Prince."

"So what is its name?"

"*Lion of the Littoral*. It had to be something with an aristocratic ring to it. Littoral refers to the coastal area."

"Where is it running?"

"In smaller races to start with since the *Lion* has never been entered in a race before. The Louisiana Derby, the Arkansas Derby, and maybe the Santa Anita Derby. That's why I know he's gone after her. He's never had time to watch any of his horses run in anything except a major race. This is just an excuse."

"Have you ever seen any of his horses run before?"

"A few times in Europe. He did take Faisal and me to the United States to watch one of our horses run in the Kentucky Derby though, the year before we left to go to Oxford."

"To change the subject, I need to get into your father's computer while he's gone."

"I'll keep my end of the bargain," she said. "I still agree that these terrorist groups need to be stopped. It could help protect our family."

Bill waited for her to continue. He knew she needed to tell him how she felt.

"Last week I cried because I knew you would be leaving soon. In a society where you are part of an arranged marriage, there's not much room left for love. You learn to love the one who's been picked for you, if you're fortunate. I knew that you were using me all along but that didn't bother me. It was when I realized that after a few weeks I wouldn't be able to be with you anymore that I cried. I suppose that means I love you."

"I never meant to hurt you."

"It's not your fault. It's just that I've never been in love before. I didn't know it would hurt so much when it didn't work out."

"I wish...."

"Don't make excuses for yourself. It was all my doing. I don't blame you for anything. You were just being yourself. Now let's go and get this done."

They headed toward the computer room and walked inside as if it was an everyday occurrence. Hassan, who had been assigned by Faisal to watch the computer, was a relative but he knew little about its operation. Khalisah told him that they were going to do some math problems on it and that it would be all right for him to leave. When he walked out they began to search for a way to disable it.

"Turn it on," Bill suggested.

"How?"

"Let's find the manuals so we can see how to start it up," Bill said.

They spent most of the next half hour pouring over the manuals until they finally found out how to turn it on.

"Now what?"

"I'm not sure," Bill said. "Let's see if there is anything that can be pulled off, broken, or disabled."

They went over the computer several times but could not find anything that looked vulnerable. *Why not disconnect the electric cord that supplied power to the computer? That would be the easiest way and it would not do any serious damage to the computer itself,* Bill thought. He told Khalisah but she said if someone tugged on the cord and it came out, the place where it had been cut would show.

"What else can we do?" Khalisah asked.

"I don't know."

He pried around the ON switch until it came loose and then he disabled the wires that were connected to it.

"I don't think an electrician will want to look at it since he doesn't normally work on computers. Hopefully, the computer technician will come quickly. Now it's time for you to do your part. Tell your relative, Hassan, what happened—we caused it to fail some way. Then call your father and tell him and shed a few tears and ask him what you can do. Without seeming to be pushy, suggest that a Honeywell technician be called to come fix it. Have your relative standing by the phone with you in case your father wants him to call them. Although knowing your father, I suspect he'll call Honeywell himself."

Unrequited Love

Bill Smith could not decide whether to wait for the computer technician to come and repair the computer or to try and leave before Prince Faisal returned. If he could contact Rhonda Gialetti somehow, she could give him an idea of how long Faisal was going to be there with her. Bill suspected that Faisal would not remain out of the country for long and when he returned he was sure to have Rhonda with him. Then he received another rose scented letter from Rhonda. It had been opened, of course, although it was not possible to tell from the physical appearance of the letter.

They are very proficient at this, he thought, *but when you open as many letters as they do, you are bound to be good at it.* When he read it, he was as puzzled as he had been when he read her last letter. Then he noticed that she had used the word, "leave," an inordinate number of times in the letter. It was time for him to go. He spread a map of Saudi Arabia out on the table before him and traced a route to the nearest country where he could catch a flight out to Europe. Qatar, to the east was the closest country and its capital city of Doha should have regular flights out.

He would need to drive east from Riyadh to Al Hufuf, then south to Salwa, and then back east across the border into Qatar and on to the capital city of Doha. He thought about getting Khalisah and her brother, Faisal, to go with him into Riyadh to shop. He could slip away and rent a car and drive on to Qatar alone. But if it appeared that they had helped him, they would risk the anger of Prince Faisal when he returned. He was sure that he was at greater risk now and if he stayed any longer, someone was going to figure out why he was there just as Khalisah had.

He packed a few clothes and hid them inside the Range Rover so that he could leave quickly. When he returned, Khalisah was waiting for him.

"Are you leaving?"

"I think I have to. It could become very unpleasant for me when your father returns."

"Yes. I thought you would be going now."

"How did you know?"

"I felt it."

She had her arms crossed over her chest and although she did not say it, Bill knew that she meant she felt it inside.

"I had a melancholy feeling come over me because I knew that my life with you was ending and there was nothing I could do about it."

"I'm sorry."

"I believe you. It doesn't lessen the pain though."

"I wish I could keep you from hurting, but I have to go."

"And you won't take me with you, will you?"

"I can't."

Khalisah started to cry and wiped her eyes and said, "I wasn't going to make a scene."

"It's all right," Bill said.

"I promised myself that I wasn't going to do this. But I feel like my life is over. What am I going to do now, Charley?" She sounded like a child asking her parent why things had gone wrong.

"It'll be all right."

"No. It won't. Not for me. Not without you. If I lose you, I lose everything."

"No. Listen, Khalisah, You will get over this."

"No! Don't tell me that! You don't know! I can't stand to see you go."

"What can I do, Khalisah? I can't go off and leave you like this."

"Let me go with you. I won't be any trouble. I promise. You won't even know I'm there. You don't have to marry me. I just can't stand the thought of not ever seeing you again."

He thought about staying around a day or two in hopes she would feel better about him leaving, but he remembered Rhonda's warning. "Leave."

"I guess you'll have to come with me then."

Khalisah looked at him as though she could not believe him. Then she turned quickly and headed for the women's quarters to pack her clothes. They left within the hour. They decided to go alone and not get her brother, Faisal, to go to Riyadh with them. Half of Prince Faisal's security force was in America with him, including the director. The half that remained was concerned about stopping a threat from the outside; not about keeping anyone from leaving.

Bill headed the Range Rover down the highway toward Al Hufuf while Khalisah gazed out the window and thought about her childhood growing up here. Tears came to her eyes but she shut them off. She was going to leave here at some point anyway; it was better to go with Charley now. It was sooner than she had planned but she could make her own way. She would find work somewhere. She wasn't worried about her standard of living being lower; that had never meant much to her anyway. Being kept hidden away had been the problem and that wasn't ever going to change if she stayed in Riyadh.

She would find a way to finish university. There was always some sacrifice involved in doing things your own way. She had not had time to tell her mother good bye. She would have to write her a long letter explaining why she was leaving. She turned and looked at the young man she knew as Charley Harper. It was true she couldn't stand to see him leave. But she was doing this for herself. She might get over losing him enough to bear it somehow but she would never be able to tolerate being cloistered in someone's harem.

Charley had offered her hope; a way out of the suffocating social system of the Kingdom of Saudi Arabia. It might have been years before she would have had the courage to leave her home. Perhaps she would have even given up and accepted life in Riyadh as something that was inevitable. She shuddered to think about being trapped in such a life. No. this had to been done and if she waited until she graduated, it would be harder to leave—not easier.

"You remembered to get your passport, right?"

"Yes, I have it, Charley," she answered.

She felt a sense of security with Charley. He wouldn't let anything happen to her. She closed her eyes and drifted off into a state of semi-consciousness. She was aware of her surroundings but her body was relaxed. She was leaving with Charley Harper and that was the most pleasant sensation she had experienced in her young life. Especially since she knew that being without him was not something she could endure right now.

Bill Smith and Khalisah Amtullah al-Saud arrived at LaGuardia International Airport in New York City late at night and changed planes to go to Minneapolis-St. Paul. He told her that his name was not Charles Harper and she said that she had realized earlier that it was not his real name.

"What should I call you then?"

"Bill will be OK."

"And what is your last name going to be?"

"Smith will be fine."

"Hum. It sounds more like an alias than Charles Harper."

"It's my real name though."

"Aren't you afraid I'll tell someone?"

"No. Besides there are no records that I ever existed; except for a couple of fake passports and a few other forged documents."

"Well, my shadowy Lothario, when are you going to disappear again?"

"I'm not. You're doing better, aren't you?"

"No. But at least now I can pretend that I am. I suppose that's a start."

"You're really something, you know?"

"Just don't disappear yet. You promised you wouldn't."

"And I won't. I plan on giving this type of life up though. It's too, too…too much."

"My, my. The one and only invisible man can't take it anymore. I don't believe it."

"That sounds more like you. I don't guess I have ever told you how much I owe you, have I? You really did help me tremendously. I don't know how I can ever repay you; I really don't. But I will try."

"Yes, that does leave you in debt to me, I guess. I'll try to think of someway for you to pay me back. I'm sure that I will need your help at some point."

"I'll do whatever you need me to do, Khalisah."

They decided not to try and hide their travel route from her father. It would be difficult and she planned to write him in a few days before he became too upset when he found that she was gone. She felt she had the perfect gambit. She would tell her father in a nice, gentle way that if he sent anyone after her to bring her back to Riyadh, she would expose his affair with Rhonda Gialetti. She was due to go back to Oxford in a few weeks anyway so she would tell him she had changed her mind about going there and had decided to enroll in a university in the United States.

And although she had left with Charley Harper, he was not the reason she went. It was convenient to travel with him and she would tell her father that he had dropped her off at a university in the United States. And, no, nothing had happened between them, she would say. On the contrary, he had been a perfect gentleman. He had left and she didn't know where he had gone—to see his fiancée, he said. She would tell her father she would have the university send the costs for her tuition and room and board on to him and that she needed him to forward her enough money to meet her expenses while she was studying in the U. S.

She would say that she was going to work hard and make him proud of her. She planned to enroll in medical school after one more year but she would come for a visit next summer when school was out. After all, she would be twenty-one in another six months and it was time for her to be on her own. She would finish by saying that she hoped he wasn't too upset but she was not able to continue on in the life that women were expected to submit to in Riyadh. He would agree to that, she felt. After all, he had no choice. When you engage in the type of behavior that he had, it made it easy for those who knew about it to do as they pleased without securing his approval.

Once they arrived, she decided that she was going to like it in Minnesota except for the cold weather. England had been cold and rainy but it was not nearly as cold as the winters were here. There were sacrifices that had to be made in every situation, she decided, and eventually "Bill Smith" would leave and she would have that same feeling of dread return. The feeling that her short time with him had ended and she didn't know what she was going to do without him. She was shaken out of her reverie when the vehicle they had rented went off the pavement and onto a dirt road. They were only a few miles from Rebecca Lundstrom's home.

CHAPTER TWENTY

Black September

Jamal Al-Gashey, also called Samir, looked over the seven men that he had trained with for the past few months. They were all good men, all good fighters, including his cousin, Adnan Al Gashey. They all had reasons for wanting to carry out this mission. It had been almost a year since Samir had escaped from the Jordanian soldiers. He was the only one to escape that he knew of. He knew that many of the members of Fatah had fought to the end and died there rather than surrender to King Hussein's troops. Others had fled and were captured by the Israelis and languished in prison in Israel.

He heard that Abdul had been taken prisoner by the Israelis. So he had suffered the same ignominious fate as the others, he thought. Samir knew that it had taken some luck as well as skill for him not to have been captured or killed. Now he and the other seven men were preparing to travel to Munich, Germany to carry out a mission to take the entire Israeli Olympic team hostage and trade them for the 232 prisoners being held in Israel. Samir and the other seven men belonged to a newly created and secret part of Fatah that called itself "Black September" after the bloody month in 1971 that King Hussein's troops had attacked the Palestinians and driven them completely out of Jordan.

He wondered how many had died in the war that became known by the month that it began. He heard that Yasser Arafat claimed that up to 5,000 Palestinians were killed during the "Black September" fighting. He knew that this was regarded by most observers as being greatly exaggerated. He had read estimates that there were 1,500 to 3,500 killed, due largely to the intransigence of most of the members of Fatah who fought to the bitter end.

Now he and the other members of Black September were following a plan devised by the terrorist Abu Daoud in a coffee house in Rome to force the government of Israel to release all of the prisoners they held in return for the release of their Olympic athletes. Abu Daoud, who planned the attack, was actually Mohammed Oudeh. Prior to the attack, he spent weeks in Germany using a false passport in the name of Saad Walli, meeting with individuals who were sympathetic to the Palestinian cause. He bought and stored weapons and material for the raid, mostly AKM assault rifles, Tokarov pistols, and grenades.

He also met with Willi Kohl, a member of a neo-Nazi group, who offered assistance in the form of manpower and financial support. But Mahmoud Abbas had already supplied all of the financing that was necessary for the operation. Now, if things went according to plan, there would be little bloodshed and the two brothers of the team leader, Luttif Afif, would be freed along with the other prisoners being held. This was the plan, despite the fact that the official policy of the nation of Israel was to never negotiate with terrorists; no exceptions.

Samir had been chosen because of his background and his experience fighting in Jordan for Fatah. Those who formulated this plan wanted hardened fighters with a deep seated need for revenge. All of the other members of Black September were Palestinians from the refugee camps along the Jordanian, Syrian, and Lebanese borders. Samir remembered the words of his father telling him not to allow himself to be sacrificed needlessly in order to bring praise to others. But the excitement of being a part of a group such as this and the thrill of finally being able to do something on the world stage had overruled his better judgment.

He had gone too far to turn back now. Samir admired the other members of the group: the leader was Luttif Afif, also known as Issa; his assistant was Yusuf Nazzal, called Tony; and the other members were Khalid Jawad, called Salah; Mohammed Safady, called Badran; Afif Ahmed Hamid, called Paolo; Ahmed Chic Thaa, called Abu Halla; and Samir's cousin, Adnan Al-Gashey, called Denawi. One of the members of the group had told Samir that he felt worthless and powerless until someone from the

PLO had given him a gun. Then he felt as though he had become a valuable part of the struggle to reclaim his homeland.

Black September took *Ikrit* and *Biram* as the name of their operation. That was the name of the two Christian Palestinian villages where the inhabitants were forced out by *Haganah* in 1948. When the members of Black September left for Munich, Yasser Arafat, the head of the PLO met with them as they were leaving and said to them, "God protect you." To familiarize themselves with the Olympic Village, Luttif Afif, the leader of the raid, and two other team members worked at the Olympics beforehand to reconnoiter the quarters where the Israeli team was staying. Yusuf Nazzal, the second in command, was actually found in one of the rooms in the Israeli section but no action was taken since he worked at the Olympic Village. The Games were in their second week when the attack occurred.

Munich was only 16 kilometers from Dachau, the first concentration camp opened in Germany in 1933. It was for political prisoners only according to Henrich Himmler, the Police President of Munich at the time, but thousands of Jews died there. Over its gate was the infamous sign, *ARBEIT MACHT FREI*, meaning *"WORK MAKES YOU FREE."* As early as 1935, children's jingles were heard in Germany saying, *Lieber Gott, mach mich dumm, damit ich nicht nach Dachau kumm.* ("Dear God, make me dumb, that I may not to Dachau come").

The irony of Israelis going back to compete in Munich only twenty-seven years after the war was not lost on the public or the German government, which allowed security to be deliberately lax to show how much things had changed. There were two hundred additional unarmed security personnel there just to show how unnecessary it was to have tight security. On September 5, 1972, many of the athletes climbed the fence and went to Munich for a night on the town. Early the next morning, they climbed back over the fence into the Village.

The terrorists dressed in track suits similar to those the athletes wore and carried their weapons in bags like those used by the athletes. They were helped over the fence and into the Olympic Village, ironically, by Canadian athletes who mistook them for other athletes. The security forces also confused them with the other athletes returning from Munich. The terrorists entered the compound at 4:30 am and made their way to the apartments where the Israeli athletes were staying. The events that followed at the Olympic Village in Munich on September 5, 1972, signaled the beginning of the *Age of Terrorism*.

The Hooded Figure

Klaus von Kleinmann awoke to a beautiful day and stood at his hotel window and looked out over the city of Munich at the beautiful scene below. Germany was certainly one of the neatest and most orderly countries in the world. Add to that the natural beauty of the German landscape and it was truly a stirring sight. He had been to Munich many times and now he wanted to watch the Olympics and relive the time he and his father had spent at the games together. It had been the most memorable thing he had ever done.

He never thought he would get to attend the Olympic Games in Germany again. He had invited his daughter and her fiancé to go with him but she had shown some reluctance so he did not insist. He had given up on the idea of getting her to come to Buenos Aires with him. Her life was here and she would never leave. It was painful to think about leaving her but perhaps she would come for a visit later on.

He visited some of the old castles nearby before the games began. He especially enjoyed his visit to *Schloss Linderhof*, built by "Mad" King Ludwig II of Bavaria, the only castle he lived to see completed. The most spectacular of Ludwig's castles, *Konigschloss Neuschwanstein* was the epitome of what a castle was supposed to look like. With its towers framed against the mountains, it was indeed a beautiful sight. It was rumored that a shipment of Reichsbank gold had been stored there briefly during the war before being moved to another location.

Even though Ludwig had paid for *Neuschwanstein* castle out of his personal funds, his other building projects had brought him to a position of insolvency and he was found one morning floating in a nearby lake. Klaus supposed that every kingdom was entitled to a madman or two and if the worst he did was embark on a building spree like Ludwig, perhaps he should be forgiven for loving beauty too much.

At the games, he went from one event to another and tried to visit as many of them as possible. The games had been smaller and simpler in 1936 and he and his father had been able to view most of the competition. Now he enjoyed walking and listening to the people talk to one another. Except for a few brief conversations, it had been 27 years since he had listened to German being spoken by native speakers. The lilting *Bayerische* accent of southern Germany was the most well-liked by the Germans themselves and the *Müncheners* expressed themselves in the Bavarian dialect to perfection since it was their own. It was far more pleasant to the ear than the Plattsdeutsch, or Low German of the Northeast, or the brusque Berlin accent, or the Swabian dialect of Baden-Württemberg.

In addition to their pleasant accent, Klaus thought, *the people of Munich were hard workers.* But in spite of that the Berliners had a saying about them: *The people in Munich are always preparing for a festival, having a festival, or recovering from a festival.*

Müncheners know how to work without causing undue stress, Klaus decided. *Berliners like to think of themselves as being the only serious and business-minded people in Germany; but that's true of the people in most capital cities, I suppose. Especially Buenos Aires,* he concluded.

He walked through the Village enjoying the warmth of the day and listening to the voices coming from the crowd until he happened to look up and see the head of a hooded figure peering over a balcony. That could only mean that violence was coming. He felt for the Walther but it was in his hotel room. There was little he could do with it at this point anyway. Then he heard the unmistakable sound of gunfire from automatic weapons. All around him people began to scurry in the opposite direction. He dropped his half-eaten *Thüringer Rostbratwurst* in a trash receptacle and walked swiftly toward the location where the sound had come from, Building 31 at 13 *Connellystrasse*.

He waited for several minutes in front of the apartment building and then suddenly the door was opened and a body was thrown out and tumbled down the steps. It was the body of a large man. He had been shot several times. When Klaus saw a uniformed policeman, he asked what had happened. The policeman did not know except that it had been reported that someone had been killed; someone in the Israeli compound, he said. When Klaus asked who had done it, the policeman replied with a shrug saying that was not clear yet. He turned and walked away quickly, leaving Klaus to speculate about the reason.

Then Klaus saw an armed force from the *polizei* move quickly into position and surround the Israeli compound. Two figures appeared in the window, apparently some of the hostages. The detachment from the *polizei* moved away from the compound as quickly as they had surrounded it. The kidnappers weren't going to allow them to stay and had threatened to start killing their hostages if they did not leave. *That is the usual turn of events*, he thought. Now there would be negotiations. Those who had taken the hostages had a list of demands he was sure, presumably for the Israeli government. They must have known that the Israelis never negotiated with people who took hostages but apparently that made no difference to them.

He knew the Israelis could not afford to negotiate with such groups. If they gave in to one set of demands, then another group would try the same thing a short time later. The only way to resolve this situation was to kill all of the terrorists. He wondered how the Israelis would try and accomplish it. They had a counter-terrorism force, he knew, which most other nations did not have since they felt little need for them. But no Israeli forces would be allowed into Germany. That left the German government to deal with the terrorist's demands.

After two hours of waiting, nothing else happened and Klaus left the Olympic Village and went back to his hotel room and followed the events of the hostage stand-off on German television. The terrorist's demand came out in the news rather quickly. They wanted 232 Palestinian prisoners being held by the Israelis to be released in exchange for the nine Olympic athletes they had taken. They also demanded that Andreas Baader and Ulrike Meinhof, members of the Red Army Faction, an ultra-left wing group sympathetic to the Palestinian cause, be released from prison by the German government.

Klaus listened as it was announced that two Israelis, a weightlifter and a wrestling coach had already been killed when they resisted and fought back against the group known as "Black September." It was obvious to Klaus that the government of Chancellor Willy Brandt found itself in a difficult situation since the hostages were Jewish. The government wanted to show how different things were now that the Nazis were gone but this opened old wounds and brought back memories of genocide. Brandt's government offered the terrorists a large sum of money on several occasions but it was always refused. No mention of it was made on the news. They offered to switch German officials for the Israelis but that was refused also.

The public learned from the non-stop broadcasts on German television that the members of the group called "Black September" were Palestinians whose families had been driven out of Jordan by King Hussein beginning in September, 1971. It only took a few hours for the German media to uncover and report the news that those refugees lived on the border between Israel and the Arab nations. They lived in makeshift camps in terrible conditions because there was no place for them to go. None of the Arab nations wanted them since they feared that Yasser Arafat and the PLO would appear in their midst and try to take over the country as they did in Jordan.

Klaus learned from the news broadcasts that that two German officials were allowed in to see the Israeli hostages briefly: the Interior Minister of Bavaria and the Munich Police Chief. An Egyptian who was an advisor to the Arab League and another who was a member of the International Olympic Committee also tried to secure the release of the Israelis, but none of them could persuade the leader of Black September to even consider it. The only good that came of the negotiations was that they persuaded the group that their demands were being considered.

Because of this, Luttif Afif, called Issa, the leader, postponed the deadline for killing the hostages several times. It was apparent to Klaus that the members of Black September were watching German television and using the news broadcasts to aid them in their decisions. Then the media reported that Luttif Afif suddenly demanded a passenger jet to take them all to Cairo, although the Prime Minister of Egypt had made it clear that he did not want them to come there and get Egypt involved in the situation.

Klaus knew what was coming next. They weren't going to fly Black September and the hostages to Egypt. Luttif Afif's demand would be granted quickly, he knew, since it fit the plans of the German officials quite well. He could only imagine one outcome; they were going to end it by launching an armed assault on the terrorists. To do this, it would be necessary to isolate them somewhere and the ideal location would be an airfield with a jet parked there ready to take them to Cairo. German television reported that the kidnappers were persuaded that it would be more practical to go to Furstenfeldbruck, a NATO airfield nearby, rather than Reims, the main airport for Munich.

From this point on the public was shut out since the plan for the assault by German forces had to be kept secret. According to the plan devised by the German authorities, when the terrorists and their hostages arrived at the airport, Luttif Afif and Yusuf Nazzal would inspect the plane. Once inside, six German policemen dressed as members of the flight crew would overwhelm them. Then the five German sharpshooters would take out the other members of the group. For the six remaining terrorists there should have been twelve snipers, two for each one of them. But there were only five snipers because the officials who visited the Israelis had only seen four terrorists, a mistake that would prove fatal for the hostages.

The details of the assault were hidden by the German government for twenty years because of the number of egregious errors that were made in attempting to carry it out. The events that unfolded on that night were not revealed until two decades later by the German news magazine *Der Spiegel*.

CHAPTER TWENTY-ONE

Blue Earth, Minnesota

"Well, we're almost there," Bill said.

Khalisah was unsure how this was going to turn out. He was taking her with him to Rebecca's home without a second thought, so she supposed she would have to make the best of it. They pulled up into the driveway in front of the small frame house with a rose trellis on both sides of the steps leading up to the porch. Her first thought was that whoever lived here was more interested in growing plants than they were in caring for the dwelling. But even though the paint was peeling in a few places, she noticed that the house was neat and well maintained.

They stopped and Bill honked the horn and Rebecca and her mother came out on to the porch. She thought that the girl would come running and jump into his arms as she had seen other impulsive Americans do, but she waited for him on the porch instead. Khalisah was wearing her abaya, black with gold trim, and felt out of place, but Rebecca and her mother greeted her warmly. Bill and Rebecca embraced and exchanged kisses. Bill had never been here either, he told Khalisah, and had never met Rebecca's mother. Rebecca introduced him to her mother and then Bill introduced Khalisah to them.

He referred to her as a medical student who planned on attending university in the U. S. He explained that he had been the guest of her and her brother in Saudi Arabia. After seeing Rebecca, Khalisah could understand why Bill was so taken with her— blonde hair, fair skin, blue eyes and a kind and gentle manner. She thought that Bill and Rebecca behaved more like they were brother and sister. But it was obvious that they were thrilled to see each other again.

Khalisah knew that she wasn't over Bill yet; not at all. It seemed strange to suddenly start calling him Bill Smith instead of Charley Harper. She didn't think that she would ever be over him, but she had to try, and she had to move ahead with her life. Maybe she would decide to be married to her work after all. She couldn't be happy with anyone else and dedication to her work seemed to be the only way to have a purpose in life. She and Bill had only been together for a few months but she thought that no one could ever make such an impression on her again.

She had decided that her attraction for him was difficult to explain; but when she put all of the things that drew her to him together, it made him seem irresistible to her. No, her life would not be an enjoyable one without him. Poor little desert flower, starved for water—she must seem very strange to them, and backward, being from a society that was still governed by tribal customs. All of the money in the world wouldn't change that. Her mood was interrupted when Bill approached her with a sheepish look on his face.

He explained that Rebecca wanted them to get married right away. She didn't know when Bill might be called away again and she wasn't going to let him go away again and not know when he was coming back. He said that he had tried to explain to her that he wasn't going to go away and do this kind of work again, but she still insisted. Khalisah thought that she would feel the same way; she would want to marry Bill as soon as possible also.

"Does she know how I feel about you?"

"No," Bill replied.

"Then perhaps I should tell her."

"If you like. She's not going to be upset by it. She will understand, I'm sure. Her mother has an appointment for a check-up in Rochester tomorrow. When we come back, we'll go up to the university in Minneapolis and have a look around. See what you think about it. It will give you something to compare other universities to."

"That would be nice."

"I need to take good care of you and try to keep your father suitable impressed, so he doesn't send someone after me."

If only you could, she thought.

Rebecca came out on the porch and Bill went back into the house. *Almost on cue*, Khalisah thought.

"We're going to eat in a few minutes. Can I get you something to drink now?"

"No," said Khalisah. "But would you mind if we talked for a few minutes?"

"Not at all. Let's sit over here. I would love to learn more about you. Bill thinks very highly of you," Rebecca replied.

"Yes, and I think a great deal of him. But I suppose you can tell that."

"Yes. I can tell that."

"I left Saudi Arabia with him because I could not stand to see him go. We were only together a few months but…I fell in love with him. I hope you can understand that."

"Yes I can."

"I was going to leave there at some point anyway. It is a very repressive society for women and when I went away to university in England, I did not want to go back home. But when Charley, excuse me, Bill, had to leave…well, I begged him to let me go with him. I think you should know that."

"I understand."

"I don't think I can stand to see him go out of my life yet. I know he loves you and you are going to be married right away. But can you understand how I feel? It may sound silly, but I just can't take it if he leaves me now."

Rebecca reached over and took Khalisah's hands in hers and said, "I understand perfectly how you feel and I want you to know that he is not going anywhere. We are all going to stay here together at my mother's home and get better acquainted."

Khalisah managed a weak *thank you* and Rebecca continued, "I hope you understand why I want to marry him right away. I know he said he wasn't going to leave again. But nothing is certain with him. I want us to be married now before something happens that could take him away again."

"Yes. In fact, I think it might be better if you do get married. It might help me to realize that I need to get started on the next phase of my life. It is so difficult to think about beginning it without…."

"Of course it is. We want to help you do that, Khalisah, and we will do everything possible to keep you with us for as long as you wish to stay. I think we are going to be close to you for a long time. Now let's go in and I want you to meet my daughter, Olivia. I think I heard her wake up from her nap."

Stokely-Van Camp

"I can't do this anymore," Bill said. "I can't leave you. I can't bear being away from you. I have to quit this business."

Rebecca listened attentively, trying not to influence his decision. He would have to decide for himself whether he could continue working for Yitzhak Kahan. Linda had enough money for them to live on but men like Bill were too proud to live off someone else, even though he had lived in poverty for most of his life.

"I went down to the Stokely-Van Camp plant at noon and they hired me. I start next week. I'd rather shovel peas onto a conveyer belt for the rest of my life than leave you and go back to doing the things I had to do to. I haven't been trained to do intelligence work, or spying, or whatever you call it," he said. "I only know one way to do it and that's to get a nice, innocent young girl like Khalisah to fall for me enough to help me steal secrets from her father. Now that she has, she will probably be miserable for the rest of her life because I'm such a heartless fellow."

"You're not, Bill. The fact that it bothers you so much shows that you're not heartless. But you'll have to do whatever you think best, Bill. I'll be happy whatever you do."

"I suppose we should wait to get married until after I get back from taking Khalisah to Minneapolis."

"I don't want to wait, Bill. But if you think it is best, we'll wait. I just don't want to wait too long."

"Neither do I. We don't really have time to arrange it until we get back though. Do we?"

"All we have to do is get a marriage license and have a justice of the peace marry us," she suggested.

"You don't mind doing it that way?"

"No. Do you?"

"Not at all. I thought you would want all of the things that go with a wedding."

"That would be nice. But all I really want is you, Bill."

"Then let's go and get the license."

"We might have to take a blood test and wait three days for the result," she replied.

"Then we could get married when we get back from Minneapolis. Can you wait that long?"

"If I have the license in my hand, I might be able to, Bill."

"Good. Let's go."

Bill felt that he needed to tell Khalisah that he and Rebecca were going to get married today. He found her in the small garden that Annike Lundstrom had planted. It was almost bare now with only a few brown plants left.

"Khalisah, Rebecca and I want to get married before we take you to Minneapolis."

"Yes. She said it would be right away."

"Look Khalisah. I can't go back to doing what I did with you. It's cruel to do that to someone as nice as you."

"You didn't hurt me, Charley, I'm sorry, Bill. It was all self-inflicted."

"Maybe so. But, look, Khalisah, I bribed two people just to get to meet you."

"I don't mind, Bill. I'm just happy to have had the short time with you that I did. Go and get married now."

"We're going down to city hall and apply for the license now. I think you'd better come with us."

"You don't want me to come. I'd just be in the way."

"I want you to come because I'm afraid to leave you alone right now."

Khalisah began to tremble and then broke into tears. "I wasn't going to be any trouble to you. I didn't mean to make a scene like this. I should have never come with you."

Bill took her in his arms and held her. She kept her head down until Bill put his hand under her chin and lifted it up. She gazed into his eyes, questioning what he was doing.

"You're going with us. I won't leave you here alone."

"You're right. I don't need to be left alone now."

They turned and started for the house and she told Bill that she wanted to change out of her abaya.

"I'm sure Rebecca has something that will fit you. You are about the same size."

When they went in, Rebecca showed her into the small bedroom where all of the clothes that Linda McIntyre had bought her were stored. The closet was full and they covered most of the room.

"I think we can find something for you here; in fact, we'll put together a whole wardrobe. I won't ever wear this many outfits," Rebecca said.

Khalisah was impressed by the sheer volume and the quality of the designer apparel.

"Here are some that you can have. Try them on. I think we're about the same size." Khalisah tried on a three outfits at Rebecca's insistence. They all fit perfectly.

Khalisah protested, "I couldn't take all of these!"

"Oh, yes you can. And several more when we have time for you to try them on. We can't even get in this room, let alone use it, if I don't find a way to move all of these clothes somewhere else."

"Your friend, Linda, does she always do things in such grand style?"

"Almost always. I wouldn't say this to her, but she is still a poor girl at heart who happened onto money and she grabs up everything she can because she is afraid that it may all disappear tomorrow."

Khalisah was still trying to make sense of everything. Rebecca was nice to her and acted as though they could become best friends. She and Bill told her everything they were thinking and wanted her to stay with them permanently or so it seemed. Was this the way things were really going to be? Or were they just trying to pacify her temporarily? She didn't have long to think about it because as soon as she changed clothes, they all piled into the car and started toward the town hall. Annike Lundstrom, Rebecca's mother, sat next to her in the back seat holding Olivia and reached over and patted Khalisah's hand.

Bill was the only American Khalisah had known and she was surprised that Rebecca and her mother seemed to accept her from the start and wanted to befriend her. It was certainly different from the society in Riyadh where everyone from the outside was viewed with suspicion. Even the British tended to ostracize anyone from outside their country. Perhaps it was just because of Bill that people seemed more congenial here. It would become clearer when she met more Americans. Surely they wouldn't all be this nice to her.

When they arrived at the small city hall, the four of them almost filled it up. She had often thought of standing with Bill and applying for a marriage license, but instead of her it was Rebecca standing beside him. She hadn't planned on a Muslim ceremony with him. It would have been like this, except now she was watching while he married someone else. Everything had happened so suddenly after they arrived that it seemed almost surreal to her. Rebecca handed Olivia to her to hold while they said their vows since her mother couldn't hold the baby standing up.

She looked down at it wondered where the baby fit it. Who was the father? Bill had not told her about a baby. The ceremony was brief and it was over more quickly than she had anticipated. They walked back to the car and headed back to the little house on the edge of town. Now what? Where were they going to spend their first night together? They would surely have to leave her now. Then she realized they were going to drive to Rochester that evening. *We will all stay in a hotel and Annike Lundstrom will have her medical checkup and Bill and Rebecca will start their life together. Then the following day, Bill will take me to Minneapolis to look over the university. If I enroll, he'll go back to Rebecca and I won't see him again until the end of the semester. I don't know if I can stay away from him that long.*

CHAPTER TWENTY-TWO

Thunder in Deutschland; the Munich Massacre

Twenty years after it occurred, the people of Germany finally
learned what took place on September 5, 1972 at the Summer
Olympics when eight members of the terrorist group known as
Black September killed two Israeli athletes and took nine others as
hostages. Knowledge of the events of the "Munich Massacre," as it
came to be called, were finally uncovered through the excellent
investigative work done by reporters from the news magazine, *Der
Spiegel*. The true account had been hidden by successive
governments for two decades after the administration of
Chancellor Willy Brandt.

Large amounts of the material relating to the hostage
situation had been hidden away for years and some of the most
incriminating documents had been destroyed. It was clear that no
subsequent administration was willing to release any of it. A
condensed account of what the investigation by *Der Spiegel*
uncovered reveals the following information.

Events of the Munich Massacre
*The hostages and the terrorists boarded two helicopters to
go to the Furstenfeldbruck Airport with another helicopter
carrying government officials leading them. From that point on the
plan to rescue the hostages began to unravel rapidly as everything
began to go wrong. First, the helicopters were landed facing the
control tower where three of the government's snipers were
located instead of parallel to the tower. This did not afford the
snipers a shot at the terrorists when they opened the doors of the
helicopters.*

Next the terrorists broke their promise and took the German helicopter pilots hostage giving them even more innocents to place in the line of fire. Finally, the five snipers were hastily recruited competitive marksman and were not trained for this type of work and did not have the appropriate weapons with telescopic sights needed for the distance that the shots required. Two snipers had been stationed on opposite sides of the landing pad but one of them was in the line of fire of the three snipers in the control tower.

However, it was the decision that was made by the members of the polizei inside the passenger jet to abandon their post that determined that the hostages were going to die. The polizei inside the plane who were assigned to overpower the two leaders of Black September when they came to inspect the plane had concluded that the plan was not going to succeed. Without informing their superiors, they left before the two leaders of the terrorist group came to check on the aircraft. It was established by an examination of the internal reports conducted by the polizei themselves that no punitive action was ever taken against those who deserted their posts.

When Luttif Afif and Yusuf Nazzal found no one present in the aircraft, they immediately moved back to the shelter of the helicopters where they could cover the hostages without any chance of them being rescued. The snipers opened fire anyway and killed three of the terrorists. All of the helicopter pilots managed to escape during the initial phase of the fighting. Armored vehicles were not called for until after the fighting started and they became snarled in traffic on the way to the airport.

When they finally arrived an hour and a half later, Luttif Afif saw that the game was up and raked the hostages in the first helicopter with his machine gun, killing all four of them. Then he threw a grenade in it, destroying their bodies. It is thought that Adnan Al-Gashey killed the remaining five hostages in the second helicopter with his automatic weapon, shooting them at point blank range. The leader, Luttif Afif, then went running out on the tarmac firing at the police and was killed by their return fire. This left four of the terrorists remaining with two of them wounded.

Yusuf Nazzal, called Tony, the second in command, climbed the fence and escaped but was located by police dogs and killed in *a parking lot an hour later. The three remaining members of Black September were taken prisoner. Jamal Al-Gashey, known as Samir, had been shot in the wrist, Mohammed Safedy was shot in the leg, and only Adnan Al-Gashey was uninjured. The fighting was over by 1:30 am.*

Memories from Milwaukee

On the day after the "Munich Massacre," Frank Logan, Assistant Director at the CIA, received a long distance call. He was sure that Golda Meir was going to call him and he knew it was her as soon as his secretary informed him that he had a call.

"Good morning, Madam Prime Minister."

"Good Morning. You have heard about what happened in Munich, Logan?"

"I have heard."

"What do you recommend?"

"You already have an order for what happened."

"And that is?"

"An eye for an eye and a tooth for a tooth."

"You are from a Christian nation, Logan. Haven't you ever read your own orders?"

"Which one?"

"Turn the other cheek."

"That was for insults. This was an act of pre-mediated murder. You should knock out all of their teeth and gouge out all of their eyes."

There was silence on the other end of the line, so Logan continued.

"You have the best people in the world to do that. You could chase them all down in two years. If you don't, it will encourage others to do the same. Don't let them live any longer than it takes to track them down. Remember that justice delayed is justice denied. Then I would start on all of the others…."

She interrupted him and said, "And what about when they start retaliating? What should we do then?"

"The same thing you are going to do with those who ordered this. Demonstrate to them that you are more than willing to help them become martyrs if that's what they are so anxious to be."

"And then we are back in the cycle of killing each other to avenge the people that the other side kills; except it will be accelerated."

"I'm afraid that is the sort of fight that you find yourself in."

"Logan. Always correct and always having the bloodiest solution possible in mind. Haven't you read the standing order given to all of us that says, *Vengeance is mine; I will repay, says the Lord*?"

"I've found that God often uses human instruments to do his work. I'm afraid that in Palestine death has been the only solution since the days of Joshua who was told by *Yahweh* to kill all of the Canaanites."

"I am not Joshua."

"No. But the whole world will sit quietly by while you dispense justice on those who planned this attack. You have nothing to fear from the West or from the Arab world in executing the ones who gave the orders. And because you will deal with them a few at a time that will make it less conspicuous."

"I would like to be able to reach you again quickly, Logan. I may need your encouragement later on."

"For you, I am always available."

"And give my love to your children. They were like my own when we were all together in Milwaukee. Those were good years. We did not realize how good they were back then. Oh, and your grandchildren! I send my love to them also."

"Great grandchildren now, *Yekarah*."

"Can it be that so much time has passed? I must go now, *Yakar*, and begin work on this."

"*Kol Tov*."

"*B'ezrat, HaShem. Mal'ach katan.*"

Auf Wiedersehen Deutschland

The next day, after the assault was over, Klaus von Kleinmann, along with everyone else, heard only that five of the terrorists and all of hostages were killed during the attack. The following day Klaus caught a plane to Buenos Aires. Elise had agreed to visit him during the summer and since he had located her he had no other reason to stay. He missed Deutschland more than he realized and he would have risked apprehension just to stay a while longer. It was painful to leave; much more than he thought it would be.

But he vowed not to return to again unless Elise had an emergency and needed him. No matter how strong the ties were and how much the land and the people still pulled at him, Deutschland was no longer home. After he had returned to Buenos Aires, Klaus read in the *Argentinisches Tageblatt* about the continuing saga of the terrorists involved in the Munich Massacre. In a bizarre turn of events, newspapers around the world reported that the three survivors, Jamal Al-Gashey (Samir), Mohammed Safady, and Adnan Al-Gashey were freed by the German government when a Lufthansa passenger jet was hijacked to force their release.

Many of the journalists reporting on the incident believed that the hijacking was a hoax to give the government of Chancellor Willy Brandt a reason to free them. In return, it was thought that the German government extracted a promise from the Black September organization not to operate anymore in Germany. An editorial in the *Argentinisches Tageblatt* reported that Golda Meir had been reluctant to exact revenge for the Munich Massacre until this occurred. The *Argentinisches Tageblatt* quoted unnamed sources that said after the three were released, she was reputed to have given the overall commander of "Operation Wrath of God" *carte blanche*. She was reported to have urged him to "…turn the dogs loose on them."

Newspaper articles began to appear about the retaliation the Israelis carried out to avenge the massacre by Black September. Numerous accounts in the press reported that Israeli war planes were sent to Syria and South Lebanon within a month to attack ten locations known to be PLO headquarters and over 200 PLO members were killed. Other news articles about "Operation Spring of Youth" in 1973, told how two leaders of the PLO and the leader of Fatah's Intelligence branch who directed Black September were killed. It was reported that this was carried out by the Israelis in a daring amphibious attack in Beirut utilizing *Sayeret Matkal* commandos.

This convinced most Palestinians that *Mossad* could strike anywhere they wanted to at any time since Yasser Arafat himself was only a few yards away when the attack occurred. The press reported that the psychological aspect of retribution by the nation of Israel seemed to be taking a toll on the PLO.

Changes at *Mossad*, *Shabak*, *Aman*, and the *Knesset*

It was a rainy day in Tel Aviv with the weather expected to be overcast for the rest of the week. Yitzhak Kahan, the Assistant Director of *Mossad*, rehearsed in his mind the factors regarding the nation's current relationship with Egypt. Gamal Abdel Nasser, the President of Egypt, had officially launched the "War of Attrition" against Israel in March of 1969 and died less than two years later. He was succeeded by his Vice President, Anwar Al-Sadat, who had turned his attention from fighting the "War of Attrition" to concentrate on rebuilding the Egyptian Army.

The reason was simple; Israel had occupied the entire Sinai Peninsula by the end of the Six Day War in 1967 and Egypt was determined to get it back. Informants inside Egypt reported to *Mossad* that Sadat had begun planning an all-out offensive against the 160 kilometer row of Israeli defenses in Sinai along the east bank of the Suez Canal known as the *Bar Lev* Line. For Yitzhak, it was a difficult time since he found himself caught between his boss, the Director, Eli Rosencrantz, and the Defense Ministry regarding the use of the information that came from Prince Faisal's computer detailing the money trail.

The Director, Eli Rosencrantz, wanted to act on it immediately. But Moshe Dayan, the Minister of Defense, felt that might bring on suspicion and endanger the source of the information, the computer, if action was taken against too many groups at once. He wanted to wait and use the information sparingly. It had been given the highest classification of *Most Secret* and no one in *Mossad* other than Yitzhak and the Director and their technical team knew how the information was being collected. Their man at Honeywell, whose name was highly classified, was a civilian not associated with the intelligence service, but he was trustworthy and reliable.

It had been relatively easy for him to copy all of the information on Prince Faisal's computer when he went there to repair it while Faisal was still out of the country. He was on call if further repairs were needed and was scheduled to go back to Riyadh once a year for maintenance. He would copy the information on Faisal's computer at least once a year and that would be sufficient to keep up with where the money was going, Yitzhak reckoned.

For his entire career, Yitzhak Kahan had been content to be "second fiddle." He was especially happy about it now since it gave him a chance to wait patiently until all of the turbulence from the recent changes had dissipated. A new head of *Mossad*, a new head of *Shabak*, a new head of *Aman*, the military intelligence service, and new members from the *Knesset* on the Subcommittee for Intelligence and Secret Services could only mean an upsurge in conflict about control. Until all of the clashes between the new personnel over territorial rights had been settled, it was best to keep a low profile.

He was on his way out in a few more years but until then he could take pride in being the longest serving member of any of the intelligence services, except for Daniel Ya'alon, of course. No one knew for certain how old Ya'alon was, but he had been around when *Haganah* was still operational. The head of *Mossad* was not willing to try and force him into retirement since his wife had already died and his two children lived in America, and he had no desire to spend his last days there. So he would likely die at his desk since he spent most of his time there.

He was still the consummate analyst and could extract information from data that others regarded as useless. He was reluctant to comment on how he reached a conclusion until other evidence confirmed what he said but his assessments about incomplete intelligence information were regarded as the gold standard. Currently, Yitzhak was busy trying to find more sources that could tell him about what was going on in the inner circle of Anwar Al-Sadat. He sent every scrap of information that became available to Ya'alon as soon as it came in. So far Ya'alon would only say that Egypt was definitely planning an attack in the Sinai sometime in the next 18 months.

That would have been enough to satisfy even the most demanding decision maker, but Yitzhak felt he needed more. He wondered if the new man Simons Grebel was using would be able to uncover anything if he were to ask him to go to Egypt. He had done a magnificent job in Saudi Arabia by gaining access to Prince Faisal's computer. Yitzhak planned to call Grebel and even go and visit him if necessary. They had not communicated by phone or in person since the time when they received word that Bill Smith had died in Vietnam. Grebel seemed to prefer it that way.

Then he received a message from Grebel that stated: NEW PRODUCT NO LONGER IN USE. No reason was given. Yitzhak replied, SEEK ANOTHER PRODUCT TO REPLACE OLD ONE. ADVISE. He received an answer informing him that Grebel only wished to use the same product and he would let him know if that one could be put back in service. *A shame*, thought Yitzhak. *We are deprived of a most valuable asset, in addition to the services of Grebel, who recruited him*. It would not be wise to ask Grebel to try and coerce his recruit in order to get him to work again. Grebel's man had to decide that for himself. Yitzhak could only wonder who he was and why he refused to work for them anymore.

CHAPTER TWENTY-THREE

Mayo Clinic

Back in Blue Earth everyone usually rose early at the Lundstrom household; much earlier than they wanted to. Annike Lundstrom had several white Columbian Rock chickens back there and a Speckled Sussex Rooster that she had named *Gregory Peck* after her favorite movie star. He announced to the world every morning at 4:30 am that he had risen. Since it was their wedding night Bill was glad that he and Rebecca were not back in Blue Earth. He definitely did not want a rooster waking them up at such an inopportune moment.

He asked Rebecca how it felt for them to finally be married and she said that she had never been so happy in her whole life. That convinced him, not that he needed any more convincing, that he was never going back to the Middle East again. After they passionately consummated their marriage, he was absolutely sure that he wasn't ever going to leave her again. He would spend the rest of his days at Stokely-Van Camp, shoveling peas onto a conveyor belt if that was what it took for him to stay with her.

When they finally arose in the middle of the next morning, Rebecca inquired about how he would feel if she called Dr. Matthew Avery. She wanted to check and see how he was doing. Bill agreed and she asked Matthew to meet them at the hotel for lunch. Bill knew that the real reason was to inform Dr. Avery that they were married now. He suspected that she also wanted Matthew Avery to meet him in order to bring about some closure to her relationship with the doctor. She told him about the emotional turmoil that they had both gone through when she was trying to help the doctor during his time of grief.

He didn't feel threatened by the close ties that Rebecca had developed with Matthew Avery while she was trying to help him. What would he have done if Rebecca hadn't helped him when he needed her? When they met in the restaurant it was a convivial atmosphere. Matt hugged Rebecca and kissed her on the cheek. He shook hands with Bill, and he even kissed Khalisah's hand in a great show of respect when they were introduced. He saved Annike for last and grabbed her and hugged her and swung her around in the air. When he sat her down he told her how pleased he was that she was doing so well.

"So you are Bill. It's good to finally meet you. Rebecca spoke of you often when she was working here at the Mayo Clinic," Matthew said.

"You worked at the Mayo Clinic?" Khalisah never considered that Rebecca might have worked there.

"Yes. Until Mother had surgery. Then we went back to Blue Earth for her to recuperate."

"That's interesting," Khalisah responded.

"I would have to say that Rebecca has a gift for helping people who are suffering emotionally. I had just lost my wife to cancer and Rebecca was instrumental in my recovery," Matt responded.

So that was what made her so desirable, Khalisah thought. *She is not only beautiful; she is also intuitive and empathetic. That may even be what attracts men the most*, she thought.

"Matt, we have something to tell you, Bill and I," Rebecca said.

"Let me see. What could it be? You didn't get married, did you?"

"Yes. How did you know?"

"Oh, a lucky guess, I suppose," Matt said, giving Annike a wink.

"Well, aren't you going to congratulate us?" Rebecca asked.

"Sure. But first, who did Bill marry? And, more importantly, who did you marry?"

After everyone had a good laugh, Matthew Avery congratulated them and they ordered lunch. *He is pretty clever*, Khalisah thought. *Even Bill couldn't do that as well*. While they were eating, Rebecca mentioned that they were going to take Khalisah up to Minneapolis-St. Paul tomorrow to look over the university and also to investigate the medical school.

"Well, I attended medical school there at the University of Minnesota in the Twin Cities, the Minneapolis-St. Paul metropolitan area, and while I would recommend it over any other school, there is a new medical school that is just opening up this year, right here in Rochester at the Mayo Clinic."

"Really?" Rebecca asked.

"Yes. I think it's going to be as good, if not better, than any medical school in the country since the Mayo Clinic emphasizes education and research as much as it does patient care. Also, they specialize in tertiary care and emphasize the integrated practice of medicine."

"Refresh my memory about the meaning of tertiary care," Rebecca said.

"That means 'difficult to treat' cases. Integrated medicine means that they do not reject out-of-hand the treatment methods from alternative medicine, as opposed to evidence based medical treatment."

"That sounds fascinating," Rebecca said.

"She might want to look at it while she's here, and interview with the Dean of Admissions. How much work do you have at the undergrad level, is it Khalisah?"

"Yes, Khalisah. I have one year at the Women's University in Saudi Arabia and two years at Oxford."

"That should be enough for you to be admitted to Mayo Medical School."

"Well, I had planned on another year at the undergrad level before applying for medical school," Khalisah said.

"It wouldn't be necessary. But where were you thinking about going?"

"I'm not sure yet. I need to attend an English-speaking institution. But I have decided not to go back to Oxford. I thought I would like to look over the university here in Minnesota instead."

"You could not go wrong by choosing either the state university in Minneapolis or the new Mayo Clinic Medical School here in Rochester."

Khalisah tried to ascertain the difference in distance between the two schools but she wasn't sure, so she asked Matt Avery.

"What's the difference in the distance?"

"From here? The university is about a four hour drive from Rochester. The Mayo Clinic is about ten minutes from here."

Khalisah knew that they had only traveled about an hour and a half from Rebecca's home to Rochester. That meant that Bill would only be 90 minutes away.

"I think I might like to enroll at a new medical school. What would it take for me to do that? Interview with the Dean of Admissions, you say? What else?"

"You should take the MCAT, Medical College Admissions Test, and write for your transcripts. Have them send me a copy also. I'll look them over and if I think they indicate that you could succeed at Mayo, or the university, I'll give you a recommendation. One from me is all you would need here at Mayo."

"That would be very kind of you."

"It would be my pleasure."

"Well, we had better get mother back home. I think she's ready to go from her looks," Rebecca said.

"Yes. I am definitely ready to go home after all those tests and the examination," Annike agreed. "Besides I need to gather the eggs."

"Bill, I think I would like to stay here and go to the Mayo Clinic and see about applying there."

"Certainly. I'll take Rebecca and Mom home and then come back and pick you up, in, say, four hours?"

"That should be enough time. Would you mind calling me a taxi to go out to the Mayo Clinic, Dr. Avery?"

"I think I can do better than that. How about if I give you a guided tour and introduce you to a few of my friends who are on staff there?"

"That would be very kind. Are you sure you have the time?"

"Certainly. Besides, you make time for important things. I think this qualifies."

The Pilgrim

As they drove to the clinic, Khalisah sat quietly looking at the scenery until they turned into the entrance leading to the Plummer Building, a tall, tan building with a terra-cotta trimmed bell tower. It was the heart of the campus and would compare favorably with any building in Riyadh, she thought. The carillon was playing Mozart's Piano Concerto, Number 21, a tune that she recognized. *This is going to be a good place to be for the next three years*, she thought. Bill said that he was through with what he had been doing in the Middle East, so he would be as close as she could get to him.

I'll need to contact Father about getting an automobile so I can go visit them on the weekends. Maybe I can get Bill to give me a few more lessons since I will be driving in city traffic instead of in the desert. I will also need to apply for a student visa, but that should not be too difficult to do. As they entered the grounds of the Mayo Clinic, Matthew Avery pointed out the *Red* Clinic Building built around 1914, and the building housing the Mayo Clinic Institute for Experimental Medicine, added in 1922. He parked and they walked across the campus listening to the carillon.

The Admissions Office gave her the application for admission to the medical school and Dr. Avery wangled an impromptu visit with the Dean who was an old friend. The Dean was interested in recruiting more qualified students for the medical school and he was suitably impressed with Khalisah since she had spent two years at Oxford. He practically guaranteed her entrance into the medical school if her transcripts were satisfactory. After visiting with Matthew Avery's close friend, Dr. Jeffrey Caine, and a few more colleagues, they toured the campus until Khalisah had a good idea about the location of the all of the buildings there.

He offered to help her look for an apartment and called Rebecca on his car phone to tell her that he would bring Khalisah back to Blue Earth himself. He took her to the Sandhurst Suites where the most expensive luxury units were located and asked her what price range she wanted to look at. Not wanting to seem pretentious, Khalisah told him if he thought she would like them, any of them would be fine. The first one they looked at was similar to Khalisah's quarters back in Riyadh. It was spacious and luxuriously furnished.

"I think I would like this one. Yes. It will be acceptable," she said.

When they went to the office to fill out the application, Khalisah asked if she could reserve it until her father could send the money to her.

"Normally, it is two month's rent in advance to reserve a suite," said the lady who managed the apartments. "Do you have any sort of information that would justify reserving this for you?"

"Here is my passport," said Khalisah. She handed it to the lady who had identified herself as *Margaret*. She looked at the name inside and said, "I'm sorry, but this doesn't give me enough information to hold this suite for you."

Matthew Avery signaled over Khalisah's head that he would be good for the deposit, but Khalisah had already begun to explain to Margaret about whom she was and why she should hold the suite for her.

"I don't wish to sound presumptuous, Madam, but did you read my name on the passport?"

"Yes."

"And you didn't recognize it?"

"Should I?"

"I suppose not."

"I'm sorry, dear, but if you are not from the U. S. that means that there will be even more problems if you can't pay cash in advance. What country are you from, by the way?"

"I am a member of the al-Saud. We are the ruling family of Saudi Arabia. We control all of the oil that comes from our country and thus all of the revenue from the sale of it."

"Yes, well, I'm sure that you are being honest, but I really can't agree to hold this suite for you because of that. But since Dr. Avery has agreed to vouch for you and put up the money to hold it...Isn't that right, Doctor? Then I will go ahead and let you sign a lease for it."

Dr. Avery replied with a nod.

"And since he is my doctor and I am due for a physical examination with the physician who is taking care of his patients now, I suppose I had better do what the doctor orders. Right doctor? Even though he never bothered to ask me about turning over his practice to someone else."

He nodded again and forced a weak smile. Khalisah was frustrated since money had never been a concern for her before, but she resigned herself to being indebted to Dr. Matthew Avery for the money necessary to reserve the suite. He was kind, she thought, and he had helped her take care of everything in one afternoon. Without him, it could have taken days to get it all done.

"I want to thank you, doctor, for all you've done for me. It could have been a nightmare without you. Please accept my sincere thanks for everything you've done."

"It was my pleasure."

"I never thought there would be a question after she saw my name. I suppose it was presumptuous of me to think that everyone in this country should immediately recognize who I am."

"A prophet is not without honor, save in his own country, but for a pilgrim it is the opposite, I guess."

"A pilgrim? I suppose I am, aren't I? Nevertheless, please know that I am grateful for your kindness in guiding me and helping me get settled here. I really had no idea that I could get into medical school now."

On the way back to Blue Earth, Khalisah noticed that she felt safe and secure with Dr. Matthew Avery, much like she did when she was with Bill. She asked him how he had known that Bill and Rebecca were married since it had only been one day.

"Well, that was a very leading statement that Rebecca made, wasn't it? But that's not how I knew. Annike Lundstrom calls me every day, usually in the evening, and tells me everything that's happened that day."

"Does she? And why would she do that?"

"I suppose she thinks I saved her life when she had a heart attack. She's been my biggest fan ever since."

CHAPTER TWENTY-FOUR

To Avenge and Then Mourn

Kidon was *Mossad's* assassination unit and one of its members, Ehud Loehbar, dried the last of the oil from his PB 6P9 pistol and put it away. It was Russian made and called *Pistolet Besshumnyj* or "Silenced Pistol." It was the weapon he favored at close range in every situation. It was sturdy and difficult to damage, and it had a two piece sound suppressor. The first part was unobtrusive and fixed around the barrel. The second part could be removed for ease of transport.

His *Shabak* unit had one officer in it which was a bit unusual. Most of the time there were none. He was glad that there was only one. They were usually a restraining force. Most of them did not consider finding and killing a target a viable occupation like those in the enlisted ranks did. Officers had other things to keep them busy. Most of them did not engage in killing in a time of peace unless there was some compelling reason. He reckoned that officers could kill just as effectively as an enlisted man but usually they did it in a more sophisticated manner than just finding a target and then gunning him down in some remote area.

Officers also slowed down an operation because they were always thinking about the ramifications of eliminating someone. They wanted to make sure that no one was killed who shouldn't be killed, especially women or children. That always brought the maximum amount of negative publicity. That didn't seem to bother the other side, but the Israelis could not afford to harm women or children. *We are already portrayed as monsters trying to annihilate those who are in reality trying to annihilate us*, he thought. *Just give me a target and hard and fast rules for how it can be done and then don't make me think about the consequences. Consequences are someone else's problem.*

He didn't relish killing anyone but it had reached the point where certain people had to be done away with to ensure survival—the survival of the nation. Ehud served in the organization known as *Shabak*, or *Shin Bet*, which was an abbreviation of its name. It was the internal security force and its Director reported to the Prime Minister rather than the Minister of Defense. After the Six Day War its responsibilities were extended to include uncovering terrorism in the West Bank and Gaza Strip. Ehud's current assignment was to be a joint operation utilizing military as well as intelligence units. That was unusual, but this was an unusual incident.

The incident at Munich was one of the most blatant slaughters of innocent civilians, done to draw the attention of the whole world to it. Now it had to be met with force so that none of those involved with it in any way escaped retribution. This operation would even involve civilians, which was also unusual since they were normally judged to be a bit too skittish when it came to eliminating someone. But the entire nation was outraged about the "Munich Massacre." Most of them would have pulled the trigger themselves if given the chance. *Yes, this was different. Some places were off limits and the Olympic Village was such a place,* he thought.

In his mind, the whole operation by Black September had demonstrated that it was an amateurish attempt at revenge. No matter how long they had trained, the planning and execution still betrayed them as amateurs. And they were amateurs, it was true; poor, infuriated refugees who had been driven out of Jordan by King Hussein. But even amateurs could be deadly, and when they lashed out against what had been done to them, they turned to their natural enemy, the nation of Israel.

On the other side, there were only certain members who could be killed; political figures like Yasser Arafat were off limits. His surrogates could be killed, but not him. Arafat didn't need to be killed. He was too easy to read to do away with. He might be replaced by someone with intelligence who knew what needed to be done to advance the cause of the Palestinians and was willing to do it. Such a new leader would be dangerous and would have to be eliminated even though he was at the political level. That would bring serious consequences.

It was better to have Arafat as the leader of the PLO since he was a terrorist and reasoned like a terrorist. *Kill the Israelis whenever and wherever you can.* Occasionally he considered the political consequences of an act of terror. But most of his methods were obvious enough to make him much too valuable an adversary to be eliminated. Random acts involving the murder of a few innocents were inevitable. The Munich Massacre was an exception.

When the violence reached the world stage as it had at the Olympics, the consequences of such acts must be demonstrated. Some targets deserved to be eliminated more than others. The other leaders of Fatah were all prime targets. The leaders of the newly created organization of Black September were also principal targets now. They were all designated for elimination when their identity became known.

As his four man squad started for the door, Ehud Loehbar felt the usual rush of excitement, but this time there was an added dimension—a sense of determination. The nation could not rest until justice was done for the families of the slain athletes. Nothing else mattered until the three remaining assassins were taken down and their status as heroes in the Arab world was changed to that of martyrs. Then the nation could mourn for their sons without having the thought of how to bring about vengeance foremost in their minds.

We Do Not Forget and We Do Not Forgive

Ehud Loehbar followed the target down a deserted street in the capital city of Abu Dhabi in the United Arab Emirates. Hassan Muhammad Jawal Al-Muhar had been identified as part of the logistical team that helped Black September enter the Olympic Village. Ehud paused briefly behind the darkened corner of a building while he screwed in the second part of the silencer on his Russian made PB 6P9 pistol. His three team members had signaled him that no one was following the Palestinian and it was clear to take him down.

He walked rapidly towards him and brought his weapon from behind his back. The target, Hassan Muhammad Jawal Al-Muhari, heard him coming and turned to see if it was one of his friends. His eyes widened when Ehud walked up with the pistol pointed at him. He did not attempt to flee; he stood there waiting for him to shoot. But Ehud wasn't going to shoot right away. Ordinarily he would have already fired without wasting any time. But that would be too easy. Waiting would give Hassan Al-Muhari time to think about the fact that he was going to die.

Ehud was going to keep his weapon pointed at him until he panicked and started running away. Then he would shoot him in the back. Hassan Al-Muhari stood waiting to be shot until he realized that his assailant wasn't going to shoot him right away. His eyes betrayed his disappointment. He was waiting to die as a martyr but it seemed that his enemies might have something else planned for him. They could take him prisoner and carry him away to be tortured to gain information about Black September. *Shabak* was rumored to have used enhanced interrogation methods on Palestinians on numerous occasions in violation of their charter.

Panic showed on Hassan's countenance when Ehud withdrew a syringe from his pocket with his right hand and held it up for him to see. It was empty but Al-Muhari did not know that. He turned and ran and gave Ehud a clean back shot. Not a fatal one; just enough to stop him. Then he shot him in both legs. Ehud walked up and stood over him and watched the fear rise in his eyes. He was going to stand over him as he bled to death. He would not have done it with anyone else but this was different. The Israeli athletes had been bound to chairs and then to each other and had waited for hours knowing they were going to die.

This was the best he could do. He waited for a few minutes, then shot Hassan Al-Muhari in the face twice and walked slowly away. A rose and a card expressing condolence had already been sent to his family before he was killed. Inside the card was written the words: *We do not forget and we do not forgive*. He thought that it was a sad act but one that had to be done. He wished that it had been Adnan Al-Gashey that he had just killed. Al-Gashey was thought to be the one who machine-gunned the five Israeli athletes in the second helicopter.

Hassan Jawal Al-Muhari was the fifth man that Ehud had killed but he did not regret putting any of them to death. They were all dedicated to killing and had deserved to die. It had become necessary for them to die so that the fragile façade of peace could be maintained. They were trying to destroy it. He was trying to preserve it. If they had not died, many others might have died unnecessarily. He and the other team members waited for months for news about Mohammed Safady, Jamal Al-Gashey, and Adnan Al-Gashey but none ever came.

It was thought that they fled to Syria or the Soviet Union out of the reach of *Mossad*. They disappeared into the shadowy world of those who fled for their lives and spent the rest of their days looking over their shoulder. Ehud learned later that Mohhamed Oudeh who planned the attack never showed any remorse about the loss of life caused by the abduction. He stated that it was not intended to be so bloody, but that he would never apologize for his part in planning and facilitating the attack. Ehud heard that he also disappeared and was rumored to have fled to Syria where he was treated as a hero.

The Source in the Inner Circle

"The Prime Minister wants to extract more than *an eye for an eye.* She wants to punish them by demanding a dozen eyes for one of our eyes, and 48 teeth for each one of our teeth," Yitzhak Kahan explained.

"And this is the school teacher from Milwaukee who is not even a *sabra* and who had to change her name so that it sounded more like a Hebrew name? And now she is giving us orders?"

"Are you simply a misogynist, Levi, or anti-American, or are you just resistant to civil authority?"

"I cannot afford to be guilty of any of those things, Yitzhak. But I think that once in our nation's history is enough," Colonel Levi Zechariah replied.

"You are speaking of Deborah, who judged the nation in ancient times, are you not?"

"Maybe."

"Then you are at least the first one of those. In addition, you do not understand that the PM can do this because she is a woman. If a man tried to exact as much retribution as she is doing, he would likely be condemned, even in our own camp, as being too cruel."

"Perhaps you are right, Yitzhak, but the major concern for me and what I fear most is that they are plotting a major offensive and that it will be too late when we find out about it. We need a source that is in the inner circle who can tell us what they're going to do."

"Yes, that is the value of intelligence work. Learning what they are going to do so that we can prepare for it. Otherwise much of what we do is wasted effort."

"I take it you have a suitable source to do that."

"Perhaps. But as you know, Levi, I could not tell even someone as reliable and trustworthy as you whether we do or not."

"Granted. But those of us in the IDF can only hope that you do. Otherwise much more than effort is going to be wasted. A large number of fine Jewish boys are going to be wasted while those of us in the army are trying to find out what plan the Egyptians are executing."

"You and those in your command and everyone in the IDF are the best fighting men, excuse me, men and women, in the world, it's true, and we do not want a single one of you to be wasted."

"Then those of us in the army can only trust that you and your colleagues have someone in place already."

"You may assume that. Because as you say, we are failing you and all of our fighting men and women if we do not."

"I will take your word for it then," Colonel Zechariah said. Then he stood and did a precise about face and exited swiftly through the door.

After Colonel Levi Zechariah left his office, Yitzhak pondered about how difficult it might be for someone to deduce who their source in the Egyptian inner circle was. Everyone seemed to realize that without having someone there, the military was virtually blind. They could build up the *Bar Lev* Line until it resembled the Maginot Line that France built on the German border after WWI. But if the Egyptians circumvented the *Bar Lev* Line as the Germans did when the *Wehrmacht* went through the Ardennes Forest, it would be just as worthless.

In his duties as the Assistant Director of Mossad, Yitzhak Kahan had reached some conclusions about the defensive line on the east bank of the Suez Canal. *I am afraid that we have not made the Bar Lev Line strong enough to withstand an all-out assault on it by the Egyptians; but we have made it too strong as a front line defense to walk away from it when it is attacked. That leaves us in an in between position which means that we will make the wrong move no matter what we do. If we stand and fight we will be overwhelmed and if we retreat to a more favorable defensive position, we will allow the Egyptians to occupy the most powerful strategic base possible to attack us from. We will lose either way. I have a bad feeling about this next war—a very bad feeling.*

He thought about the source that *Mossad* had inside the Egyptian inner circle. Ashraf Marwan was married to Mona Nasser, the daughter of the late President of Egypt, Gamal Abdel Nasser. Marwan's handler reported that despite Nasser's death, his son-in-law would be aware of any impending strike against Israel and seemed willing to relay the information on to him. This was the only source of human intelligence they had that was capable of giving them any sort of advance warning of an Egyptian attack. They would have to rely on information about a buildup of the Egyptian armed forces on the western bank of the Suez Canal for corroboration.

A very delicate balance exists in judging between what Ashraf Marwan tells his handler and the evidence of an increase in military activity, Yitzhak thought. *If only the will exists in the government to take another preemptive strike before they overrun us.* He remembered the misgivings of his friend, the retired American intelligence agent, Simons Grebel, about the danger of waiting until they were attacked in the next war. *We may lose the war or suffer a grievous loss of security because the mystique of our invincibility will be shattered,* he thought. *What could be worse?* He sunk back in his chair, despairing about his lack of ability to do anything to change the situation for the better.

CHAPTER TWENTY-FIVE

In Rhonda Gialetti's Hotel Room in the U. S.

"And what do you think those technicians that you hired to bug me were doing while you were up there in my apartment, Faisal? Putting in earplugs and pulling on blinders? I don't think so! I am not going to be spied on! Not now! Not ever!"

"But I didn't know about it…."

"And I'm Rita Hayworth!"

Then Rhonda Gialetti curled up in a ball on the couch and *sulled up* like a possum, as they say in the South. It had always worked better than anything else when she wanted to get a man to do something for her.

A Civil Ceremony

"Charley, I have a message for you from Simons Grebel," Rhonda Gialetti said. "It is a brief one. He said that 'your other friend' already had someone in place at Honeywell that could repair the appliance that needed to be worked on. Your other friend had never used him before but it worked extremely well and the appliance is fixed now, thanks to you."

"That's great news, Rhonda. Now if no one finds out about what we've done…."

"Don't worry. I've had to keep a lot of secrets in my lifetime. No one is going to find out from me."

"Thanks. I know I can trust you. How are things between you and your suitor?"

"Well, you were right, Charley. Faisal came and got me. He came all the way to Tifton, Georgia. He looked funny, even in western clothes. My relatives gawked at him and at first they thought he was a movie star. But when they saw all of those body guards with him, they were certain he was a gangster. What a laugh they had!"

"You didn't go back to California?"

"Are you serious? I couldn't afford to live out there now. After I paid my taxes, there wasn't much left, since you advised me to throw the little checkbook at him before I left!"

"Sometimes you have to sacrifice for the greater good. He came and got you, didn't he?"

"I suppose you were right. But it was not a lot of fun living with my aunt in her little shotgun house till he came. It brought back memories of my childhood and made me almost sick to think about going through that again. I've decided to treat him especially good from now on."

"I'm glad for you. What now?"

"I am going to live in Qatar when we go back, Charley, in the capital city, Doha. It's lovely there. He showed me some pictures of our home. It's beautiful. Oh, and I am pregnant."

"Are you married to him yet?"

"No."

"Has he discussed it with you yet?"

"Yes. He wants me to convert to Islam and have a Muslim ceremony so that his child will not be considered a heretic and illegitimate."

"If you do that you will disappear like all of the other women there."

"I've never been visible to anyone there anyway."

"That's true, but if you become a Muslim you will be subject to Sharia Law and won't be seen by anyone and can't go out of the house unless a male family member is with you."

"No, I don't want that. What should I do then?"

"Make him marry you in a civil ceremony in a western country. I suggest England since he went to Oxford."

"I can't make him do that."

"You can if you play it right."

"How?"

"Tell him if he doesn't marry you in a civil ceremony, you'll take the baby and he'll never see either of you again. I'm sure you've convinced him by now that you're tough enough to do that. Tell him that you love him and don't want to live without him but that he must do this for you. Otherwise you are condemning yourself to a life that you could never submit to."

"Love? I'm not sure I love him. I haven't thought about whether I could love him or not."

Bill didn't answer. He waited for her to think it through.

"He's sweet enough, he's kind, he's handsome, and he's even romantic most of the time when he's around me."

She paused and then continued, "Marriage has always been a decision I've had to make based on economic necessity. It's never had anything to do with love. I don't guess that I've ever had the ability to decide about anything based on love."

"You won't be able to this time either. But make sure he understands that if he keeps you he has to marry you in a Western civil ceremony. After all, he's not going to take you back to Riyadh to live since he can't make you one of his Muslim wives."

"No. He'll come to Qatar on weekends and once or twice during the week."

"No need for you to convert then."

"No. I guess you're right, Charley. How is it that you are always giving me advice? Even though I need it and it is always correct. I'm older than you. I should be the one giving you advice."

"You gave me some of the best advice I've ever had. *Leave Riyadh.* It got me out of there just in time. Does he ever say anything about me?"

"Not a word. Charley, you'll come by and see me if you can, won't you? Or I'll meet you somewhere. I need to talk to you regularly."

"It's probably not safe to meet. He'll have a detail on your trail wherever you go."

"Oh, I've got to see you. We'll work something out. I'll tell him I'm going to see Khalisah. She's still with you, isn't she?"

"She's enrolled in medical school."

"Where?"

"She'll have to tell you. I'll give you her number when she gets settled. I have to warn you though, she doesn't like you."

"Oh, I'll find some way to make her like me. I need a reason to come here to the U. S. You'll still talk to me on the phone, won't you, Charley? I need to talk to you. You're the only one I've ever been able to trust."

"If you can get to a line that you're absolutely sure has not been bugged. You know I enjoy talking to you."

"You are sweet, Charley. Don't let me down. How can I know where to call?"

"I'll get someone to call you and then you can go to a safe line. We'll need to work out a signal so you'll know it's from me when I have someone call you."

"That will be wonderful. How will I know?"

"How about using the word, *rose*? If you hear anything about a rose, you'll know it's me and you can call me back. You have my number now."

"I'll be waiting to hear from you, Charley."

"And do what I told you now. You have to, you know."

"I know. Don't wait too long to call."

"I won't."

"Bye. Love you."

"Bye, Rhonda.

My Little Bird

A week after she had moved in, Prince Faisal and Rhonda Gialetti appeared unexpectedly at Khalisah's apartment. Matthew Avery had just come to check on her to see if she needed anything. When they walked up the door was open and Dr. Avery was standing in the doorway talking with Khalisah.

"What do you think you are doing here with my daughter? You are ten years older than her," said Faisal.

"More like a dozen," replied Matthew Avery.

"Even worse. You will be an old man while she is still a young girl," Faisal responded.

Rhonda and Khalisah looked at each other and thought of the contrast in Rhonda and Faisal's ages.

"Besides she is a Muslim. She is promised to a Muslim back in her own country."

Again the contrast was obvious. Faisal was not married to an American yet but judging by Rhonda's profile it should be done soon. No one spoke and they all shuffled about nervously. Faisal looked as though he wanted to attack Matthew Avery physically.

"Actually, Sheik...."

"Wait, Dr. Avery. Father, he is a physician who is going to give me a recommendation to enter medical school here. He is just a friend," explained Khalisah.

"Why here?"

"Because the Mayo Clinic is here. It is world-renown for its advanced methods of treatment in almost every field. It is the best possible place to study, even better than Oxford."

"But you are here talking to him without a family member present...."

"I am sorry Father, but I told you many times that I was not going to stay in Riyadh after I was old enough to leave. If you won't help me live and study here then I'll work and apply for a scholarship. But I am staying here and I'm not coming back to Riyadh except for visits."

"No, no. You won't have to do that. Everything will be taken care of."

"As I told you in my letter; you did get my letter didn't you?"

"Yes. It was forwarded on to me."

"I'll work hard and make you proud of me, you'll see. I want to do something that will help people, especially the people of Saudi Arabia. I cannot stay at home and do nothing. You understand don't you?"

"Yes. Yes, I understand. You have always been my little bird that chirped the loudest. I will see to it that you have everything you need to succeed."

When she looked at him closely, she could see that he was trying to hide his tears. It was the first time that Khalisah had ever seen her father cry. *Why, he's crying because I'm leaving him*, she thought. *He's crying because it hurts him to have me leave him. I didn't know that he wouldn't be able to bear it if I left him. How thoughtless of me.*

They embraced and both of them wept and then Khalisah said through her tears, "*Baba*, I did not mean to hurt you! I never thought that you would miss me so much. Please don't cry. I'll go back to Riyadh with you. Just let me pack my clothes. It will only take a minute. Wait right here. I'll hurry."

Prince Faisal continued to hold her, and spoke softly to her, "No. Your place is here in school, where you want to be. Just promise me that you will not forget me. Promise me that you will come to visit me regularly. Then I think that I will be able to make it, from one visit to the next. Promise me that you will call regularly. Your mother will need to see you and speak with you regularly."

"I promise! I promise!"

He kissed her on the forehead and turned to Dr. Matthew Avery and said, "Look out for my little bird, please, Doctor. She is my most precious possession. If I were to lose her…there could never be another to replace her."

"Yes sir. I will look out for her."

"Thank you."

A look of Understanding

As Matthew Avery was taking Khalisah to a restaurant later that evening, she asked him what he thought "looking out for her" meant.

"I believe he was speaking in a strictly paternalistic sense, don't you? *In loco parentis.*"

"What? Oh, yes. I suppose," Matthew Avery responded.

"Surely you don't think he meant anything else, do you?"

"Ordinarily, I would say no. But when he looked at me, I caught a certain look in his eyes."

"What do you mean?"

"Sometimes, not very often, I would even say rarely, I have seen that look in a person's eye—a patient or a close friend. It is a look of understanding. They suddenly grasp the meaning of the situation. As when someone suddenly realizes from what you have told them that they are going to die. I saw that same look in my wife's eyes even though I had not said anything to her. She understood at that moment that she was going to die. I held her and we cried but from that point on, she began to be very indifferent towards me. I think it was a defense mechanism; that and an attempt to spare me from as much of her suffering as possible. She seemed to be trying to slowly withdraw from me so that I would be hurt as little as possible by her death."

"I certainly don't want to take anything away from what was clearly in the nature of an epiphany for you and her, but wouldn't you say that *a look* is more akin to anecdotal evidence than anything else? Do you know of any studies that have been done about what's involved in causing that sort of reaction? There doesn't seem to be any scientific basis to what you have concluded."

"That's true. I agree with you that it would be difficult if not impossible to conduct a double blind study on *a look*."

"Then what makes you believe that those looks meant what you thought they did?"

"Because the few times that I have observed them, they have been entirely accurate."

"I suppose it is difficult to argue against that."

"Yes. Sometimes in arriving at a diagnosis, you see indications of what is happening without understanding the mechanism that triggers the symptoms."

"So what do you think my father's look meant?"

"I think he realized at that moment that he had lost you for good. It was as though you had died. You could never go back to being the way that he had loved you the most—as his little girl.

"You're going to make me start crying again."

"Sorry."

"So you don't think that what he said to you was not just a sort of generic statement when he asked you to take care of me?"

"What do you think?"

"I asked you first."

"I'm not sure."

"You're evading the question."

"Sometimes that is the best option."

"I don't want an option. I want an answer."

"Why do you need an answer?"

"Because…you know why there needs to be an answer to that…."

"What if I'm wrong?"

"We'll worry about that later. Tell me what you think it meant."

"He could have meant it literally."

"You mean take care of me completely?"

"I suppose that could have been what he meant."

"But he doesn't even know you."

"What was that you said about your Father a few days ago? That he always has people figured out, usually right after meeting them."

"Do you think that he figured you out enough in such a short time to trust you to take care of me?"

Matthew Avery shrugged his shoulders and leaned back against the car seat.

"I'm flattered that it would even occur to someone of your stature to consider that as the meaning of his request."

"Thank you. But I am just attempting to answer your questions about what just happened."

Khalisah wondered how he would feel if he knew that she had come here because she couldn't bear to see Bill Smith leave her.

CHAPTER TWENTY-SIX

First Love

"Hello, Khalisah?"

"Yes. Hello, Bill."

"Did you see in the paper what happened at Munich?"

"No. I've been too busy to read the newspaper. What is going on at Munich?"

"The Olympics."

"Too bad I've been missing them. I know that we don't have any female athletes from Saudi Arabia at the Olympics and our men don't seem to do very well there."

"It's not about what happened in the games, it's about an act of terrorism that took place there."

"Terrorism? Oh no."

"Eight terrorists took nine Israeli athletes as hostages."

"What happened, Bill?"

"The Germans tried to rescue them and all nine Israelis were killed in addition to two others the terrorists had killed earlier."

"Oh, no! Where were they from, the terrorists?"

"They were part of the Palestinians who were driven out of the West Bank in 1967 and then driven out of Jordan by King Hussein in September of last year."

"You were right about terrorism, Bill. I'm glad we did what we could to try and stop it."

"Yes. But these terrorists were not from the Wahhabi schools. Fortunately, they were not connected to…to anyone we know."

"What happened to them?"

"Five were killed and three were captured."

"I'm glad...."

Bill interrupted her and said, "I'm sure that your father's people are watching out for you and taking good care of you."

"Yes. You're right. I'm sure they are."

"What are you doing now, Bill?"

"Working. I have a job at Stokely-Van Camp shoveling peas onto a conveyor belt. It's great exercise. I enjoy it. It's the first honest work I've ever done, on a permanent basis, that is. I have a record now. I'm no longer a shadowy figure without roots. It's kind of nice."

"It seems as though you ought to be doing something with that brilliant mind of yours."

"Oh, I'm studying Russian now, and Hebrew. It keeps me occupied."

"Bill, I must tell you that I believe I am in the right place now. The Mayo Clinic is ahead of almost any other medical treatment facility and the medical school is excellent, even though this is the first year."

"That's great. I must say that I am not going to make the mistake of underestimating you anymore. You are really something."

"Coming from you that is a great compliment. You know how I feel about you. I also think you are really something. Maybe you won't have to work there for very long."

"We'll see. There's no one that I like better or feel closer to than you. And I owe you more than anyone else, much more. Thanks, Khalisah."

"It helps to hear you say that. I guess you're the only person that I know here that even resembles a family member."

"We are family, *okhty*."

"I'm glad you think of me that way. I still don't think of you as *akh*. You're more like a marriageable cousin to me. Except you're married now."

"Oh, Rhonda Gialleti wanted me to tell you that she wants to talk to you and even come to see you periodically. I told her how you felt about her and your father but she insisted. She wants to become friends with you. I have her number if you want it."

"Oh, she's not so bad, I suppose. I've already met her. She was with my father when he came to visit me. I knew he wasn't here to watch our horse run, even though *Lion of the Littoral* won the Louisiana Derby and placed in the Arkansas Derby and the Santa Anita Derby. He's entered in the Kentucky Derby this year but my father probably won't even bother to come and watch him run now, since he has what he came over here to retrieve."

"I had no idea that you had already met her."

"Well, I have. It may surprise you to know that my father married her in a Western civil ceremony while they were here in the U. S. She is already beginning to show, so I suppose I will have another sibling before too long."

"Really?"

"Yes. And if I didn't know better, I'd think that you had something to do with it, William Smith. It just sounds so much like something you would think up."

Bill remained silent, not wanting to lie to Khalisah.

"It had to be my father's idea though. He never does anything that he doesn't want to. I suppose that somehow he thinks he loves her."

"Maybe he does."

"I still think it's about the money for her, however."

"I guess it has to be, doesn't it?"

"Oh, and my brother, Faisal, married Elizabeth Farnsworth-Smythe, his English girlfriend. He convinced her that he would never take another wife and that they would always live in England. I suppose he thought he had to act now while our father was not in a position to disinherit him. She was one of my best friends. I hope they are happy. I miss them both."

"I wish them the best. By the way, how are you liking the med school at the Mayo Clinic?"

"I am really enjoying it. It is wonderful being here, close to you...and Rebecca. In fact, it's time for class now, although I'd much rather skip class so I can talk to you."

"You'd better go to class."

"All right. I'll go. I'm fixin' to go to class *dreckly*, Bill."

"Don't make too much fun of Occidentals. Especially us guys from the South. We are very insecure. You might hurt our feelings."

"Hah! No chance of that. I'm not sure that you have any 'feelings.'"

"I do, and you're deeply entrenched in them. You are coming to stay with us this weekend, right?"

"I may need to study all day Saturday. But I could come on Sunday."

"That would be great. I'll come get you."

"Wonderful. Call me more often. I miss you."

"I miss you too."

"Thanks. Love you."

"Love you too, Khalisah."

Well, at least he said it, she thought. *I don't doubt that he meant it but there is no way to transfer it into anything tangible. I was not wise enough to keep from falling in love with Bill Smith and I suppose I'll always have deep feelings for him. He was my first love, after all. It must be true that your first love affects you more deeply than anything else and you don't understand why,* she thought. *He and Rebecca are the only ones I know here. But that's enough. I can make it with Bill close by.*

Farewell Blue Earth

Yitzhak Kahan called Simons Grebel and inquired about his man who had done such great work in Riyadh. Would he be interested in working again? He had several places where he needed someone like him to work. Someone not associated with us, Yitzhak said. Since he had done the impossible in Saudi Arabia, Yitzhak said that he hoped that Grebel's recruit might have changed his mind and be willing to work for them again.

"I'll have to ask Bill." Grebel replied.

"Bill? Is that the name of your new recruit?"

Grebel paused then said, "It's Bill Smith. He's still alive. He didn't die in Vietnam. He showed up on my doorstep a few months later."

"You didn't think it was necessary to tell me?"

"It was his choice. He didn't want to because he felt that he had failed you."

"Uhm."

"He was more than a little bit messed up from his experience over there."

"Understandable."

"I hope you're not offended."

"On the contrary, Simeon, it would be good to work with him again if he will agree. He is excellent. Look at what he did in Arabia. I knew that he had good instincts."

"But we haven't asked him and he hasn't agreed yet."

"That's true. Perhaps it would be best not to push him. He needs to decide this on his own."

"Agreed. I'll get back to you if he decides to work for you again."

"Wonderful, Simeon. I would rather have him than anyone else."

"I'll inform him of that. My gut feeling is that he will agree to work again, even though everything is against it. He's married now and his wife is expecting."

"That changes things."

"For the better I think. He'll have more reason to come back safely."

"Yes. It may make him more skittish and afraid to take risks. But that's good. It will be much better if he is careful and does not act rashly."

"That's true."

"He learned from the best, Simeon, when he learned from you."

"But I'm out of the spy business, Yitzhak. I just support Bill now."

"Are we ever out altogether, Simeon?"

Simons Grebel grunted and waited for Yitzhak to continue.

"You know, Simeon, If he agrees, it occurs to me that his wife should come to Tel Aviv so we can protect her. Where is she staying now?"

"In a small town in Minnesota, named Blue Earth."

"Our men would stick out like the proverbial 'sore thumb' there. It is imperative that she come here if Bill works for us again."

"She and her daughter live there with her mother."

"Um, they would need to come also."

"And there is a rooster that his mother-in-law will not part with, I am told. The laying hens she might be persuaded to leave with her neighbors, but not the rooster."

"There is always room for one more rooster here in Israel."

"I'll see what he says."

"Excellent. Thank you, Simeon. Come by and see me some time. I miss our discussions."

"It's better this way, I think. I'm out of it and visiting you would only make me want to get involved again."

"Are you sure you don't miss it, Simeon?"

"Maybe. But I enjoy it better the way things are now."

"I understand. Well, *Shalom*, Simeon."

"*Shalom*, Yitzhak."

Bill Smith listened to Simons Grebel explain to him on the phone what Yitzhak Kahan wanted. His reply was terse.

"You can only give what you have to give. You can't give what you don't have. I don't have anything to give anymore. Tell Yitzhak that I'm sorry. I like him but I don't think I can do the type of work he wants me to do anymore."

"Well, I should inform you, Bill, that you may not be safe where you are."

"Why not?"

"Yitzhak just told me that he sent some agents to keep watch over you and bring you back here to Tel Aviv if you decided to come."

"And?"

"They've picked up on some people who have been keeping you under surveillance. And they've been watching the Lundstrom house when you're at work."

Bill felt a lump in his throat. "Any idea who they are working for"

"Not yet. But they're working on it."

"Let me know as soon as they find out anything, Simons."

"I will. Do you have any idea who it might be? No one knows about you except Yitzhak and me. Is there anyone else who might be interested in finding you?"

"It could be Prince Faisal."

"Why would he be looking for you?"

Bill hesitated and then said, "I left Riyadh with his daughter."

"That puts you in a very dangerous spot. Sheiks kill without blinking an eye when someone abducts their daughter."

"It couldn't be helped. She wanted to leave there."

"Did she leave because she wanted to come with you?"

"Yes, but…."

Simons let Bill think about the situation, then said, "If it is someone that the Prince has watching you that would be the best situation. It is much better than finding out that someone else in the Middle East that we don't know about has uncovered your identity."

"You're right. That would be much worse. I guess I don't have a choice, do I Simons?"

"Doesn't look as though you do."

"I can leave right away. I just have to give notice where I'm working."

"Don't do that."

"I won't, if you say not to."

"And Rebecca and the child and her mother must come with you."

"When?"

"They can fly you out tonight. It's not safe to wait any longer. You could have someone descend on the house at any time."

"Then tell Yitzhak's men we're ready to go tonight. I guess you told him that I'm still alive."

"Yes. It was necessary for me to tell him. It's the only decision you can make, Bill. Otherwise you're putting everyone there at risk."

"You're right. Annike won't leave here without a struggle but she has to go even if I have to carry her out."

"They'll be there at 1900 hours, your time."

"We'll be ready. Thanks, Simons, for looking out for us."

"My pleasure. It will be good to see you again. I'll meet you at the airport when you arrive."

Indian Summer

It was one of the last beautiful days during the brief Indian Summer in Minnesota. Khalisah Amtullah Al-Saud cruised down the highway in the new silver Jaguar XKE convertible she had just purchased. She sang lines from the poem, *Description of Love* by Mawlana Jalaluddin Rumi in Arabic as she flew along the road between Rochester and Blue Earth with her dark black hair blowing in the wind.

> *Explanation by the tongue makes most things clear,*
> *But love unexplained is clearer...*
> *Naught but Love itself can explain love...*
> *None but the sun can display the sun...*
> *The lover's cause is separate from all other causes*
> *Love is the astrolabe of God's mysteries...*

She was so excited that she could hardly stay below the speed limit. She wanted to surprise Rebecca and Bill and show Bill that he wouldn't have to come and pick her up on the weekend any more. She had received a letter that week from the National Bank of Commerce in Rochester informing her that an account had recently been opened in her name. She took a taxi down to the bank early the next morning and a few hours later drove back to her apartment in the new Jaguar.

When she pulled off onto the gravel road leading to Annike Lundstrom's small Craftsman style home a wave of emotion swept over her when she thought of how surprised and proud Bill would be to learn that she had driven from Rochester herself. He would be pleased that all those hours of driving lessons that he had patiently endured on the back roads around Riyadh had not been in vain. The house seemed deserted but that was not unusual; it had looked that way the first time she saw it. She parked and ran to the door and knocked impatiently on it.

When no one answered she stepped off the porch and walked around and peered in one of the windows. She was unable to see inside the house and returned to the front yard where she noticed a sign lying flat on the ground. It had "For Sale" written on it. She suddenly realized that the chickens were gone and the grass needed mowing. Did they have an emergency? She had spoken with Bill on Monday—only five days ago. She wanted to surprise them and didn't call before coming today. *What could have happened? Where could they have gone?*

A sick feeling developed in the pit of her stomach. She waited for over an hour and began to cry when she realized that Bill was gone—gone for good. Then she started the engine and headed back to Rochester. On the way through Blue Earth she stopped at Hansen's Grocery and inquired about the people at the Lundstrom household. They had been gone for about four days, the clerk said. No, no one had any idea of where they were going. They left without telling anyone anything.

Khalisah drove back to Rochester and cried again on the way back. She had no idea what she was going to do now. *Anything but return to Riyadh*, she thought. *I'll stay here for now if I can keep my mind on my studies. Bill is gone forever; I'll never see him again*, she thought. She felt betrayed. She just hoped her father hadn't found out who Bill Smith really was.

CHAPTER TWENTY-SEVEN

Farewell to the *Son of Life*

Isaac Ben-Chaim (*Son of Life*) felt more relaxed than he had in recent memory. He had an unusual sense of peace as he thought about what had been accomplished by the network of informants that he had set up almost single-handedly in the USSR. The Summer Olympics in Munich were exciting and he was enjoying the games. He had only one contact to meet with while he was here.

Downtown, an athlete from the USSR sat in a movie theater nervously awaiting the arrival of a man he knew only by the name of Pavel Bresnovski. The athlete's event was the high jump and his tall, lanky frame did not fit well in the small theater seats. He had to slump down to allow the patrons behind him to see, so he always sat on the back row to avoid the problem. There were other Soviet athletes watching the movie and he began to worry about how he could meet with Bresnovski without giving himself away. He had been instructed to go to the restroom at 1500 hours to meet with Bresnovski but when he went there, he waited for ten minutes and no one showed up.

He decided to stay until the movie was over and then leave with the other athletes and forget about the meeting. It was too dangerous despite the promise of a large sum of money. He was being recruited for the future since he had been assigned to a low-level position in the Soviet space program when he retired from competition after the Olympics. The launch of *Sputnik* in 1957 had set off a bitterly contested space race between the United States and the USSR and any sort of information about the Soviet space program was deemed to be extremely valuable. The Israelis felt they needed to keep abreast of the progress made by both sides.

Two KGB agents who were not known to any of the Soviet athletes had followed the high jumper up the stairs to the restroom and waited until he came out. They had already searched the facility thoroughly and knew that no one was inside. They moved out of view when he exited and were satisfied that nothing had transpired. The information they had received from one of their most reliable sources about Josef Storchev's plan to meet with a Soviet athlete at the games had not produced any results. The situation would require further investigation, they decided.

When word of the hostage situation reached Isaac Ben-Chaim, he had just checked his watch and was about to leave his hotel room to meet with the Soviet athlete at the movie theater. He could not believe his ears when he listened to the announcer on German television hurriedly relate what was happening. His experience and instinct told him to leave as quickly as possible and forget about the meeting at the movie theater. Usually he remained composed in the face of tragedy and did not let himself be affected by a crisis such as this; but this time he could feel the rage rising within him.

Something had to be done. This could not be permitted to continue, he thought. Without any idea of what he could do to help the hostages, he rushed to the Israeli athletes' quarters. When he arrived, he saw the body of an Israeli athlete lying motionless on the steps of the apartments. Behind Ben-Chaim, a figure in the crowd followed his movements closely. Grigori Morostev was trying to determine the best way to carry out the strike on Isaac Ben-Chaim. *It would be more difficult now because of the hostage situation*, he thought. The *polizei* were everywhere.

He had followed the man registered under the name of Pavel Bresnovski from his hotel here to the games. He had found him hidden in plain sight in the most expensive hotel in Munich, the *Bayerischen Hof*. Finding him was different from hunting targets during the war but not too different from locating the members of the thieves' world. Grigori had spent many hours every day comparing faces to the photo that he had. He canvassed the best hotels and ignored the less expensive ones. He let his accomplice, Karl-Heinz Dietrich, supplied by Dmitri's man, scour those.

It was a calculated risk based on what he thought the target would do. But it had worked and now he could stalk him until an opportunity presented itself. If none arose then he would have to force the issue and that would involve some risk. Grigori's accomplice, Karl-Heinz Dietrich, was German and he could converse in a halting manner in Russian. After the hostages were taken he was spooked but insisted that they stay and pursue Ben-Chaim. Grigori agreed since he wasn't ready to abandon his target yet. The plight of the hostages would attract everyone's attention and could work to his advantage if Ben-Chaim ever ventured into a deserted area. He had to be patient and follow Ben-Chaim without being detected.

After waiting in front of the Israeli athletes' apartments for almost two hours, Ben-Chaim walked to his automobile, and Grigori and Dietrich trailed carefully after him. When he drove away, they followed a few car lengths behind him. He did not seem to be aware of their presence. He stopped after about ten kilometers and went into a *leihhaus*, a pawn shop. When he returned he was carrying a small package. He headed out of Munich going west.

"What do you think he bought?" asked Karl-Heinz Dietrich.

"I don't know but the package was about the size of a hand gun," said Grigori.

After 20 kilometers, Karl-Heinz said, "He's heading toward the French border."

"How far is it from here?"

"About 320 kilometers. The A8 goes toward the *Schwartz Wald*.

"He may turn south toward Switzerland before then," said Grigori. "Keep him in sight."

The *Schwartz Wald*, or Black Forest, was a wooded mountain range in the state of Baden-Württemberg in southwestern Germany. It was the place of legend where tall conifers block out the sun and the mountains add to the shadows. The mighty Danube River rises from the *Schwartz Wald* and travels across central Europe before emptying into the Black Sea.

The Schwartz Wald would be a good place to act if he goes that far, Grigori thought. *But he will turn south before then, probably toward Zurich.*

Grigori turned his thoughts to his driver and interpreter, Karl-Heinz Dietrich. He seemed innocuous enough and too frightened to be a threat to anyone, but perhaps he was edgy for a reason. Grigori had not yet been able to determine if he was carrying a weapon. Grigori still thought that he had been marked for elimination after he carried out this assassination, but it did not seem likely that Karl-Heinz Dietrich would be the one to do it.

Isaac Ben-Chaim drove west until he passed through Augsburg, the last city on the A8 autobahn. He continued until he reached the border of Bavaria. Just before he reached the city of Ulm inside the *Schwartz Wald*, he turned south toward Austria. Shortly after he came through the town of Leutkirch, he turned west again toward Friedrichshafen on the shore of Lake Constance.

"He's going to the airport at Friedrichshafen," said Karl-Heinz Dietrich. "From there he can catch a flight to Stuttgart or Zurich. He could also fly to Vienna or even Paris."

"I will take him when he exits his car to go into the airport. The light should be satisfactory there. It seems quiet tonight and there should not be many people around."

"What is our escape route? Do you have a safe egress in mind?"

"I have added a sound suppressor to this weapon so we should be able to leave without haste and go back the way we came."

When Ben-Chaim started driving down the incline to the airport Grigori said, "Pull over here at the top of the hill where the trees are."

Grigori exited the vehicle quickly and removed the custom made sniper rifle from the boot of the automobile. He pushed the brace to rest the weapon on into the ground and set up for a kneeling shot. Dietrich stood behind him, watching for anyone who might come their way. Grigori adjusted the scope and was ready to fire by the time Ben-Chaim pulled into the parking lot.

"He is about 900 meters away," he told Dietrich.

When Grigori chambered a round, he looked into the scope and the street lights gave him a clear view behind him. He saw

Karl-Heinz Dietrich's reflection in the scope and watched as Dietrich bent down and pulled a small hand gun from one of the fashionable Italian boots he was wearing. Then he tucked his hand behind his leg.

So it was Dietrich after all, he thought.

He knew that Dietrich would not shoot him until he had eliminated Ben-Chaim. He would need to distract Dietrich somehow. He decided to tell Dietrich that he had missed the target. Then he would move his hand to the *Stechkin APS* he had holstered under his left arm.

One three round burst ought to do it, he reasoned.

Ben-Chaim was aware that he was being followed but he had not yet decided what to do. Whoever it was, he knew their presence meant trouble and it was likely that an attempt on his life was imminent. He pulled into the parking space that was the closest to the entrance to the airport lobby. When he surveyed the parking lot there was no one in sight. He slid across the seat and opened the door on the passenger side and exited the vehicle. He decided to sprint for the entrance. Before he could start running, Grigori squeezed the trigger gently and the rifle made a soft hissing sound as it fired. He watched as one of Ben-Chaim's arms flew outward and his body jerked forward suddenly and disappeared behind his vehicle.

To throw Dietrich off, Grigori said, "I missed him!"

But Dietrich was looking through binoculars and he replied, "No, I think you hit him."

Grigori chambered another round and carefully moved his hand to the *Stechkin APS*, the *Automaticheskij Pistolet Stechkina* he had holstered under his left arm. It was set on the fully automatic mode and the barrel was pointed behind him toward Dietrich. He squeezed off a three round volley from under his arm that went through his jacket and then he heard Dietrich moan. Grigori jerked the *Stechkin* from the holster and whirled around to see if he needed to finish him off. Dietrich had fallen on his right side was struggling to get his right arm out from under his body. When he did, the eerie sound of a silencer punctuated the quiet as Dietrich's pistol spat out a round. Grigori felt a sting in his left side just above the heart.

Grigori fired another burst, this time at Dietrich's head, and his body flopped over and lay still with his legs twisted beneath him. But Dietrich's round had found its way through the arm hole of Grigori's bullet proof vest and into his armpit. The pain made him unable to move at first. When he could use his hands, he tried to grasp his wound with his left hand but could not. He squeezed his left arm against his body and used his right hand to crawl back to Dietrich. He had a bullet hole in his forehead and when Grigori laid his hand on Dietrich's chest he could feel the body armor. *I had not counted on that*, he thought. He began crawling toward the road. He was bleeding badly and he knew if he did not get someone to stop it he would be dead shortly. He could not drive himself so his only hope was to get a car to stop for him.

Ben-Chaim lay on the ground for a moment until the pain subsided a bit and then began to crawl toward the Airport. The body armor that he had purchased in the pawn shop in Munich had not stopped the round but it had saved his life. The bullet had torn into his side and he could tell that he had a couple of broken ribs and was bleeding. But he thought he would live. He staggered for the pay phone next to the building and fumbled for some coins. He called Pieter Schmidt at the safe house and then sat down on the ground and held his right hand firmly against the wound on his left side.

"I am wounded, Pieter. Can you come get me at the airport?"

"Yes. I'll be there right away. What happened?"

"Someone shot me."

"Did you see who it was?"

"No. It was from a distance."

"A sniper. Where are you now?"

"At the phone near the building. Please hurry."

"Don't let him get another shot at you. Hide somewhere."

"Yes. I will. I'll watch for you."

"Stay hidden until you see me. I'll be there within 15 minutes. Will you be all right till then?"

"Yes. I'm bleeding but I'll be all right until you get here. Is Dr. Scheide around?"

"He's gone fly fishing. I'll bring Braun. He's trained in first aid."

"Good. Hurry."

He hung up the phone and crawled to the nearest car and sat curled up beside it. *I can't go into the airport; I am bleeding and in too much pain. It would attract attention and they would call an ambulance and the polizei. But Pieter will be here soon,* he thought.

Pieter Schmidt drove rapidly along the road into the airport and told Gerhardt Braun to look closely along both sides of the road for any movement. He did not want Ben Chaim's assailant to get another shot at him if he could stop him. When he reached the top of the hill going down to the airport, a figure staggered out in front of his car and collapsed on the pavement. Schmidt jammed on the brakes and skidded to a stop just before he hit him.

"Help me," the figure cried in German.

"Who are you?" Schmidt asked in German

"Help me," came the cry again.

Schmidt exited from the vehicle and drew his Beretta and peered around the fender while Braun did the same. A man was sprawled in front of the car clutching a pistol.

"Help me," he said again in German.

"Who are you?"

Grigori had exhausted his vocabulary in German and could not understand the reply so he moaned for help in Russian. Schmidt was stunned to hear him call out in Russian. He questioned him in Russian.

"Who are you?"

"A fellow Russian. Help me!"

Schmidt said, "Drop your weapon."

The pistol clattered on the pavement and Schmidt said, "I will shoot you immediately if you make any sort of move."

He crept around the vehicle and retrieved the hand gun. Then Braun searched him for other weapons. Schmidt took his handkerchief and pressed it against the man's wound to staunch the flow of blood. He told him to hold it tightly while he and Braun lifted him into the car.

"You need a doctor," he said.

"Yes. Please help me."

"Who shot you?"

"He's dead."

"You need to tell me what is going on before I take you to a doctor. And you'd better hurry because there is not much time. Where is the person who shot you?"

Grigori nodded in the direction he had crawled from and Schmidt told Braun to tend to the Russian while he took a quick look. He hastened into the brush and found a dead man sprawled on the ground holding a hand gun. He removed the dead man's wallet and looked at the driver's license. It identified him as Karl-Heinz Dietrich, a German citizen. He took the dead man's hand gun and started back toward the vehicle.

His foot hit a large object and he stooped down and felt for it. He lifted it up and saw that it was a rifle—a very expensive sniper rifle. *This must be the weapon that was fired at Pavel*, he thought. *It must have been the Russian.*

He took the weapons and went back to the car to question the wounded Russian.

"There was a sniper rifle up there. The dead man was a German named Karl-Heinz Dietrich, according to his papers."

When Grigori did not answer, Schmidt said,

"He was holding a hand gun."

Grigori feigned unconsciousness, but Schmidt said, "You haven't passed out from a lack of blood yet. I need to find out which one of you is the sniper. So I'm going to save your life for now."

He drove quickly down to the airport and located Isaac Ben-Chaim and he and Braun lifted him into the seat.

"I think I have your sniper here in the back seat, Isaac," Schmidt said.

Ben-Chaim turned and looked at him and said, "He looks dead."

"No. I think he'll live."

"If he does, we can find out who hired him."

"Yes. And he had an accomplice with him. I found him dead in the woods nearby."

"What happened to him?"

"I don't know yet, Isaac. But we can find out if the sniper lives."

"What did you do with the body?"

"I left it there."

"Should we take it with us?"

"Not unless you have a good reason, Isaac."

"Just to tie up loose ends, I suppose. Where is the body?"

"Right out there," Schmidt said. "About twenty meters into the woods."

"Stop the car," Ben Chaim said. "I think we should take him with us."

"We can stuff him in the trunk, I suppose," said Braun.

"Let me go see him."

"But you are wounded, Isaac."

"You're going to have to go get him anyway. I want to go with you and get a look at him. You and Braun can help me get there."

When they arrived where the body was, Ben-Chaim took a look at the German and told them to wait.

"Don't take him yet."

It occurred to him that the dead man was about his size. Ben-Chaim thought that no one could identify him by his physical appearance. *This fellow could easily pass for me*, he thought. *If someone is trying to have me killed, it might throw them off if it looked as though the attempt was successful. Why not trade identities with the dead man? I have nothing to lose by trying. I have a passport in another name and a set of identity papers hidden in the false bottom of my suitcase.*

He told Schmidt to take the dead man's wallet.

"Now take the cash out of my wallet and leave it lying on the ground nearby."

It had his identification papers in the name of Pavel Bresnovski in it. Then he told Schmidt to remove the dead man's coat and take off his body armor to make it look more like a robbery.

"The name on his driver's license, Karl-Heinz Dietrich, has to be an alias since he is obviously an assassin also."

"It would seem so, Isaac."

"And he would have kept his true identity well-guarded. I don't think anyone will claim the body."

"No. I wouldn't think so," said Schmidt.

"If it was reported that Pavel Bresnovski, a. k. a. Josef Storchev was dead, it might give me breathing space for a while," said Ben-Chaim.

It would be good if Tel Aviv also believed I'm dead, he thought. *That would make the deception complete.*

"The ruse might work if the murder is not investigated too closely," Schmidt said, "and even the *polizei* in Friedrichshaufen are preoccupied with the Munich Massacre now."

"It's worth a try."

"But right now, we have to get you to Dr. Scheide. I sent someone for him. Perhaps the Russian will not die and we can get the whole story out of him."

"How do you know he's a Russian?"

"He spoke to me in Russian. I questioned him in Russian. I think it is the only language he understands."

"Help me back to the car, Pieter. I am feeling weak."

CHAPTER TWENTY-EIGHT

Death in the *Schwartz Wald*

Two days after the Munich Massacre, a brief article appeared on page ten of *Der Spiegel* about a murder that took place in the shadow of the Black Forest. It was eclipsed by the acts of terrorism that had unfolded at the Olympic Village in Munich, but it accomplished what Isaac Ben-Chaim wanted.

Pavel Bresnovski, a. k. a. Josef Storchev, Vilnius Ilyich Lovinovich, and Gerhardt Schroeder, was found shot to death near Friedrichshaufen, Germany on September 5, 1972. He was known to have also used numerous other aliases. The polizei are treating it as a robbery. His wallet contained no cash and was found lying on the ground near his body. No other motive has been established. He died from a gunshot wound to the head and the body was found by police acting on a report by an anonymous source. No witnesses have been located thus far. The body has not been claimed and it remains in the custody of the Friedrichshaufen polizei. He was known to have occasionally acted as an agent for professional athletes in several countries. Anyone having any information about the incident should contact the Friedrichshaufen polizei immediately.

The Wounded Hunter

Pieter Schmidt looked at the sleeping figure on the bed in front of him with tubes attached to both arms. He was a hated Russian. They were the only ones that Pieter hated more than Nazis. He would probably be out hunting down escaped Nazis if he did not hate the Russians so much. But it was difficult to do the Russians any harm now. Schmidt was a Hungarian whose real name was Jan Piewysciez. He was raised in an orphanage without knowing who his parents were. He was large and muscular, and had become a member of the resistance movement in Hungary once the Soviet Army began to push the Nazis out of the country.

He escaped to West Germany when the Soviets moved in and started killing all of those who had collaborated with them against the Nazis. They would form the nucleus of a resistance movement against them, the Soviets reasoned, and there was no reason to keep them around any longer after the Nazis were defeated, so they began killing them. Schmidt was aided in his escape by a man he had never met. He learned later that the man was his father. *At least the man who fathered me kept up with my whereabouts and was willing to help me escape when the Russians came rolling into Budapest,* he thought.

Schmidt ran a tavern now in Friedrichshaufen named the *Taverna Budapest.* Even though the food was recognized as being excellent, it was a little too spicy for the German palate and the tavern barely turned a profit. It did not matter since Isaac Ben-Chaim regularly used it as a safe house and his money provided a satisfactory income for the owner, Pieter Schmidt. When Grigori began to stir, Schmidt turned to Gerhardt Braun and whispered that they would find out now just who this fellow was. When Grigori awoke he could feel that there were tubes attached to his arms and he saw that he was bound to the bed by several cords.

"You will recover," Schmidt said. "Although you may not have full use of your left arm."

"Where am I?" mumbled Grigori.

"In a safe location," said Schmidt. "What is your name?"

"Does it matter?" Grigori asked.

"I suppose not. We know what your papers say. But they are obviously false."

"My name is Grigori Morostev. What are you going to do to me?"

"I think you are the assassin and the other fellow was your accomplice," said Schmidt.

Grigori did not answer him.

"Why were you trying to kill Pavel and who are you working for?"

"I didn't try to kill him. It was the other guy."

"He was holding a hand gun. He couldn't have hit him with that. One of you used the rifle. We'll keep you here until you remember."

"I don't know why."

"Who hired you then?"

"Someone named Dmitri."

"Dmitri?"

"That's all I know."

"Well, you are of no value to me. It would have been better if you had died. Now I can't keep you and I can't let you go. You might come after Pavel again. I will have to decide what do with you in the next few days."

"No. I wouldn't come after him again."

"Why not?"

"The people who paid me tried to have me killed to cover it up. I won't work for them anymore and I won't come after him again."

"Even if I believed you, it still wouldn't matter. You are an assassin and killing is your work. And now you are the only one who knows what Pavel looks like."

"I would not be so sure of that."

"Why not?"

"I was shown three photographs of men who could be him. One of them was an older photo but it was possible to recognize him from it."

Isaac was right. He does need to disappear. Permanently this time, Schmidt thought. *His identity has been uncovered by those who are the most determined to get rid of him. If he does not disappear, the attempts on his life will only increase.*

"Where did you learn to shoot?" Schmidt asked.

"In the Great Patriotic War," Grigori replied.

"How many Nazis did you kill?"

"Four hundred and seventeen that I saw fall, with three hundred and fifty-one being confirmed and about two dozen more recorded as probables."

"I'm impressed. How many since then?"

"Forty-six."

"And who were they?"

"They were all members of the crime syndicates in the USSR. They pay me to kill each other."

"I'm even more impressed. But what should I do with you now? I could turn you over to the *polizei*, but you would probably tell them things we did not want them to know. Or I could shoot you myself but I would have to go to the trouble of finding a way to dispose of your body."

"I won't say anything."

"What should I do with you then?"

"Let me go. I want to go back to Kazan in Russia, where I was born."

"If I turned you loose what assurance would I have that you would not try to kill Pavel or any of the rest of us again?"

"I will be running for my life and won't have time to try and harm any of you. I will have to stay in hiding for the rest of my life. I can only speak Russian, so I cannot leave the USSR for very long."

"That doesn't convince me. I still think you might come looking for Pavel again."

"No. I won't."

"Why not?"

"Because no one will pay me to kill him now."

"Maybe I should turn you over to the KGB then. They will know how to deal with you. But it would be difficult to transport you there."

"Just let me go. If you let me go I won't bother you anymore and you'll never see me again. You won't regret it. I am a man of my word."

"The word of an assassin. How reliable is that?"

"Do you not have any gratitude for those who fought in the Great Patriotic War and helped defeat the Nazis?"

"I suppose I should. But now the USSR has become an even greater oppressor than the Nazis. It has become the greatest oppressor of them all."

"So you will not let me go?"

"Because you killed so many Nazis, I think I might let you go, just to be rid of you. As soon as you are able to travel. That will be your reward for killing over 400 of those Nazis murderers. You can go back to the Soviet Union and start shooting members of the crime syndicates again. It would be better if you could shoot Andropov and some of his agents in the KGB."

"No one would pay me for that. But if you let me go I will not bother you again."

You do not realize that you are being released because Isaac Ben-Chaim's ruse worked and the people who hired you believe it was him who died instead of your accomplice. And you will not go back and tell them any different, will you? No. I think not. If you showed up they would do away with you to cover up what they paid you to do. Just like they tried to have your accomplice do. Isaac does not want anyone killed who does not have to be, even though you were trying to kill him. He thinks it is safe to release you despite the fact that you are a hired killer since you have no reason to try and kill him now. From now on you will have to remain in hiding from the thugs sent by the people who hired you. Things seemed to have worked in your favor this time, hunter. Perhaps because you killed so many of the right people— Nazis and Russian criminals.

Replacing the *Son of Life*

In Tel Aviv, Yitzhak Kahan informed Simons Grebel that Isaac Ben-Chaim, also known as Josef Storchev, had been killed in Germany near Lake Constance. Since Ben-Chaim's network of informants was leaderless now, Yitzhak wanted to find someone to replace him who could keep it functioning. He thought that William Smith would be an excellent fit. Grebel concurred and told Yitzhak that the only thing that remained was to get Smith to agree.

"How much direction do you plan on giving him this time?" asked Grebel.

"Very little," said Yitzhak. "Mostly information. After all, who else could have done what he did in Saudi Arabia? That was brilliant. It was one of the greatest intelligence coups in the brief history of our body politic. Now we know where all of the money is going."

"Yes. It was an excellent piece of work," said Grebel.

"He will have as much financing as he needs now that I am involved. However, most of the funds used to pay off clients will still come from Isaac Ben-Chaim's man in London, who shall remain nameless."

"You know, Yitzhak, he could have just been very lucky in Arabia. Don't you think it might be better to keep in closer touch with him this time?"

"Ah, Simeon. You sound like a father talking about his favorite son. I am in favor of just turning him loose and getting out of his way. He seems to do his best work when he initiates something himself, as he did in Arabia. If we contact him there is always the possibility that we could inadvertently expose him."

"It was just a thought, Yitzhak. You're probably right. I'm used to more command and control when dealing with assets."

"Understandable. You will still be willing to receive communication from him when he has something to report, won't you?"

"Yes. I'll keep you notified. I need to find a means for him to contact me without having to call Tel Aviv, however. It's probably better if I'm the only one who knows what it is."

"Agreed. And we will arrange for Charley Harper to disappear so that the people Faisal has investigating him will be able to report his death to the Prince. They were the ones carrying out the survellience of him in Minnesota."

"I thought it was probably them. It seems you have thought of everything, Yitzhak."

"You understand how necessary it is to be meticulous in our work, Simeon."

"And you are one of the best at doing that. Bill will be in good hands."

"And we think that he will continue to be as successful as he was in Riyadh."

"It seems he has a way of getting to the heart of a situation. At least he has been able to do so thus far."

"He was a great find, Simeon. Well, I must go. There is a great deal of work to do. It seems we will have another war to fight right away. Just as you predicted."

"I wish I had been wrong, Yitzhak. *Shalom*."

"*Shalom*, dear friend."

A Marriage of Convenience

Charley Harper was dead, or so she had been told. Khalisah Amtullah Al-Saud could not decide whether that was the truth or a ploy to keep her from trying to find him. Either way, it meant that he was gone for good, she decided. She would never see him again. She asked Dr. Matthew Avery to pull over and stop in a park near the Mayo Clinic.

"Marry me," she said.

"Are you sure?" he asked.

"Yes. Do what my Father asked you to do and take care of me."

"What about Bill Smith?"

"What about him?"

"Do you know where he is?"

"Dead I'm told."

"Who told you?"

"It came in a letter from my brother. My father told him that Charley Harper died in a plane crash near Birmingham. If that's true then Bill Smith died with him."

"England?"

"No. Alabama. That was his home."

"How did your Father know?"

"Faisal said Father had a detective agency tracking him to find out who he really was. Now he'll never know. But Faisal said

Father was truly saddened by his death. He saved Father's life when there was an attack on our compound."

"Was anyone else involved in the accident?"

"Not according to the report. Just him and the pilot. But that makes me somewhat suspicious. He and Rebecca were inseperable. He wouldn't have let her out of his sight."

"Are you sorry?"

"Yes. Of course. He was a good friend to Faisal and me."

"Is that all?"

"Why? What do you mean?"

"Was he more than a friend?"

"Yes. I suppose he was. What made you think that?"

"I watched your eyes when you were around him."

"You're very perceptive, Doctor."

"You learn a few things after observing patients for as long as I have."

"Yes. Bill Smith was my first love. But he married Rebecca and now he's gone. And whether he's dead or not, I won't ever see him again. Does that disqualify me from consideration because I fell in love with him?"

"Not at all. Is there anything else that you think should be discussed before we make a decision?"

"What about Rebecca Lundstrom Smith?"

"She's married now."

"Not if Bill Smith is dead."

"But you don't really believe that he is dead."

"I don't know, but since I won't ever see him again, he's dead as far as I'm concerned."

"True. And I will never see Rebecca again."

"Did you love her?"

"I told her that I couldn't even think about starting over with someone else after my wife died and at the time I meant it. But I would have married her if she had not already been committed to Bill."

"So we are both in the same predicament. In love with someone we will never see again. That could be the most difficult obstacle of all to overcome."

"What do you think we should do about it?"

"I've already made my decision. If you don't concur that's

your prerogative."

"I haven't had any time to think about it. You just now asked me. I need some time to make a decision that important."

"We've know each other long enough. Either you want to or you don't."

"Despite the adjustments that we would need to make?"

"I can make them. If you can't or don't want to…."

"I'm just pointing out that there are some significant differences to consider."

"Yes, Matt. I know. There's the age difference and the cultural difference. But I'm willing to do whatever we need to do about those. Is it because I'm not attractive enough?"

"Hardly. You're a very beautiful girl. One of the most beautiful that I've ever met. You are as beautiful as I could ever want my wife to be."

"What is it then? Did I make it sound too much like a marriage of convenience?"

"No. Although every marriage is that to some degree. I suppose you have been conditioned to accept marriage as that."

"Yes. I have. But that doesn't mean I couldn't love the person that I married as much as they needed me to."

"Khalisah, I will be extremely pleased to be married to you. So don't think you have to overcome any opposition that I have. But over here, the man initiates the proposal, so allow me to do that."

"You're right. It is so much the man's prerogative back home that I suppose I am trying to go completely counter to that century's old tradition. Pardon me for taking the initiative. I will leave it all to you."

"I think we have a lot of things to talk over and decide about first but let's proceed on the basis that we are planning to be married."

"Is that a proposal?"

"No. That's just establishing the hypothesis. When I propose, you won't have any doubt about it whatsoever."

"How very logical of you, Doctor. I feel a great sense of assurance that we will thoroughly investigate everything beforehand, lest we do anything that might not fit in the theorem that you construct."

With that she jabbed him in the ribs and he laughed and reached for her. *It was going to be all right with Matthew Avery,* she thought. *And it would be much more than a marriage of convenience. So much more.*

"You know Matt, I know more about romance in the West than you do."

"How's that?"

"Well, it's obvious that you know little or nothing about how romance works, in the West or anywhere else."

"You're right. I tried to emulate my parents by staying so busy that there was little time for romance. I thought finding someone to love would take care of itself because I would be so preoccupied saving other people's lives. And by some strange coincidence Natalie came along and it happened that way. That made me think that it always happens that way. But of course, it doesn't. You're right. I was clueless then, and still am, I suppose. How did you learn about romance in the West?"

"By reading all of those western novels."

"The British ones?"

"No. The British are in more of a strait jacket about love than the Saudis are. Just in a different manner."

"I think we are going to be very happy together. I have a lot to learn from you, Khalisah."

"Yes, Doctor. And I'll try to be very patient with you."

"Please do."

Yes, it was going to be pleasant with Matthew Avery, she thought. *It could turn out to be even more of a love match than they envisioned. Father somehow sensed that when he told Matt to take care of me. He knew that I was going to need someone when Charley Harper disappeared. I don't know how you are able to know about such things, Baba, but thank you.*

Helsinki

William Smith and his wife, Rebecca, her daughter, Olivia, and her mother, Annike Solvang Lundstrom, touched down in Tel Aviv aboard El-Al Flight 321 the day after leaving Minnesota.

Gregory Peck, the Speckled Sussex rooster, tolerated the trip well in the cage hastily purchased for him by one of the members of the *Mossad* Unit sent to take them out. But later that evening, he started crowing as though it was time for the sun to rise rather than time for it to set.

After speaking with Grebel for three days about what Yitzhak wanted him to do, Bill agreed to go. He did not want to leave Rebecca for an extended period of time but felt he had no choice. He found himself in a familiar position; out of work and out of money. If he went, Yitzhak would see that Rebecca had a home here in Tel Aviv and everything she needed. She felt that this was home now and she would be happy here. Her mother had never been out of Minnesota and wouldn't be happy anywhere else, but she couldn't return to Blue Earth now.

If Rebecca bought her a few chickens, that might help, Bill thought. Jim and Linda McIntyre would return soon from Colorado and Rebecca would be surrounded by those she considered to be her family, he decided. As for him, he concluded that coordinating an entire network of informants would be difficult at best and impossible if he had to begin without any prior knowledge of the organization. Then he realized that it was not an organization at all; just a fragmented collection of individuals who were willing to divulge what they knew if they were well paid.

He began to formulate a contingency plan to keep the information coming in. For now, he would let the woman known as Oksana run things since she was already in Moscow. She could report to him wherever he decided to locate. He would not attempt to travel into the Soviet Union. It was too dangerous, especially since he didn't speak Russian. After looking at a map, he decided that Finland was the closest western country to the Soviet Union. The capitol, Helsinki, was only a short distance from Leningrad, which lay across the narrow Gulf of Finland.

Helsinki was also closer to Moscow than any other western city. In Helsinki, he would be as close to the Soviet Union as he dared to be. He discovered that there were only five million people in the entire world who spoke Finnish and the language was considered to be the most difficult western language to learn. It seemed it was necessary to grow up speaking Finnish to be fluent in it. He hoped Helsinki had enough English speakers to allow him to function there.

Just how cold does it get in Helsinki? He wondered. *At least it's not the Arab world. I think I had rather freeze than be scorched at this point. I suppose it doesn't matter since I'm going to be miserable without Rebecca and I'll still be lying to people if I get anything accomplished. There just doesn't seem to be any other way.*

Thunder in Sinai

While Egypt's *War of Attrition* against the nation of Israel was continuing, the storm clouds were forming for yet another epic struggle between the two nations in the Sinai Peninsula. Because the Sinai is a cross roads for both north and south and east and west, the ruts of war chariots have crisscrossed the peninsula since the time of the Hyksos. Those Semitic invaders from the east introduced two-wheeled battle chariots into Egypt during their conquest of the Nile delta in the Old Kingdom. They ruled Egypt for 150 years and then were driven out and disappeared as suddenly as they had come.

Now modern war chariots of steel were being prepared to do battle across the Sinai, beginning on the Day of Atonement. This time the conflict was to be for control of the Sinai itself, part barren desert and part desolate mountain ranges. Life is difficult in the Sinai under the best of circumstances as evidenced by the harsh life of the Bedouins who have lived there for centuries. The victor would possess an inhospitable and unforgiving land where scorpions and asps guarded the access to *Jabal Musa*, the Mountain of Moses, believed to be either Mount Sinai or Mount Horeb. It was on *Jabal Musa* where the prophet wrote that *Yahweh* descended in fire to give notice to man that he was accountable.

Made in the USA
Charleston, SC
21 July 2014